ADAM'S FALL

PAUL FAIRALL

ADAM'S FALL

THE UPRISING

Tate Publishing & Enterprises

Adam's Fall
Copyright © 2011 by Paul Fairall. All rights reserved.

No part of this publication may be reproduced, stored in a retrieval system or transmitted in any way by any means, electronic, mechanical, photocopy, recording or otherwise without the prior permission of the author except as provided by USA copyright law.

The opinions expressed by the author are not necessarily those of Tate Publishing, LLC.

Published by Tate Publishing & Enterprises, LLC
127 E. Trade Center Terrace | Mustang, Oklahoma 73064 USA
1.888.361.9473 | www.tatepublishing.com

Tate Publishing is committed to excellence in the publishing industry. The company reflects the philosophy established by the founders, based on Psalm 68:11, *"The Lord gave the word and great was the company of those who published it."*

Book design copyright © 2011 by Tate Publishing, LLC. All rights reserved.
Cover design by Kristen Verser
Interior design by Nathan Harmony

Published in the United States of America
ISBN: 978-1-61739-372-3
Fiction: Religious
11.07.15

This book is dedicated to God; Jesus; the Holy Spirit; my wife; and my children.

PREFACE

Over a period of several years, I felt that the Lord was showing me different ideas for this story. He didn't give them to me all at once, but instead revealed them a piece at a time. One day, I was flying on a business trip and felt the leading to start writing these ideas down. The finished work is held between the covers of this book. I feel that the Lord was able to communicate many valuable principles and lessons through it, and I am blessed to be a part of that.

In the end, the purpose of this book is twofold. The first is that this story, filled with action and adventure, might appeal to a secular audience. My hope is that this might provide a window of opportunity for someone to share the message of salvation. The second purpose is that this book might be used as a wholesome form of entertainment for the Christian community.

I pray that you and others are blessed by this book.

CHAPTER 1

"Forty Years since the Great United States Pandemic." The bold black text stands out against a pale white page. The words stare coldly from an outspread newspaper that hides a mysterious figure. Judging by the hands that firmly grip the sides of the paper, the person is probably between fifty and sixty years old. The newsprint closes to reveal the hidden stranger. Indeed, he is an older man, as is apparent by his gray hair. He refocuses his eyes, which previously had been immersed in one of the many articles, and scans the room. The deep wrinkles around his eyes and on his forehead bear witness to a hard life, yet his gaze is so peaceful. Within those two vibrant round spheres is a spark. It is a spark of love, tempered by years of wisdom, gained through the overcoming of many hard trials. His perseverance and patience through those trying times in life had built an impeccable character. It was that character that emanated and flowed from every fiber of his being. Still, his body had not been able to escape the grip of time. Riddled with spontaneous aches and pains, his joints reminded him of that fact every day. He peers down at his leather-banded wristwatch through metal-framed glasses. He then carefully folds the newspaper in half and in half again and finally lays it on an already crowded end table.

The paper comes to rest beside a half-full cup of coffee, a vintage looking table lamp, and a bowl of soup with just a few remaining drops drizzled around the bottom. He looks out around the dimly lit living room, which is cluttered by people on couches and chairs. A young man is setting out folding chairs for the overflow of unfamiliar faces that continue to wander in. The hearty aroma of homemade vegetable soup fills the air.

We sure have a lot of new folks here today, he thinks to himself. *I hope we have enough soup.*

He can see that a number of the people there have just started supper. The whole place is buzzing with chatter and movement from the flurry of people. Some are sitting and eating, while still others stand and make small talk. Children are laughing and playing games on the floor, too wrapped up in conversation to focus on eating. The old man leans back in his green, plush, overstuffed chair and lets a relaxed sigh escape from deep within his chest as he takes in the whole scene. A tug on his pant leg startles him out of his cozy state. He jerks his head forward to see what has grabbed his leg. As he looks down over the top of his glasses, he finds the culprit. It's one of the boys who had been playing at his feet. The child appears to be about nine years old with sandy blond hair. His cheerful eyes rest on a pair of puffy round cheeks. The boy stares back at the old man, making him wonder what the little one was up to.

"What is it, son?"

"We want to hear one of your stories," the boy quietly replies.

Scanning the rest of the floor to see who "we" is, the gentleman sees a group of children from seven years old all the way up to teenagers staring expectantly back at him.

"One of my stories, huh?" the old man questions back.

The floor comes alive with commotion as some of the younger kids start to chime in.

"Yeah, a story."

"That'd be sweet!"

"Tell us a good one!"

The old man glances at his watch again, making sure to pause just long enough to build the children's anticipation. He scoots up in his chair and says in a loud voice, "Okay, we have some time before we need to get started. Everyone gather around."

The children all scoot forward, crowding to get a better seat. The adults squeeze in around him as well, some even sitting on the floor, like the children. All eyes focus on the steadfast old man as they wait with quiet expectancy. He looks around at the crowd again before he starts to speak with a slow and deliberate voice.

"The plan was simple, but it took twenty-five years to complete. This story is about dark times, times that shook many souls. It is still to this day the darkest part of history known to man. It all started with a terrorist group. They called themselves the Al-Qaeda, and the task of tracking its members was virtually impossible. In fact, at one time, the government believed that they had permanently dismantled the evil organization. As time would reveal, however, the truth was just the opposite. The group went underground. They disappeared from the face of the earth, and they started plotting against our country. This unseen force declared a holy war on the United States, because of the large number of Christians living there.

"You see, the Al-Qaeda believed that their god wanted them to kill Christians. In fact, these terrorists were willing to give their very lives to destroy the Christians and often employed tactics of self-sacrifice, including suicide bombings.

"One of the top advisors to this militant group was a man by the name of Mohamed Achmar. He was a genius when it came to military strategy. And looking back through history and over time, it has become clear that he was the mastermind behind an idea that would ultimately change the course of the world forever. This leader devised a plan—a plan that brought the United States to its knees.

"He proposed that Al-Qaeda send thirty carefully selected families to the United States. The families would first be conditioned to ensure they had the best odds possible of completing their mission. Only after this intense training were they allowed to work undercover for the terrorist organization. The group spent a substantial amount of time identifying and preparing these families for the work that lay ahead. After all, they were the foundation—the key to destroying America.

"To avoid suspicion, the families were to claim that they had been political refugees running from government persecution. With the new open borders policy of the United States government, it didn't take much for the immigrants to be welcomed with open arms.

"The Al-Qaeda had given each of these families large sums of money, most of which they were allowed to spend however they pleased. The Al-Qaeda also offered the families a great life in America. Unlike others before them, however, they didn't even have to die for their cause. Instead, they were to have children. The only requirement that the terrorist group put on them was that they dedicate their firstborn son to Al-Qaeda.

"Each family raised their first son within the culture of the United States but filled their hearts with hatred toward it. They also preached false promises of an unending supply of virgins, feasts, and riches in eternity. They corrupted their sons' innocent hearts as they spoke of a place that would bring pleasure beyond description—a place that would fulfill every carnal desire.

"A portion of the wealth that the terrorists gave to the families was used to ensure their sons were educated in the finest military and political institutions. With degrees from schools like Harvard, West Point, and Princeton, the sons of Al-Qaeda had no problems getting internships with the top military and political organizations in the United States. The genius of the plan was that these well-educated men had been born in the United States, and therefore, they were citizens. This helped them avoid the scrutiny that was placed on non-citizens applying for such high profile positions.

"Throughout their upbringing, the families continued to brainwash their sons, training them for one purpose and one purpose only. Their destiny was to kill. 'Kill and you will live forever,' they were told. These men were to sacrifice themselves for the ultimate benefit of Al-Qaeda and their god. In doing so, they would kill millions of their enemies—the Christians.

"The United States had focused on keeping terrorists out and monitoring potential threats that had immigrated into the country. But there were more and more foreigners flooding into the United States who actually were fleeing persecution. They didn't think to keep track of those persecuted immigrants, much less their children. Even if they would have had the foresight, I doubt that the government would have tracked them for nearly twenty years.

"Finally, the day had come. The plan had been successfully and diabolically orchestrated. There were now terrorists working at the Pentagon, the White House, and at top military headquarters around the United States. The imposters then infected themselves with a deadly disease that was engineered from a virus. The original strain of virus was called the H1N1 virus, more commonly known as the swine flu. The initial reaction to the virus resembled an ordinary flu. It usually began with a runny nose, a cough, aches and pains, and a fever. Therefore, the host would not show any life-threatening symptoms for several days. After that, however, the infected person would begin to experience trouble breathing and would have an extremely high fever. Once the telltale signs showed up, most people who were infected would die in a matter of weeks. The mortality rate was over sixty percent.

"It took quite a while before the hospitals figured out that this was no ordinary flu, and by that time, the virus had already spread across the nation. Most of the government was wiped out, since that is where the virus was first released. The Al-Qaeda had ensured that their undercover terrorists held key positions in government organizations. Since the infections started in those areas, they were the hardest hit. A large portion of the population was infected as well. What ensued was chaos. People died by the millions.

"Businesses lost employees to sickness or death, and in turn, they couldn't stay open any longer. This was a hard blow to an already staggering United States economy. A domino effect ensued that started with the food manufacturers. They couldn't get enough raw produce or meat to keep supplying an adequate amount of food for the nation. There wasn't even enough food coming in for the steadily decreasing population. With a dwindling supply from the manufacturers and stockpiling from consumers, the few grocery stores that were still open couldn't stock their shelves.

"It was then that the looting started. The police force wasn't large enough to stop any of the rioting. At this point, there were only disorganized remnants left of the once mighty organization. After the starving masses cleared any remaining shelves in the stores, there was absolutely nothing left to feed the populace.

"It didn't take people long to figure out where the food was coming from. The looters turned their attention to the distribution lines. Any trucks that carried food were hijacked and stripped clean. The criminal element formed into localized gangs inside the cities. In reaction to this, other groups of people banded together in pockets to protect their homes and families.

"Starvation set in for many. What was left of the government set up truck routes for food shipments. These trucks were accompanied by armored guard units with heavy artillery. This ensured that the food reached its intended destination. A portion of the food was then rationed out on a first-come, first-served basis. The United Nations sent us relief supplies and aid, but most of the damage had already been done.

"The leaders of our once great nation searched for a solution to the grave situation. In an act of desperation, they opened up communication with Al-Qaeda. The terrorists said that Christians were to blame for the war. They said that Christians were preventing peace, because they believe that Christ is the only way to heaven. Their argument was that this narrow view was causing division and standing in the way of world peace. 'How could the world ever fully unite if judgmental, narrow-minded Christians were allowed to have a place in it?' they asked. They threatened that worse was to come and that they would not rest as long as Christians were allowed to practice their closed-minded religion in the United States.

"The citizens were desperate, hungry, and worn down. They were tired of war and chaos and longed for the life they once knew. A devastated and dwindling American population turned their anger and hatred toward the Christians. A flood of people began calling for the current president to be immediately impeached. The leaders bowed their knee to the overwhelming support for a new president. Elections began quickly and ended almost as expeditiously with the same reckless abandonment of reason as when they had begun. The people elected a Muslim president into office. They believed that he would be more in tune with the terrorist group and therefore be able to negotiate a swift and painless end to the war. His name was Mahjub Matloob. President Matloob's first act in power was a sweeping resolution meant to keep the terrorists at bay. He issued an executive order making Christianity an act of treason. The order was made into law, and the punishment for breaking it was death. With the passing of this law and after several months of negotiations, Al-Qaeda signed a peace treaty with our nation. The American people were overjoyed."

A teenage girl with short brown hair and freckles pipes up from the floor. "Is that why we're not supposed to have Bible studies today?"

"Sadly, yes," the old man replies. "The police would put us all in jail if they knew we were meeting here tonight to study God's Word."

"My mom told me that the police used to help people," the teenager responds innocently.

The corners of his mouth turn up slightly. "Let me tell you the rest of the story, and I think you will understand why some of the things are like they are today. You asked about the police.

"This new anti-Christian government empowered the local police forces to end Christianity. The government replaced anyone in a position of authority who did not agree with the new law. This ensured a united front against the religious traitors. The police forces grew again, but now their purpose was something different. They had an agenda. Their main mission was to search out all Christians and stop them from practicing by any means necessary. Initially, it seemed that they would wipe the Christians from the face of the earth, but then the police forces came under fire themselves. They had more trouble on their hands than just the small remnant of Christ followers.

"One source of disruption was from the local gangs who had taken over parts of the urban districts during the riots and looting. They were still deeply entrenched in the cities. It was almost impossible to track them down, because they would take refuge among the endless rows of deserted buildings. Communications were down for most of the city as well, making coordinating attacks more challenging.

"Some of the people who had banded together to protect their families during the riots were still together. They became impatient with the lack of support from the police. Eventually, some of these people began to form right-wing militant operations. They knew that they were no match for the government in open warfare. Their strategy was to use guerrilla tactics against their enemies. To the average person, any one of these members appeared to be just another everyday citizen. It was commonplace that the families of the militant members would not even know about their hidden life.

"Most of these groups met in the urban areas, where they were better fortified. The government-appointed troopers were always trying to find the meeting locations so that they could disband the rebellion. That's why the city was so dangerous. They most frequently fought against the new police task forces while warding off attacks. Their arsenal typically consisted of small weapons, rifles, and makeshift explosives. Despite a growing focus on these groups, they were still able to coordinate effective strikes within the rural areas. They would plan attacks on police patrols, headquarters, and anywhere else where they could easily disrupt government operations. Sometimes the militant groups would secure large munitions, such as rockets or grenade launchers from their raids. These types of heavy explosives were reserved for when the group could attack high-profile enforcement agency members.

"The gangs were constantly pushing past the limits of the cities, and the right-wing militia groups relentlessly disrupted operations. With the eye of the police turned to other matters, some Christians were able to continue meeting in their towns, undetected by the preoccupied policemen. We all thought that the persecution would end. It didn't though. In spite of the obvious immediate threats that the other groups posed to the force, their main mission remained. Ending Christianity was at the top of their priority list, and it seemed that would never change."

The old man leans back in his chair and reaches for his cup of coffee. The group of people crowded around his chair listens intently as they wait for him to continue his story. He takes a sip of his coffee. The cup clanks against the wooden table as he sets it down again. As he begins to speak, the boys and girls can smell the strong scent of coffee lacing his breath.

"Nine years after the treaty was signed and in the middle of persecution, God chose a teen named Joseph to lead many to Christ. In fact, a lot of the Bible studies we have today were started because of him. This is the story of Joseph.

"There was a change in the weather. It was that time of year when the heat of summer is gone and God staves off the cold of winter with his hand. The air is cool, the leaves show their brilliance, and the sun shines warmly down on the earth from heaven. It was during this season, a little over thirty years ago, that Joseph started his change as well.

"There was going to be a Bible study, much like this one." The old man looks around the room and chuckles softly. "Only with a lot fewer people. Bible studies were illegal then, just like they are now," he explains. He winks at the young girl who had pointed that out just a few moments ago. "And Joseph had been invited by one of his friends, who was named Sarah, over to a secret Bible study at the Jansen's house. But Sarah wasn't the only one doing the inviting. Joseph had asked someone to attend himself."

CHAPTER 2

"Hey, wait up, Joseph," Zaphin says as he pushes his way through a stream of slow-moving juniors. He can barely make out Joseph's gel-filled, messy brown hair. It is bouncing up and down through the tide of students. The school hallways are packed with teens. All of them are trying to get to class before that dreaded dull buzz rings out.

As full as the hallway is, there's no mistaking that hair. Zaphin didn't know how someone could spend so much time on their hair just to make it look like they hadn't even touched it. The teen's styling reminded Zaphin of when he used to take a bath as a little kid. He would wet his hair down and then shape it into different clumps sticking up, down, and every which way.

Zaphin gets another glimpse of the suspect moving through the crowd. His suspicions are confirmed. It is Joseph. Joseph is a medium-build junior. His height is about average for his class, which made him even harder to spot. Zaphin can see that Joseph is wearing the usual zipper-up brown fleece vest with a long sleeve beige T-shirt underneath. The shirt has some sort of emblem showing on the front. He can't see it from where he is standing, but Zaphin is sure it has something to do with extreme sports. And don't forget the designer khaki pants and top-of-the-line kicks.

What is he thinking with that? Zaphin wonders.

Zaphin's hair, on the other hand, hangs down to his chin. It is straight, black, and quite a bit longer than Joseph's. He is a skinny boy with a thin face, which makes his cheekbones stand out. His brown eyes begin to dart back and forth as he pushes through another mess of walking backpacks. *There he is.*

"Joseph Garrison!"

Joseph hears him this time. Turning to see who just called his name, he sees Zaphin headed straight for him. He appears as though he really needs to get something off of his chest. A smile cracks across Joseph's face as he adjusts his backpack strap further up onto his shoulder. He sarcastically cocks his head sideways.

"Zaphin Lane, what are you doing here so early?" Joseph says with a puzzled look on his face.

"Early? That stupid buzzer is about to go off."

"That's what I mean. Don't you usually show up around third period?"

Zaphin rolls his eyes at Joseph and grants him a half-hearted smile for the attempted joke.

"Real funny, man. Real funny," he says.

"Sorry. I couldn't resist."

"So count me in for the—you know," Zaphin says. He nods his head, as if he is trying to coax the answer out of his friend.

Joseph's blue eyes brighten as he tries to fight back the enormous smile that is already growing on his face.

"That's great news!" he exclaims. He tries hard not to show too much excitement. "So do you remember when?"

"Sure. Tomorrow evening. I'm supposed to meet you at your house, and then I'll just follow you to the Bible study."

Joseph winces, as if the words pierce him through the heart. His smile isn't there anymore. In fact, in its place is a defined frown. He quickly puts his finger up in front of his lips, signaling Zaphin to stop talking. Joseph glances around the hallway, combing the area for anyone who may be listening.

They both stand quietly for a moment, as if they are waiting for the secret police to break through the windows and helicopters to descend on them. It's Zaphin who finally breaks the silence. "Look, I'm out of here. I'll see you Saturday. Cool?"

Joseph regains his composure and starts slowly nodding his head. "Cool."

Joseph watches Zaphin walk off down the hall. His black T-shirt and baggy white zippered pants bob in and out of the stream of teens until he loses sight of his new friend in the crowd. Joseph drifts his attention through a window to the outside world of sun, trees, and grass.

Wow, he thinks to himself, still surprised by Zaphin's news. *So he's really going to come.*

He never thought in a million years that Zaphin would accept his invite to the Bible study. After all, he had just met him a couple of months ago. What perplexes Joseph even more is the age difference. Zaphin is a year older than Joseph, but he is a senior.

How cool is that, friends with a senior. I never thought he would want to hang out with me, and go to a Bible study, no less. Everyone knows that you can go to jail or worse, just being caught at one of the meetings. On top of that, Zaphin's parents aren't Christians either. All the odds were against him saying yes, but still he accepted.

What an opportunity to reach him. Zaphin might get his parents to check it out too. What if they get saved? Of course, Zaphin has foster parents. And they don't live with him anymore. Come to think of it, they kind of don't get along with each other either.

Joseph picks at a piece of loose paint on the window frame as he continues to go over everything in his head.

Joseph's own parents aren't Christians either. In fact, they are outspokenly against Christianity. They're nothing like his real parents. They had adopted him when he was just six years old.

My parents would—Joseph's train of thought is interrupted by the mind-numbing clanging of the school buzzer. He breaks away from his window daydream and spins around, only to find that he is all alone in the hallway.

"I'm late again!" he murmurs under his breath as he trudges down the long corridor. Finally, he reaches the end, where a closed door awaits him. Joseph contemplates ditching the class, but instead, he takes a deep breath and turns the handle. As he opens the door, he hears his biology teacher already starting in on him.

"We've been waiting for our honored guest to arrive," the teacher squawks. "And here is a ticket for our honored guest." She hands Joseph a slip of paper. Joseph's teacher is one of those pompous know-it-alls that thinks she has everything all figured out. She's the kind of person who likes to hear herself talk and rarely affords anyone else that luxury. After all, there wasn't a thing that anyone could tell her that she didn't already know. Or at least that's what she told herself.

"What's her problem?" Joseph silently grunts as he looks down at the colored piece of paper that he is now holding in his hand. "Detention!" Joseph's face burns red as he crumples the paper in his fist and jams it into his pants pocket. The teacher looks quite pleased with herself as she begins to speak again, picking back up where she had left off.

"So the law of thermodynamics states that things in a system will become less complex over time, unless new information is introduced into the system by an outside source. How does that..."

Her words fade as Joseph drags his feet across the white speckled vinyl floor while he passes between the aisles of desks. He plops down into an open seat at the back of the class. Without a word, he lets his backpack drop off his shoulder. It crashes to the floor, producing a dull thudding noise from the weight of the books.

Joseph is so irritated by her arrogant attitude that he zones her out for the rest of class. Instead, he starts daydreaming. He begins replaying some of the events of the previous weekend over and over in his mind. Of course, he had been with his friends competing in extreme sports. He started getting into them as a hobby right after his parents died. Joseph was eight when he first tried messing around with skateboarding. That's what jumpstarted him on the road to other extreme sports. Not only did he skateboard, but he also went rock climbing, rode dirt bikes, and began rollerblading. Joseph was into pretty much anything that would give him an adrenaline rush.

He was pretty good at all the sports, but there was one extreme event that really caught his attention. Joseph used to watch people do unthinkable things, relying solely on their own body strength and agility. Sometimes they would spring from the top of one building to another or scale up what was seemingly a flat wall. The more he watched it, the more he wanted to do it. He would practice jumping off small walls or leaping over the hood of a car. His parents tried to redirect his interest away from the dangerous obsession by enrolling him in martial arts classes. Not only did this fail to curb his enthusiasm for the extreme, but it actually had the inverse effect. Studying the art form actually encouraged him. The martial arts taught him techniques that improved his speed, flexibility, strength, and balance.

When he was ten, he was good enough to start attempting harder stunts at home. He would hop from limb to limb in his tree or shimmy down his two-story house on the gutter. When he was thirteen, he joined up with a local group of teens that informally call themselves the MagiX. People who participate in these extreme sports are also known as *urban ninjas*. As an urban ninja, Joseph performs very dangerous stunts without any safety nets or ropes. As soon as he got into the sport, Joseph loved it. He couldn't get enough of it.

The MagiX isn't just a group of independent competitors though. The urban ninjas are more like a group of brothers. They have a very good mentoring program for less advanced members. Although most of them employ the teaching style of "practice by doing," they at least ensure that their *protégés* are at the acceptable skill level before performing any higher risk tricks. By the time he was fourteen, Joseph was already doing some of the most dangerous stunts. He would do things like dart across the tops of light support beams fifty feet off of the ground, hang on the outside ledges of parking garages and then drop from level to level, or execute back flips off of ten foot ledges with ease. As his reputation grew, so did the list of places that he was banned from. Although what he was doing wasn't illegal, the shopping malls and stores were afraid that someone would get hurt and sue.

He has come a long way from that unsure eight-year-old boy. He is seventeen now and pulling off stunts that nobody has done before. This past weekend, he ran on top of a handrail and leapt from one building to another one over twenty feet away. The building that he landed on was one story down from where he had started. He narrowly cleared the railing, rolling into the open door on the balcony. Just a couple of feet in either direction would have meant broken bones for sure, and five feet shorter would have ended his life. The weekend before that, he got a running start in a parking garage, hurdled over the guardrail, and caught a light pole in midair, five feet away from the balcony. He shimmied down the steel pole as the crowd of MagiX teens cheered him on from below. What a rush! Joseph was trying to think of new tricks that would top the already unbelievable stunts that he was pulling off. The bell rings again, bringing him back into the reality of the dull and musky smelling classroom.

Finally, he thinks as he snatches his backpack off of the ground and scoots out of his chair. Joseph ignores the teacher, pretending that he doesn't see her condescending stare as he walks past her desk and heads out the door.

The next class is science. He really enjoys that class for two reasons. The first is that he likes learning about different forces that God put into existence when he created the earth. It amazes Joseph to learn about things like the human body, cells, and DNA. Like how all of the cells in a human body start out exactly the same, but some of them decide to become heart cells, and some decide to become an arm. The exact same cell—the cell that splits and splits and splits is an exact duplicate of the other. There's no information inside the cells themselves that tells them what to become. The only explanation is that something outside the cells is telling them what to change into.

The teacher's explanation is always one of evolution. That doesn't make sense to Joseph, though. He had a hard time buying into the whole evolution thing. On the one hand, his last class is teaching about the law of thermodynamics. That is a well-documented and accepted law demonstrating that things in a system get less complex over time, unless something outside of that system injects new information into the system. But the evolutionists teach that everything came from pond scum or the Big Bang. So they're contradicting the law of thermodynamics. They're saying that things started out very simple and became more complex without any new information being injected into the system. Not to mention that no one has seen any evolution in the thousands of years of documented history.

As Joseph walks to class, he remembers when he had brought up the topic of evolution with his parents. It didn't go well. They immediately started in on him about his "faith."

"Don't you start getting caught up with all those fairy tales," his foster dad had said in an irritated voice.

"You know that there are steep punishments for anyone who teaches that nonsense," his foster mother had agreed.

"You say that I believe that God created everything because of my faith," Joseph had responded. "It's true that I have faith, but what about you? You believe that some ball of mass was just always there, exploded, created the sun and planets, and beat out millions of statistics to create and sustain life on this ball of dirt."

"Yes," his foster dad had answered. Joseph can still remember the look on his father's face—how he had raised his eyebrows and pursed his lips in a matter-of-fact way, almost challenging Joseph to continue.

"So where did the ball of mass come from? Who created it? I believe that a being beyond my understanding who has always been and will always be created everything. So tell me, which takes more faith: to believe in a ball of inert mass that always was, or a being beyond our understanding that always was? I would say that you have more faith than I do, it is just misplaced."

Joseph rubs his cheek, remembering what happened next. His mother had fumed as she quickly swung her open hand, connecting with his face. Joseph hadn't retaliated. He had just rubbed the side of his head and looked over at his foster mother, who still had tears running down her face. Without saying a word, Joseph had retreated up to his room. He had never brought up the subject again.

Joseph shrugs off the unpleasantness that lingers from the memory and refocuses on the second reason that he looks forward to this class all day. Even more than the science, he liked seeing Sarah Jairus. There's something about her that he finds very attractive. Sure, she's stylish. Zip-up sweaters are the "in thing" for this year. She's always wearing the latest styles, so of course, she is sporting one at all times, along with her faded blue jeans. That isn't why he likes her though. He enjoys being around her because they get each other. Joseph can really talk with her about stuff. Sarah isn't bad to look at either. She isn't overweight, but she isn't a skeleton. He likes the way her white cheeks have just a hint of pink that play across them, like she has been out walking in the chilly air for too long. And jasmine—Sarah's brown hair is about shoulder length. It smells of sweet jasmine, and Joseph is intoxicated by it every time he is near her. It must be the shampoo that she uses or her perfume. In any case, he really likes that about her. The memory is so strong that he can almost smell it as he strolls through the hallway.

Although she has large pouty lips, they almost always form a gentle smile on her face that accentuates the bright twinkle in her blue eyes. Joseph enjoys hanging out with her too. She's funny and sweet, and conversations come so easy with her. Of course, he said yes when Sarah had asked him to go to the Bible study. He wonders if she had noticed how nervous he was.

"Maybe she'll just think that I was scared that my parents would find out," he tells himself. "She's lucky that she doesn't have to worry about that."

Sarah's parents are Christians, so they completely support her. She doesn't have to hide anything from them. They consistently encourage her to read the Bible, pray, and to reach out to others. Joseph, on the other hand, has to tell his parents that he's going over to a friend's house. That isn't a lie, because the Christians he meets with are his friends. It isn't exactly being honest with them either though.

"I hope Sarah doesn't mind that I invited Zaphin. After all, it's not like it's a date or something. We're just friends," Joseph tries to convince himself as he makes his last turn down a short hallway. "Here we go."

Joseph follows a group of giggling teenage girls into a classroom that is filled with pictures of planets, animals, and plants. A model solar system sits by the window among the microscopes and miscellaneous "bugs in a jar" that clutter the table. Various drawings and formulas on large flip charts line the wall opposite of the windows. The vague stench of formaldehyde seems to seep from the cabinets behind them. Today, however, Joseph is oblivious to it all. He hones in on a table in the back of the classroom next to the window, searching for her. A smile breaks across his face. The stress of the morning seems to fade out of existence. Sarah is already there.

"She's waiting there, sitting at our lab table."

He hadn't really hung out with her before this year. They had bumped into each other every once in a while, but they had always run in different circles. At the first of the class, the teacher had assigned everyone a lab partner. It was fate that Joseph and Sarah were paired together. Initially, Joseph was hardly enthusiastic about having to sit next to her for the whole year, but they ended up hitting it off right away.

Sarah sights Joseph coming through the doorway. She quickly looks out the window, pretending that she hasn't seen him come in the classroom. She would be just utterly humiliated if Joseph knew how much she looked forward to seeing him in class every day.

What's the big deal? So I look forward to seeing my friend. There's nothing wrong with that. Sarah reassures herself as she fights back the shy smile that is slowly pushing the edges of those pouty lips up.

"Hey, Sarah."

She turns her head toward him, flipping her hair over her right shoulder.

"Oh hey, Joseph. How's it going?"

"Couldn't be better. After all, it's Friday."

Joseph scoots the hard metal and plastic blue chair out from under the desk and sits down.

"So are you still coming to the Jansen's?" Sarah asks.

Joseph leans over to whisper in Sarah's ear, taking in the strong jasmine fragrance.

"Yeah, I wouldn't miss it. What are the Jansens going to go over in the Bible study?"

Sarah leans over as well so that no one else can hear their conversation. "We're going to study Joshua from the Old Testament."

"That's cool. I hope you don't mind, but—"

The buzzer clamors again, signaling the end of freedom and the beginning of the next class.

Joseph stops talking as the teacher stands up from his large wooden desk and turns to write on the board. Sarah looks over at

Joseph and holds out her flat, open hands as if to say, "Well, are you going to tell me?"

Joseph cups his hand around his mouth to further deaden the sound of his voice. "I'll tell you later."

"Whatever."

Mr. Becker, the science teacher, has finished writing on the board. He turns around to address the rows of floating heads and blank stares. On the board is a drawing of a group of many interlocking circles with one little dot on each circle. There is one cluster of dots in the center of all of the circles as well. It resembles a number of individual planets orbiting around another group of planets that have all been mashed together.

"Does anyone know what these are?" he questions.

Sarah's hand shoots into the air. She's sitting straight upright in her chair with her arm reaching for the ceiling. It reminds Joseph of a gymnast who has just stuck a perfect landing. Trying to provide as much height as possible to her outstretched arm, she arches her back as well. Her face beams with confidence as she pleads to be called upon.

"Yes, Sarah," the teacher says, giving his approval for her to answer.

"It's an atom."

"You are correct as usual, Sarah. This is an atom. All matter on Earth is made up of these atoms. Would anyone care to guess how many atoms lined up in a row it would take to make just one little centimeter?"

A few of the students feel up to the challenge and raise their hands. The teacher surveys the room with his eyes, giving more students the chance to raise their hands.

"Okay. Just call out some guesses."

"Five hundred thousand," a boy responds in the back, who incidentally had not raised his hand.

"One million," a girl in the front row blurts out.

"Ten million," a girl adds as she leans back in her chair.

"One hundred thousand," another boy says.

The teacher raises his hands, calling for the class to quiet down. "A row of one hundred million atoms would be one centimeter long. An atom contains a dense nucleus of protons and neutrons and a very large cloud of electrons surrounding the nucleus."

The teacher points to the middle of the drawing on the chalkboard. "As you can see, all the protons and neutrons are clumped together in the middle. This is the nucleus."

The teacher points to what looks like the orbiting planets that circle around the nucleus. "Do you see these large circles around the nucleus?"

Some of the students are finally showing signs of life and are now at least responding by nodding their heads.

"All these little dots are the electrons that make up the large cloud around the nucleus. These electrons in the cloud are bound to the protons in the nucleus by an electromagnetic force. Electrons have a negative charge, and protons have a positive charge. Since they are opposite, they work like opposite poles of a magnet and attract one another. It is this magnetic attraction that holds the cloud of electrons the correct space away from the nucleus. And empty space is what makes up the majority of the atom. In fact, if an atom was the size of a football stadium, the nucleus would be as big as a grape."

Joseph raises his hand, trying to impress Sarah by contributing to the discussion. "Is it possible to change the makeup of an atom?"

The teacher is delighted by the intriguing question and doubly so that it has come from Joseph. "Quite an interesting question, Joseph. Yes, it is possible to change the makeup of an atom. In fact, scientists have created new ones that they call *super-heavy atoms*. They have only been made artificially though, and they do not serve any practical purposes."

"Why not?" Joseph inquires.

"Because of their short half-lives. These atoms start to decay in just a few milliseconds." The teacher pauses a moment, surveying the room. "Does anyone else have any questions?"

No one raises their hand. In fact, most of the students appear as though they have lost interest again.

"Very well," the teacher bellows. "Since you have no questions, I must have done a very good job teaching you. Take out a sheet of paper, and write a one-page essay on what we have learned so far this week."

Moans go up from the classroom, which is now filled with sounds of crinkling paper and a roar of dissenting chatter. Chairs screech across the floor as students grumpily slide them closer to their desks.

"Quiet please, or I might think you have so much time you could write a two-page essay," the teacher warns. Again, a hush falls over the room.

The rest of the class seems to fly by as Joseph steals glances at Sarah in between paragraphs. Of course, Sarah is one of the first students to turn in her essay. As she walks back to her desk, she tries to get Joseph's attention. Finally, he glances up at her. Getting the upper hand, Sarah teasingly mouths the word *loser*, making sure to keep her back to the teacher. Joseph smiles wryly up at her. As she takes her seat beside him again, Joseph takes the opportunity to jab back at her.

"Nerd."

He waits for her reaction, but she doesn't respond. Instead, she just opens up her science textbook and starts reading the next chapter. Joseph barely finishes and turns in his essay before the buzzer goes off.

As they walk toward the door, Joseph tries to make small talk with Sarah.

"So did you see me last weekend?" he asks clumsily.

"No, why?"

Joseph holds open the door for her as they pass through it. "No reason. I only pulled off the most crust stunt ever." "Crust stunt?" Sarah asks, with a confused look on her face.

"Yeah. You know—"

Joseph tries to follow her but is compelled to continue holding the door for some girls exiting behind him. Sarah keeps walking, unaware that her lab partner has been detained. He offers a polite and impatient nod to the young ladies as they exit the classroom. Taking advantage of the break in the line, he dodges some oncoming teens and slides through another line. Catching up to Sarah, he continues. "You know—the crust—as in the upper crust of all stunts. It means the best of the best."

"Very impressive," she says with a monotone voice as she continues walking down the hallway.

As they round the corner and come into the main hall, they notice that a group of kids are peering out of the window frame doors that lead to the main entrance of the school.

"What's going on?" Sarah asks one of the girls at the back of the crowd.

"They found a Bible in Daniel Parson's locker. You know what that means."

Sarah's face changes to a pale white color as she turns away from the glass door. She leans into the wall with her shoulder to steady herself. Joseph stands up on his toes, stretching to get a glimpse of Daniel. What he sees crushes his spirits. Two troopers are putting him into a patrol car. Rays of sun reflect off of the cold silver handcuffs that bind his arms behind his back as they bend him down into the backseat of the police vehicle. Joseph sees another car in front of the one that they just loaded Daniel into. This is no ordinary patrol car though. It has the words "Senior Captain" printed in black lettering down the side of the vehicle. That means there must be a captain in the car. Joseph's eyes immediately fly up to the passenger seat. He doesn't know why, but the figure that he finds in the front seat sends a bolt of fear down to Joseph's very core. The figure's head comes up to the top of the window. Judging by how large he is compared to the car, he must be at least six or seven feet tall. He looks stocky too, from what Joseph can see. He's wearing a velvet red beret with a royal green cape. His eyes are cold and dark, like two black onyx spheres encircled by only a sliver of brown. A thick black mustache accentuates the man's grim frown. An elbow-high glove that hides his arm hangs slightly out the window. The captain raises his hand into the air, motioning for the car with the prisoner in it to pass by him. Joseph watches helplessly as the car takes Daniel away. He keeps watching until it is completely out of sight.

As the mob of onlookers disappears, Joseph hunts around for Sarah.

"Where the heck is she?"

Joseph is clearly unsettled. He's nervously combing the halls for her when he runs into Ashlynn. Ashlynn is one of Sarah's friends. She always has such an upbeat and positive attitude, not to mention quite a bubbly personality.

"Ashlynn," Joseph calls, gently grabbing her sleeve.

"Hey! What's going on?"

"Have you seen Sarah?"

"No, why? Is something wrong?"

Joseph can hear the genuine concern in her voice. Just then, he spots Sarah out of the corner of his eye. She looks as though she's in a trance as she slips out of the bathroom and into the hallway.

Joseph hurriedly breaks off the conversation. "Okay, thanks," he blurts out as he rushes off to meet Sarah. "Wait up!"

Ashlynn watches as he runs over to Sarah. Seeing that she is fine, she turns and heads off to her next class.

Sarah looks up to see Joseph coming toward her. She discreetly brushes her eyes with the back of her sleeve, trying to wipe away any leftover tears.

Joseph gently lays his hand on her shoulder. "Are you okay?"

"Yes, it's just that…" Sarah stumbles to find words as she fights off the urge to cry again. She crosses her arms and turns away from him. Taking a moment, she regains her composure. In a low voice, she says, "It's just that I gave Daniel that Bible they found in his backpack."

It clicks. Concern gives way to compassion as Joseph's face softens. Sarah starts to cry again as she turns back around to face him.

"He's going to go to the correction facility because of me. It's because of me! You know that people are never the same once they come back from there. That's if they even come back."

Joseph examines the hallway for a second time. No is paying attention to them, let alone close enough to hear what they are discussing.

"So it was one of the red Bibles?" Joseph asks.

"Yeah," Sarah whimpers.

"Did anyone see it besides the cops?"

Sarah briefly reflects back on the events of the day. "No. The cops found it during class, and they didn't show anyone."

Joseph seems relieved. "That's good. Some of the kids here know that we have red Bibles. I would like to think that nobody we know would turn us in, but you can never be sure. I know that some might be tempted to, especially if they offer a reward or something."

Sarah shakes her head in agreement. "Poor Daniel," she faintly whispers.

Both Joseph and Sarah stand there quietly for a moment until he changes the subject.

"So are we still on for tomorrow, or did you want to cancel that now?"

The tears that were streaming down Sarah's cheeks dwindle as resolve begins to displace her sorrow.

"We're still on all right," Sarah says in a steadfast voice. She uses the sleeve of her zip-up sweater to dry off her face again. "Daniel was going to come. I know that he would want us to have it." Sarah seems calm now. "I'll see you tomorrow, Joseph."

"Right, see you then."

As Sarah turns to walk away, Joseph raises his hand to call out to her, but the words don't come.

She'll be okay, she's a tough girl, Joseph convinces himself as he watches her walk away.

CHAPTER 3

After school, Joseph hops in his car and speeds off toward home. He still can't believe what had happened to Daniel.

"I wonder how they knew he had a Bible."

Joseph can't stop mulling it over in his head. It seems like more and more Christians are getting caught. Things are getting so bad that sometimes he wonders if it might be easier to run away to the city.

Wake up, Joseph, he thinks to himself.

He would have to be insane to do that. It's just too dangerous there. Nobody went into the city, especially after dark. Even the trooper units stay clear of certain sections. The gangs and militant groups are so entrenched in those areas that it's a suicide mission to try and attack them. Most people live in the suburbs or the country where it's safe. After the outbreak, the government and law enforcement agencies had been able to secure a perimeter around the city. This kept order in the suburbs, but the Troopers still didn't have the resources required to actually take back the urban districts completely.

As he fixes his eyes upon the outline of the broken city, he wonders how Daniel is holding up in what must be an unbearable situation. A crushing weight as heavy as that patrol car that took him away feels as though it's sitting on Joseph's chest. An unseen bolt of sadness seems to tear his very soul in half. The color leaves his face. His lunch churns uneasily inside his stomach. What would he do if he was in the same situation? After all, it could have been any one of them.

"It can still be any one of us," he admits to himself.

On the other side of town, a trooper car pulls up to a heavy, wrought iron gate attended by several armed guards. The bars are reinforced with thick metal plates, preventing anyone from seeing into the complex. The men immediately draw their weapons on the vehicle, surrounding it on every side. A lone trooper emerges from a barricaded guard shack. He marches directly to the driver's window. The guard bends over, studying the people inside. Immediately, he stands erect and salutes the car, making sure to stare straight ahead. He avoids making eye contact with any of the passengers. The armed guards encircling the vehicle stand down as well. Yet another trooper from within the guard shack opens the massive gate via an electronic control panel.

"Drive," the captain commands from the passenger seat.

The car carrying the prisoner follows them through the opening. Daniel timidly looks up at his destination from the backseat. It's a walled fortress. Razor sharp barbed wire hangs down across the gray rock exterior of the building. It appears to be an old church. The grand steeple juts into the air, like a narrow finger stretching up to touch the sky. What was once a beacon of hope now only casts a shadow of despair across the land. Pieces of wood, along with a few loose shingles, hang from the top of the unkempt structure. It menacingly towers over the whole complex. He can see that the bell has been gutted out. Some sort of heavy artillery gun now juts out from that point, the barrel of which appears to be following the car as it moves closer. Behind thick black steel bars, hollow dark holes now replace what where once beautiful stained glass windows. The cavities recess deep into the building and out of sight. Dark gray clouds hang heavy in the sky above the structure, denying any sunlight to fall upon it. Several birds hover high in the air. He can't make out any details on the winged beasts. They appear to be more shadow than real.

Closer to the base of the building in the distance, Daniel can see that there are several helicopters resting on dirt landing pads. As they make their way across the grounds, he becomes aware of the many bunkers that infest the acres of grass along the driveway. The only thing giving away their positions are the drab olive green helmets sticking out just above the ground. They too follow the movement of the car as it creeps by them. Once they have passed by, the helmets turn again toward the gate or disappear back into the trenches. Daniel twists his wrists inside the cold metal handcuffs. Because his arms are behind his back, it's even more difficult to try and work his hands free. As they journey deeper and deeper into the complex, the more the reality of the situation begins to set in.

The road ends at a circle drive. Several more troopers are waiting there for them. They stand at attention, waiting for the car to arrive.

Daniel hears the eerie sound of the brake pads squeak as they bring the car to a halt. The men in red and green uniforms march forward in unison and stop in a row beside the passenger doors. Again, they stand at attention. This time, they await their captain's orders. One of the officers approaches the first vehicle. He opens the door for the captain. A black leather boot swings out of the car and onto the concrete. The sound of the gravel crunches and pops under the captain's heal as he twists it in order to swing his other foot out of the car. The giant of a man stands up from the vehicle and walks in between the troopers to the end of the line. He towers over the average size men, who are clearly intimidated. A breeze rolls in through the passenger door of the other vehicle as one of the men opens it. Daniel can smell the mold from the moss growing up across the building. There's also another smell mixed in. It's the rich smell of wood. The scent triggers his memory. It's from when he was a very young boy. His grandparents went to an older church, and he remembered when he used to go there with them. He must have gone to their Christmas Eve service at least five years in a row. The aroma of the old wooden pews used to saturate the entire sanctuary. It even overpowered the many other good smelling perfumes and colognes that the people would wear. He remembers the hymnals too and the visitor cards that he would inevitably end up doodling on with the pencils that were stuck in the small holes. Those services were always so magical. The nativity plays, the songs—just being together. It was a luxury that he could no longer enjoy.

"Take him to the holding cell, Alex," the captain commands. He shoves Daniel's red Bible into an unsuspecting man's chest, who grunts from the force of it. The captain continues on into the building. Lieutenant Alex snaps his fingers. Two guards open the door. They grab Daniel and pull him from the backseat.

Outside of the car, he stands momentarily in front of the building. He gazes at the massive structure, tilting his head back to judge the distance to the top of it. The agitated lieutenant walks around behind Daniel.

"Move, maggot!" Alex yells as he places a foot squarely in the middle of Daniel's back. He pushes off with the full force of his body. Daniel flies forward with his arms still handcuffed behind his back. He struggles to turn his shoulder into the ground in order to save his face. The Christian, however, is only partially successful. The side of his head slams onto the hard walkway. Laughter erupts from the guards and echoes up through the ornate arches of the once holy place. Two guards pick the teenager up by his arms. Each one takes a side of his body as they drag him up the stairs and in through the entrance. Alex follows closely behind them as they pass under the elaborate crown molding. The reinforced doors knock loudly as the guards close them, sealing Daniel in the stone mausoleum.

The troopers drag him through several hallways and narrow corridors that spiral down flights of stairs. The building must be even larger than it appears on the outside. As they descend into the lower levels, the smell of mold becomes more pungent. It feels damper and even slightly cooler than when they were traveling through the main floor. Daniel notices that the outside of several rooms have been reinforced with iron bars that stretch the entire length of the wall from the ceiling to the floor. Every so often, he can hear something as he passes a cell. It sounds like the frantic scurrying that a dog makes when running from a cruel master. Daniel knows what's inside the cells though. He knows that people are inside those cells. What's in store for him? What sort of torture and injustice can reduce human beings to live like rats?

They continue on through another passageway and into a long corridor. Trash litters the unkempt walkway. Puddles of foul, stagnant water line the sides of the rock path. The stones curve in overhead. The weight of the entire building seems to be crushing in on Daniel as he moves deeper into the bowels of the church. The guards finally arrive at the end of the tunnel, where a thick wood door defiantly stands against the men. The lieutenant pulls some keys from his belt and proceeds to open a shiny brass padlock, which contrasts sharply against the old, rusted iron latch. Pushing the door open, they drag him into the room. A solitary metal chair is situated in the middle of the barren prison cell. Its legs are fixed to the ground with sturdy bolts.

The trooper to his left directs a gun at Daniel's head while Alex uses a key to take off his handcuffs. He can feel the blood flowing back into his hands as they are released from the tight steel rings. His mind tells his body to run, but before he can react, the men thrust him into the chair. Quickly, the two guards strap his wrists down against the fortified armrests. He tries to fight against the men, but it's too late. There is no escape from their clutches. He kicks violently as the lieutenant simultaneously tries to secure his feet.

"Ugh," Alex moans as Daniel successfully lands a foot squarely into his chest.

Both of the guards back away. The injured man slowly stands up, holding his rib cage. He rolls his shoulders backward toward his shoulder blades and strains his neck from side to side. Slowly, he pulls out a leather strap from his pocket, making sure that Daniel can see it.

"You want it that way?" Alex spits through his clenched teeth. "Then let's see how you do without any air."

Daniel kicks again, twisting against the straps. He arches his body against the chair. His eyes widen as the lieutenant disappears around behind him.

Without warning, the strap swings down in front of his face and comes firmly up against his neck. Daniel struggles to breathe, but no air comes. The trooper leans back, putting his full weight on the restraint against Daniel's neck. His body starts to convulse for air, but there is no reprieve.

"Please, God," is all that he can pray, just before his body goes limp.

Alex releases the strap, revealing a bright red indentation on Daniel's neck where it has dug into his skin.

Something is breathing slow and deliberate breaths. The methodical rhythm is soothing… an undertow of peaceful swishing sounds like waves sliding over the sand. Daniel steadily becomes aware that the breathing he hears is his own. *Am I alive or dead?* he wonders. Daniel slowly opens his eyes. He is disoriented. The only thing that he can see is a black veil of nothingness that seems to melt and swirl around him. He tries again, blinking several times. As he begins to stand up, he realizes that he is strapped down. He remembers where he is. His legs are now fixed to the chair along with his arms. His eyes slowly begin to adjust to the darkness. As they do, he notices a dim light coming out from beneath the heavy door. His ears also become attuned to a faint noise. It's some sort of tapping. No, it isn't tapping. It's footsteps. The noise becomes louder and louder until he can also hear the muffled sound of murmuring voices. Shadows of feet begin to appear at the base of the door. Daniel can't stop the gripping fear that's engulfing him. He panics as he hears the dreaded sound of the padlock.

"Please save me, Jesus. Please give me the strength I need. Please, Jesus. Protect me. Please," he prays in desperation.

A bright light flickers on, momentarily blinding him. As he squints, he catches glimpses of the troopers entering the room, carrying an object. They are followed by the outline of a large man. Daniel hears the sound of the bulky door closing once again. As he begins to regain his sight, the images crystallize. Standing in front of him is the captain himself. He twists his head, straining to see what's behind him. The guards are holding a contraption that resembles a large diving helmet. He turns to his left, spotting the lieutenant. He holds a covered brown plastic box out away from his body.

"Daniel, is it?" a calm voice with a thick accent booms from in front of him.

He directs his attention back to the captain. "Yes," he timidly responds.

"How do you like the facility?"

Daniel doesn't answer. Instead, he just stares skeptically back at the man. The captain begins to speak again.

"As you see, we have state-of-the-art weaponry. In fact, we have the only three helicopters in the entire region. We have hundreds of soldiers that are located within this very compound." He pauses for a moment, letting his words sink in. "So if you are hoping that you can somehow escape, even get out of this room, then let me assure you that you are mistaken." Turning his head sideways, he displays a crooked-toothed smile at the young man. "Can I be frank with you, Daniel? I am very disappointed in you." The captain rubs his thumb up and down across his pointer finger as he speaks. "Do you know why I am disappointed in you?" he asks.

"Because you found my Bible?"

Adam's Fall • 45

The captain begins to speak straight away, barely allowing Daniel to finish his sentence. "I am disappointed because you have chosen to be a traitor to your own country, Daniel." He clenches his fist closed as he enunciates the word *traitor*.

"I'm not a traitor."

The captain's arm moves with unbelievable swiftness, clutching Daniel around the neck before he can react. Daniel can sense the immense strength in this man's hand as the captain forces the teenager's head from side to side. The evil man displays an inquisitive look, almost as if he is intently studying every feature of Daniel's face. He releases his grip from the Christian's neck and places his hands behind his back.

"I believe you, Daniel," he says. "So tell me. Where did you get this Bible?" The captain points to his right, in the direction of a guard. The trooper holds up a red Bible, displaying it for the room.

"From a friend."

"I assure you that whoever gave you this wretched thing is not your friend. Now I will ask you again. Who gave you that Bible?"

"What are you going to do to them?" Daniel asks, his voice quivering.

The captain leans forward, his lips purse in anger. "You should be more concerned with what I am going to do with you, little rat."

Daniel is silent. After several seconds, the captain stands upright again. His glare seems to relax as he begins to speak.

"Very well. I thought I might have to convince you."

The captain motions to the two guards holding the large glass helmet. They advance on Daniel, straining as they lift the contraption. The two of them affix the helmet to a pair of hinges that are attached to the back of his chair. Daniel moves his head around trying to avoid it, but they force it through the opening. Quickly, they latch the front down onto two bars that jut out from the front of the chair. The troupes reach in through an opening in the top of the glass cage. They secure a Velcro flap together around his neck. The collar comes to just under his chin, similar to a turtleneck. This completely seals his head into the device. Daniel looks around nervously as the captain begins to speak again.

"You see, I don't have the patience for your types of people. Do you know what is in that box over there?" the captain asks.

Daniel strains to see the box from the corner of his eye. The captain does not wait for a response. "That, my friend, is a box full of ants."

The guards pull off the covering of the box, revealing a mass of tiny tangled legs and red bodies. "But they are not just any old ordinary ants. You see, these are a special breed of fire ants. They crave flesh. Oh, they aren't too particular what kind. They start off just crawling around, feeling out the skin. Then they begin to dig in. From what I hear, the pain is excruciating. We have fed our little helpers enough to know exactly how many to put in. They will devour the flesh on your face overnight. Don't worry. They won't kill you," the captain booms. "We did underestimate their hunger on the first couple of experiments. When we came back the next day, not only had the ants eaten away the flesh from their faces, but they had completely hollowed out their skulls. That shouldn't happen to you as long as none of them travel up into your ear canals. At least, not on the first night." The captain laughs.

He is still smiling as he reaches forward, popping open a hatch at the top of the helmet.

"Now this is your last chance, Daniel. Tell me who you got the Bible from. Then you can go home."

Sweat begins to roll down Daniel's forehead as he stares helplessly up at the open hole. "I know you're not going to let me go. I heard the other prisoners in the hallway. There's no telling what you are doing to them. If I tell you, then you'll just be torturing two of us instead of one."

"Ooh, you're just too clever for me, aren't you, boy? You will tell me—after the ants have eaten off half your face. We'll see you in a couple of days. You'll do anything I ask by then."

Alex brings the box over to Daniel and hands it to the guards.

"Not too many. Only dump in half," the captain instructs. "We'll come back in two days. That will give him more time to think and more time to suffer."

The lieutenant slides on a thick gray glove and scoops out half of the ants, dumping them in with Daniel. "Where is your God now?"

The Captain puts his hands on his hips and lets out a loud, burly laugh.

"See you in two days, Daniel."

The men leave the room, shutting off the light. They padlock the closed door behind them. Unable to see once more, Daniel can hear the little creatures scurrying around on the vinyl below his chin. He is utterly helpless.

CHAPTER 4

Completely unaware of Daniel's situation and on the other side of the suburbs, Joseph continues his journey home from a rough day at school.

"What is that?" Joseph says as he catches a glimpse of something in his rearview mirror. That truck looks familiar, and not like he has just seen it once before. He's seen that same truck the last several times on his way home from school. Joseph slows down. He turns onto a side street and pulls over next to the curb. The brown truck follows him. It speeds up, squealing its tires as it races past Joseph. He strains his eyes desperately, trying to make out the driver, but all that he can see as it whizzes by is his own reflection in the black tinted windows. Joseph takes a deep breath. He slowly exhales in relief. "They're going to admit me to a psych ward if I don't cool it. I've got to stop thinking the whole world is out to get me." Joseph shifts his car into first gear and chirps his wheels as he takes off for home.

Minutes later, he arrives at his house. He slows down as he pulls his Mustang into the driveway. The panel garage door begins to automatically open. His foster parents had installed an automatic proximity sensor in his car that triggers the door to open if the vehicle is moving toward it. Once the car is clear of the door and is moving away from it, then the sensor closes the door. One thing that he'll admit about his foster parents, they sure live in a nice house. Okay, it's more than nice. It's really nice. It's like *Lifestyles of the Rich and Famous* nice. His foster parents have loads of money, and they spoil him with all kinds of stuff. Joseph has the best clothes, a nice ride, and all the latest gear for his urban ninja hobby. Sometimes they can be real jerks, but then again, they can be really cool too. Even when they're being nice though, it still isn't the same as having his real parents around. He misses them so much. They had been martyred for being Christians when he was just a little kid. He can remember bits and pieces of it, but most of the horrific event is locked away deep in his subconscious. He can't remember their actual death, even though he was supposedly there.

His new parents don't believe in Jesus. In fact, they are decidedly against the idea and openly speak against Christians. They remark about how stupid people have to be to believe that nonsense or how the world would be a better place without "those Christians" and their narrow-minded doctrines. That certainly is in line with what the government keeps pushing.

What would my foster parents say if they knew that I was going to a Bible study tonight, Joseph wonders. *Oh well. What they don't know…*

The deep roar of the engine disappears as he finally turns the key and pulls it from the ignition. Hopping out of his ride, he gives the car door a solid push. The teen walks up to the entrance to the foyer and tries the handle. As usual, his foster parents have left it unlocked. Joseph strolls into the house. He flings the door closed as he goes through it. The solid wood rectangle slams shut against the frame. Wham! Joseph stops dead in his tracks, cringing from the sound that is still ringing in his ears.

Oops, he thinks.

A low voice comes from the living room. "Joseph. How was school today?" "Dad, is that you?" Joseph pokes his head around the corner of the kitchen, surprised that his foster dad is home.

"Yeah, it's me," he calls back.

Joseph wanders into the living room. His father is sitting on the couch, reading a book.

"What are you doing home so early?" questions Joseph.

"One of the militant groups attacked the government building across the street from my office. They sent us all home, just in case there were more attacks planned. Those idiotic bleeding heart guerillas should all be put in jail or executed. Can't they just live in peace and leave us alone?"

Joseph walks across the polished wood floor and places a hand on the ornate railing at the base of the stairs. His curiosity, however, stops him from going up to his room. He turns, facing his foster dad. "Why would they risk going so far out of the city? Did they take anything?"

Loosening his tie, he peers up from his novel with a cynical look on his face. "You know I can't give you secure intel like that." He slowly shakes his head in disapproval as he turns his attention back down into the pages of his book.

"Sorry, Dad. I was just trying to make conversation. My bad." Joseph's eyes sink to the ground in disappointment. Reaching out, he grabs hold of the newel post. He pats it a couple of times, still looking at the floor. The disheartened look is unmistakable. Reluctantly, he starts to climb the stairs. His foster father glances up at Joseph again. His slow pace has only carried him halfway up the staircase so far.

"They stole some high-powered explosives and a rocket launcher," his dad says, raising his voice.

His father continues to speak while pretending to read his book again. "And I wouldn't be surprised if they used them tomorrow. These gangs just keep coming farther and farther out of the city. Pretty soon they'll be in our backyard."

"Thanks, Dad," he says with genuine gratitude.

His father looks up again, this time offering a smile. "Just keep it to yourself, or they might be hauling me off to jail."

Joseph laughs and treads up the rest of the stairs to his room.

It's Friday night, and the MagiX are getting together at the old water park to practice some tricks. Joseph has been looking forward to this all week. He peels off his backpack and tosses it into the corner by his desk. The bedroom floor is cluttered with sports equipment and clothes. The walls are adorned with pictures—typical of any normal teenager's room. His posters, of course, all consist of people competing in extreme sports. It doesn't matter if it's BMX or skydiving. If it's extreme, then it is worthy to hang on his wall. On the way to his bathroom, he stops at a poster where the edge has begun to curl down. It's a picture of a young man jumping a motorcycle between two buildings. The bike is sitting upside down, caught in the middle of a flip by the camera. He straightens the edge of the thick paper and pushes the tack back in, holding it firmly in place. Joseph steps back and examines it again, surveying his handiwork.

"They'll be making posters of me someday," he mumbles proudly.

Joseph leans over the bathroom counter. He stares into the mirror as he runs his hands across the tips of his hair. It can definitely use some more gel. Joseph pours out some goop in his hand and massages it into his hair with his fingers. As he reshapes the small clumps, he begins to think about what lies in store for him. They're doing something really cool tonight. He can hardly wait. It's going to be so sweet, although it didn't seem to impress Sarah at all when he had told her about it.

Joseph finishes molding his hair. He chuckles at his own image in the mirror. Now that he thinks about it, it's actually kind of cool. Sarah really seems to like him for who he is. She doesn't care about all that other stuff. "That settles it. I'm going to ask her out," he promises himself as he pulls one final clump of hair together.

Joseph runs down the stairs to the dining room. He finds his foster mom and dad already there with supper waiting.

"Thanks, you made my favorite—lasagna."

"I'm just glad you could stop by in time to wolf some down, honey." His foster mother doesn't seem very happy. Joseph looks at his foster dad, who promptly raises his eyebrows as if to say, "Your mom's just having one of those days."

Joseph pulls out a chair across from her and politely sits down. He pretends to dig around in his food with his fork as he says a quick, silent prayer. He barely finishes before shoving a fork full of cheese, noodles, and sauce into his open mouth.

"So what are you doing tonight, Joseph?" his foster mom asks.

He finishes chewing the lasagna before answering her. "Me and the MagiX are going over to the old water park."

His mom slams her fork handle onto the table. "Now, you know I don't like you doing all that dangerous stuff."

"I know. I know. You only worry because you love me. And I appreciate that. I really do. Don't worry about me though; I'll be fine. I promise I'll be careful," Joseph says, waiting to see what her response will be.

His foster mother's face softens. "I know, honey. I just worry about you."

"I know."

Joseph finishes up supper, sprinkling in some light conversation every so often. They discuss the riffraff that are moving into their neighborhood and how the people next door won't keep their dogs off of their lawn. Joseph places his fork and napkin on his plate and gets up from the table. "That was great."

He walks over to his foster mom and kisses her on the head. Then he smiles at his foster dad from across the table. "Take it easy."

"Be back before ten," his dad says sternly. "You know that it's illegal for teenagers to be out past ten-thirty without a pass, and you've been out later then that every weekend for the last month."

"I'll be back by ten, Dad."

"You better be, or we're going to ground you from your car."

Joseph slouches his shoulders and sighs. "I told you—I'll be back by curfew."

"Just be careful," his mom interjects.

"Okay," Joseph yells back as he heads out the door to the garage.

CHAPTER 5

"Why are they always riding me?" he complains.

Joseph starts his car and puts it into reverse. The garage door opens as he slowly backs toward it. Once his car is clear of the door, Joseph speeds out into the bright sunlight. The warm rays beam down on him through the glass. It feels so good on his arm. Joseph lowers his windows as he zips down the tree lined street. He's on his way over to Raedun Silverman's house. Raedun is a friend of Joseph's. They met through the MagiX organization. That's when they found out that they live relatively close to one another. Both of them thought that it was a good idea to just take one car from Raedun's house over to the water park. Raedun is a short and stocky guy with naturally curly, sandy blonde hair. Joseph gets along great with him, most of the time. He has to admit, however, that Raedun can be pretty cocky when he wants to be. That's how he earned the nickname "Bags" from some of the MagiX. They said that he didn't just have a chip on his shoulder. He had the whole bag.

Joseph pulls up to Raedun's house at six o'clock, just as planned. Raedun is already sitting on the stairs in front of his house. He's relaxed and all laid-back. One leg is stretched out down along the stairs, and the other one is bent up toward his chin. His left hand is behind his back, which is keeping him from falling over while still allowing him to strike his pose. When he sees Joseph drive up, he flashes a quick wave with his free hand.

Joseph rolls down his window. "Hey! Don't get too excited about going."

Bags pretends to laugh violently. Then he abruptly stops, giving Joseph a very serious look as if to say, "I'm not amused."

"Just get in," Joseph yells.

He hops up and jogs over to the car, bending down to the passenger side window so that Joseph can hear him. "I wanted to take my car. I just got new wheels."

Joseph grabs the steering wheel and jerks the keys out of the ignition.

"Whatever, man, let's just go."

He leaves his parked car in front of his friend's ranch-style home and hops into Raedun's ride. "Those wheels are really sweet. No wonder you wanted to drive. Where did you get them?" Joseph asks.

"I salvaged them."

"What does that mean?"

"I got them off of one of the parking garage cars in the city," Bags replies, boasting of the feat.

"What?" Joseph yells. "Are you insane? Nobody goes into the city." Joseph turns in disgust toward the window. He watches the blur of houses go by as they drive. "You're going to get killed one of these days."

"I know my limits," Bags replies as he hits the accelerator.

Joseph mouths those same words, mocking his friend. Bags is just plain crazy. There's no denying it. I guess if he wasn't off his rocker, then he wouldn't be Bags. Joseph laughs off the uncomfortableness of the serious moment. "Well, at least we'll make it on time," he chuckles.

When Joseph arrives at the water park, all his friends are there. Twenty-five or thirty of the MagiX are already practicing tricks. Some are running straight up five-foot walls and doing back flips off of the top. Others are leaping over the hoods of cars or balancing on large, abandoned water tubes. Bags revs his motor, cranking the RPMs. He does this several times, showing off the power of his engine. Raedun turns off the car and slips the keys in his pocket, exiting the vehicle first. He runs and jumps onto the back of an unsuspecting friend, who almost falls over from the force. Joseph shakes his head.

"Freak," he jokingly mumbles under his breath as he steps out of the car as well. Joseph is promptly greeted with high fives and a variety of special handshakes from the MagiX, who have come over to welcome him.

The whole group starts migrating across the broken concrete lot. Grass and weeds fill the cracks that spread through the pavement. It's obvious that no one maintains the grounds here anymore. The teens stop in front of a large waterslide where a number of the other MagiX are already standing. As Joseph walks, he turns his attention toward the mountain of twisted pipes and steep slides. The tubes open up over a barren pool, whose water was drained out quite some time ago. Every so often, the pipes are open from the top. They crisscross back and forth underneath one another, disappearing as they intertwine. The butterflies start turning in his stomach as he follows the longest tube with his eyes. It ends abruptly in a hard concrete pit.

"Listen up!" a voice comes up over the crowd. Joseph turns to see John Brennan, the leader of the MagiX, standing on the stairs to the tower. The group of teens becomes silent and crowds around him as he begins to speak again.

"The rules are simple, the fastest one down the tube and up the incline to the end of the pool wins. You can use whatever you want, but remember, that is one hard stop at the bottom."

Joseph looks around at the others standing in the parking lot. He studies the faces of his fellow urban ninjas. Some look confident and excited, while others look like they're about to puke their guts out.

"Let's go!" John bellows out with commanding force. His finger is outstretched toward the stairs of the tower.

Higgy and Ray Ray run to the flight of steps to be first in line. Not Joseph though. He plays it cool. He wants to gauge just how fast the tubes are. The openings in the pipes will give him a good indication of how fast he might get going. He'll be able to watch them and see how quickly they slide through the cylinder. The first victim reaches the top of the huge tower and proudly thrusts his arms into the air.

"*Yeah!*" Higgy screams as he crosses his arms over his head, forming an X. A roar of cheers floats on the breeze high up to where he's standing. Reaching down, he grabs a greased sled and quickly walks forward to the opening of the tube. He studies it for a few seconds, uneasy about the stability of the old structure. Then he rocks his body back and forth, as if he's waiting for the gun to go off in a race. With a burst of energy, Higgy leaps forward into the tube, placing the sled under his body as he jumps. Joseph watches the openings as the sled screams down the tube.

Not very fast, Joseph thinks to himself.

The rumbling starts to get louder near the bottom of the pipe. Finally, the sled flies out of the hole with Higgy still on top of it. It connects with the concrete as sparks fly from the metal underside. The teen holds on for another five feet until it comes skidding to a halt. He jumps to his feet and races up the incline toward the end of the pool. John is waiting at the top. Holding up the stopwatch, he exclaims, "Twenty-eight seconds. That sucked, man." Higgy doubles over with his hands on his knees, panting hard. With a look of defeat, he throws his head back and stares up into the sky.

"Crap!" he gasps. Higgy staggers over to a wall and leans against it before finally plopping down on the ground.

"Next!" John yells.

Ray Ray is the second person in line. He's already moving up the stairs toward the top. Scanning the platform, he takes a quick inventory of the various pieces of equipment that are spread out across the concrete. There are so many things to choose from. He examines another sled that's sitting next to the opening. *This didn't work too well,* he thinks. *Let's see what else we've got here.*

Ray Ray moves on to the mechanics creepers and then to the rollerblades. He passes by some more sleds that have been greased before finally studying the skateboards. He leans over the edge, looking to his friends for encouragement. To his surprise, Bags is already making his way up toward him. Ray Ray can hear the multiple zippers from Raedun's pants clanking against the metal as he climbs up the stairs.

"I guess I better hurry up," Ray Ray nervously whispers. He heads back to the mechanics creeper seat and grabs one. Then placing it in front of the tube, he readies himself for the drop. "This will have to do."

Ray Ray sits down in the middle of the padded board. It begins to roll forward as he slowly scoots toward the front. Carefully, he lies down on his back, like a mechanic preparing to slide under a car. He raises his hands and slams his wrists together, forming an X. The crowd cheers enthusiastically from below, just as they did before. Ray Ray lowers his arms, signaling John to start the stopwatch. His hands grip the sides of the creeper as he shifts his weight forward. The wheels turn slowly at first. Once it is halfway in the tube, however, it rapidly speeds up. His weight rockets him down through the pipe. It's almost as if he's free falling.

Joseph watches the openings again. *That's a little better,* he thinks to himself.

As the teen progresses closer to the end of the pipe, everyone becomes silent. *He's going fast enough all right, but can he stick the landing?* Joseph wonders.

The rumbling grows louder through the hollow cylinder. Then another sound starts hissing from the end of the tube. It's some sort of scraping sound. Then, without warning, the mechanics creeper seat shoots out of the tube. It travels over ten feet in the air before gravity crashes it down onto the hard concrete slab.

"Where is Ray Ray?" Bags pants, looking down from the top of the waterslide.

"There he is!" John shouts, pointing at the tube's opening. Ray Ray slides out of it and rushes up the incline to the finish point.

He must have slowed himself down by jumping off of the creeper seat. Then he just slid down on his back. That's why the board flew out ahead of him, Joseph reasons in his head. That strategy gives him an idea. Now he knows exactly what he's going to do to win this thing.

John clicks the watch and holds it up to reveal the results, even though no one can see it from that far away. "Sixteen Seconds," he yells. The crowd of teens claps, expressing their approval of the performance.

"Next!" John yells again.

Joseph is now starting up the stairs behind Bags, who's already digging through the equipment at the top of the waterslide. Just as Joseph is about twenty feet from the top of the tower, he spots something. It's something in the parking lot. It looks like—like a little girl. He stops climbing and squints his eyes, trying to focus them in the fading light of the day. "They must have been playing tricks on me," Joseph says while he rubs them. When he removes his hands, he does spot something though. There are a number of cars coming in from the entrance. *Something's strange about those cars,* he thinks to himself. *But what is it?*

Then it dawns on him. *They don't have their lights on!* They're coasting into the driveway, one after another. Suddenly, the procession of vehicles cuts on their headlights, blinding the group as they speed into the parking lot. Flashing blue and red lights blast through the darkness, like fireworks against the night sky. The cars swiftly surround the startled MagiX.

"R and Gs!" Joseph yells at the top of his lungs from the stairs. Everyone knows what an "R and G" is. It stands for red and green, and it's the street name for the trooper units. They got that nickname from their government issued red and green uniforms, of course. The teens standing around the pool start to make a break for

Adam's Fall • 61

it but quickly realize that there is nowhere to go. A sea of red and green uniforms pours out of the cars. As they file out, they form a perimeter around the teens and stand at attention. It's almost as if they're waiting for some sort of signal. Then a menacing figure in a long, green trench coat emerges from the lead car.

Joseph's heart stops. He remembers this dark figure. He remembers the uniform, but most of all, he remembers his towering height and massive chest. It's the captain that arrested Daniel at school earlier that day for having a Bible.

"You're all trespassing." The figure turns and looks at John. His cold stare pierces straight through the leader's cool demeanor. John glances around to assess the situation. It looks grim. The captain starts to speak slowly and deliberately. His accent is thick, but Joseph can't place it.

"You all will lay down on the ground with your hands behind your backs. You are all going to the correction center."

Dead silence consumes the group of teens as they look on in disbelief at the poised troopers.

"Very well," the captain says as the cold edges of his mouth start to rise, as if he is amused at the defiance. "Take them!"

The troopers fly into action, coming for the teens with batons drawn. The first trooper reaches John, drawing back his stick to deliver a blow. John lunges forward, letting the stopwatch fall as he positions his body under the trooper's center of gravity and throws him over his back. The trooper crashes to the pavement before the stopwatch lands at his feet. As the second trooper arrives, John sweeps his leg in one swift motion that knocks the surprised trooper to the ground.

The R and Gs are intermingled with the MagiX now. Batons fly, cracking arms and backs, while the teens push forward with a flurry of dodges, roundhouse kicks, and punches. Seeing what's happening, Bags grabs one of the skateboards and places it under his back. He scoots forward and drops down into the tube. Joseph starts sprinting up the stairs. When he arrives at the top, he just barely catches a glimpse of something as it passes through one of the half open sections. It's Raedun flying down the spiraling pipe.

Joseph moves his attention to the bottom of the waterslide, watching for Bags to emerge. The skateboard shoots out of the tube with tremendous speed. It levels R and Gs as it crashes into a group of them. Bags hops out of the tube. The dazed and surprised troopers can't react fast enough. He sprints up the incline, and Joseph loses sight of him as he plunges into the sea of MagiX and troopers.

"They're coming out of the tube!" a trooper shouts as he helps up some of his comrades who have been knocked down. "Stay clear of the tube. Wait for one of the teenagers to come out of it, and then go after him." A group of angry troopers move away from the opening and wait for Joseph to come sliding out.

Down this waterslide is the only way out of this, Joseph thinks to himself. He quickly finishes lacing up the rollerblades that he has pulled on. Without hesitating, he grabs a skateboard. He places the skateboard under his back and propels himself forward. The pitch black of the hole engulfs him as he's sucked downward. His breath leaves him, still somewhere in the tube behind him. Joseph plummets straight down the shaft. A tight turn in the cylinder sends his skateboard up the wall, but he still hangs on. The wind whips at his face and hair as he flies around the corners. Joseph can feel his speed building as he takes another turn. The periodic openings provide flashes of light as he flies past them.

That was the fifth turn, Joseph reminds himself. *After this straight section is the concrete pit. This is where all the others must have jumped off.* Joseph sees a light—the end of the tunnel. The light grows exponentially larger as he races toward it. His heart feels like it is going to explode. "This is it," he gasps.

Joseph rockets out of the tube, still lying on the skateboard. Time seems to suspend as the troopers look up in amazement. Joseph uses the momentum to bend the top of his body upright. With his hands, he pushes the board down and out from under him. He hangs in the air, frozen in time. The only thing moving is the ground that's rushing toward him. He clenches his teeth, preparing for the impact. Joseph tilts his rollerblades to match the incline, bending his knees just as he connects with the concrete. Time blurs forward, trying to catch up with the previous few lost seconds. He can barely make out the shapes of people as he tries to keep his balance.

The force continues to hurl Joseph up the incline and past the remaining troopers. As he reaches the top of the pool, he uses the lip as a ramp to jump into the air. Joseph straightens his body out. He can see the battle raging below him. His arms extend out in front of his head, reaching for freedom. Sailing over the crowd of troopers and MagiX, he just barely misses them. Joseph curls his body into a ball, channeling his forward momentum into a roll. He hits the ground hard and tumbles forward several times before stopping facedown on the concrete. The teen lies there, trying to regain his composure. He moans as he crawls to his knees, his body still shaking from the landing.

Joseph looks up to see a fat trooper grab John from the back. He locks his hands around John's chest and squeezes hard. John gasps for air. Two more troopers advance on him with sticks drawn. The taller of the two swings hard at his head in a downward motion. John anticipates where the strike will land. He looks down at the grizzly hands that are squeezing the life out of him. John grabs the trooper's thumb. He bends it back hard toward the R and Gs wrist. The Trooper releases his grip, caving to the extreme pressure. At the same time, John ducks to the right. The trooper's thumb snaps as John jerks down hard on the front of the red and green uniform, pulling his captor directly into the downward blow of the taller trooper. *Crack!* The stick strikes the pudgy man squarely on the head, knocking him out. John thrusts the fat, limp body of the unconscious man on to another trooper, stopping his advance.

Now free, he strikes the taller man in the throat and follows up with a fist to his jaw. The trooper falls to his knees and drops his baton, struggling to breathe. John snatches the stick off the ground and springs off the back of the kneeling trooper in one swift motion. As he descends, he swings the baton hard and catches yet another trooper off guard. The armed man tries to dodge the swing, but it is too late. John lands on the ground with the baton still in his hand, just before the trooper's body falls onto the concrete.

Joseph starts to move forward to help his friends when he comes face-to-face with the giant. It's the captain. He appears to be headed straight for John.

He should be able to take that trooper, no problem, Joseph reassures himself.

John sees the massive man coming and sets his feet in a fighting stance. The captain seems unfazed. He simply continues his slow, deliberate strides. His lifeless expression shows no sign of fear, only determination. John lunges forward and leaps off of a tube into the air, driving his leg into the side of the captain's face. The captain's head whips around from the force, but his feet stay firmly planted. John swings the baton at his head, but the captain catches it mid-swing and rips it from his hand. Without missing a step, John throws an uppercut at his enemy's head. The captain, however, swings his arm down, breaking the punch before it even starts. He grabs John by the shirt and lifts him up with one arm. Joseph watches on in disbelief.

"Impossible," Joseph utters to himself.

Ray Ray runs up behind the captain, wielding another one of the troopers' batons. Still holding John in the air with one hand, he drives his other hand backward into Ray Ray's chest. Ray Ray flies back several feet, landing on his back. The captain tosses John up like a small child. He remains motionless for a split second, calculating where to direct his blow. Then he spins around and delivers a roundhouse kick to John's side in midair. The force knocks the breath out of him. He lets out a horrible moan as his body flies over the crowd of people and into the empty swimming pool.

Joseph is paralyzed. He doesn't believe what he has just witnessed. His confidence turns to fear as he realizes that there's nothing that he can do for his friends. John is the best fighter out of all the MagiX, and the captain obliterated him without even breaking a sweat. He has super human strength—even inhuman strength. As his body catches up with his mind, Joseph turns toward the exit. He races out of the parking lot on his rollerblades and heads back toward his house. As he speeds down a small neighborhood street, he looks down at his watch. "There's no way I'm going to make it home by curfew. I can't take the highway. The troopers will be patrolling there. My parents are going to ground me for sure!"

It's already nine o'clock, and there's no daylight left. Joseph knows that he can't go home without his car. He'll have to go back to Raedun's house and pick it up. He wonders if Bags has been arrested too or if he made it out okay. Joseph coasts down the street to his friend's house at 10:05 p.m. As his car comes into view, he catches the taillights of a dark-colored truck pulling out of the driveway. It's gone before he can see who's inside. To his surprise, Bags is already home. *How in the world did he make it here already?* Joseph ponders as he approaches the house. He skates up to the porch where his friend is sitting.

"How the heck did you beat me back?" Joseph blurts out.

"Some dude gave me a ride on the highway," he responds nonchalantly.

"I can't believe what just happened at the water park," Joseph says, shaking his head.

He glances up at Bags, who doesn't seem upset at all.

"Aren't you even a little pissed off at those stupid troopers?"

"Not really," Bags coolly replies. "Survival of the fittest, bro." He chuckles and smacks Joseph on the back.

"Right. Whatever, man. I'm out of here." Joseph turns and skates over to his car, which is still parked on the right side of Raedun's driveway. He opens his door and collapses down onto the driver seat. Joseph forcefully unlaces his rollerblades and throws them into the passenger seat. Bags jogs up to his window. Joseph, who is obviously upset, slams the door shut. Raedun takes a step backward, caught off guard by Joseph's brash attitude. He bends down to talk to him through the open window.

"Did Sarah call off the Bible study?" he asks.

"No. Why would she?"

"Because Daniel got busted for having that red Bible in his backpack."

Joseph, who had been ignoring his friend for the most part, turns and glares at Raedun. He stares directly into his eyes. He doesn't say a word. Joseph doesn't even blink.

"What did I say?" Bags seems puzzled by Joseph's reaction.

"How did you know the Bible was red?" Joseph asks with a cynical look on his face.

Raedun searches for words, clearly not expecting the line of questioning. "Just what are you saying, man?"

"I'm not saying anything. I just want to know how you knew what color the Bible was."

"I can't believe we're playing twenty questions over this. The only Bibles that I've ever seen are the ones you have, and what color are they, genius?" Bags studies Joseph's face. He still doesn't look convinced. "Look, for all I know, those Bibles could have been purple. I didn't know there were different colored ones. Do you think I'm a Bible spy now? You got me, man. I give up."

Joseph faces the windshield again, staring off into the distance. He glances back at Raedun, analyzing his facial expressions. His eyes don't offer even a hint that he might be lying. Joseph shakes his head and forces a smile across his distressed face. "I've just had a hard night. I'll catch you later."

Joseph shifts into reverse and starts to back up.

"I didn't mean what I said about the survival of the fittest and all. You know I was just kidding around. I'm just as stressed as you are, and they're my friends too. I just joke about things instead of having to deal with them." Bags tries to justify his actions as he follows the car down the driveway.

"I know," Joseph replies.

Raedun stops walking and watches the car pull out of his driveway. The tires peel out as the car zooms away and into the night.

CHAPTER 6

Joseph rolls into the driveway and cuts the engine as he coasts into the garage. He looks down at the clock. 10:37. Joseph opens his door and steps out quietly onto the concrete floor. He lifts the car handle and softly pushes his door closed, following it up with a hard nudge to engage the latch. Standing in the darkness of the cool room, he tries to discern if there are any voices coming from within the house. He tiptoes up the wood stairs and places an ear to the door. Still nothing. Turning the handle slowly, he cracks it open and peers into the dimly lit room.

"All clear on the first floor," he says under his breath.

Joseph moves quietly through the living room. His steps are uneasy, and he winces with every squeak in the floor. When he is just about all the way to the staircase, he hears something. Spinning around, he sees … nothing. It's still just an empty room with no signs of life. Joseph stands there for a second, listening intently. The only audible sound is the rapid clicking of a clock in the kitchen. He can't believe that his parents didn't wait up for him. "They must have had a little too much wine tonight," Joseph says to himself, trying to explain away the unusual behavior.

Walking a little easier, he climbs the staircase to the second level of the house. He enters into his bedroom and closes the door behind him. *I wonder what happened to my friends,* he thinks. Joseph undresses down to his boxers and hops into his bed.

"Dear Father. Please, oh please, help my friends. Protect them if they're out there, still trying to get home. Please strengthen the ones that weren't able to escape. I pray that you would heal them and give them peace to endure whatever is in store for them. Please forgive me for falling so much and for not doing the things that I know I should. Please allow me to share the gift of your Son with others. Please strengthen me so that I can stand when I need to but so that you are glorified. Please forgive people that have hurt me, and please allow me to be an example to them. Talk to them. Change their hearts, and change their lives. Show them your grace and mercy, like you do every day for me. I ask these things in Jesus' name. Amen."

Lying on his back, Joseph opens his eyes and stares blankly at the ceiling. He replays the events of the day over and over again in his head. How the heck did the captain know that the MagiX would be at the water park anyway? No one lives around there. There's no way that it can be a coincidence. No one ever goes out there. Someone must have told them. But who would do that? Joseph thinks to himself. All of the MagiX hate the R and Gs. At least he knows it wasn't John. Man, he got it bad. Joseph wonders if he got out okay. He had never seen someone throw people around like that. His thoughts swirl around in his head as he closes his eyes. Soon, dreams replace conscious thought. But not just any dreams—these are particular dreams that Joseph has quite often. These are more dreams from his childhood, or more accurately, they are nightmares.

Joseph can hear muffled voices. The sun is shining brightly, and the breeze is cool on his face. Distorted objects and blurred lines take shape. He can see buildings now and people crowded around him. The voices become a little clearer. He can hear a man and a woman yelling over the commotion of a crowd. Joseph can see them now. It's his father and mother. They're preaching on a street corner with a large group gathered around them.

His mother looks down and smiles at him. His father is saying something about Jesus and love. His face is beaming with kindness and sincere compassion. He also glances down at Joseph and sneaks a gentle wink before continuing to preach. His words echo out over the sea of faces, but to Joseph, it's still somehow muffled. He strains to hear what his father is saying.

Please not again, Joseph thinks. On some subconscious level, he realizes that he's in a dream. He can't stop it though. It's already started. A hazy fog materializes, swirling through the crowd. The cloud surrounds him and engulfs the onlookers. A group of armed men dressed in red and green military uniforms break through the fog. They push the people who have gathered away from Joseph and his parents. The men seize the couple. Two troopers hold Joseph's parents, placing their arms behind them. The R and Gs force the couple to their knees. Another trooper picks up the little boy and drags him through the multitude of people and away from his parents. Joseph screams, kicking and fighting to break away from the man.

He yells for his parents. "Mommy. Daddy!" No matter how hard he tries, however, he can't escape the man's grasp. The trooper turns around and stands the boy up. He grabs him by the back of the shirt and bends Joseph's arm up and around behind his back. The boy desperately tries to break free, but he isn't strong enough.

A dark figure walks up through the masses. Joseph struggles to see him, but the group of people gathered around is in his way. The figure stops walking when he reaches Joseph's parents. He pulls out his weapon, without hesitation, and fires twice. Joseph's point of view changes abruptly, and he is now an onlooker in the crowd. He sees himself—the small, frightened boy fighting to escape from the trooper's grasp. Tears are streaming down his face as he blindly kicks and punches at his captor. He's screaming *"No!"* over and over, but Joseph only hears a faint plea. It's almost as if he's yelling from deep within a cave. The boy finally stops fighting against the trooper, his body collapsing from exhaustion.

"Mom! Dad!" he cries in one last act of desperation.

The dark figure looks over at Joseph. He makes the connection now. The menacing figure turns and walks slowly up to the boy. Joseph is now back in the trooper's clutches. The man stops in front of him. His face is out of focus. The only thing visible is a pitch-black abyss. As Joseph's eyes adjust, he discovers that he's looking down the barrel of a gun. He cringes and closes his eyes.

From behind him, he hears one of the troopers say, "Shooting a boy might start a riot, sir." Joseph's heart stops as he listens for the reply.

The dark figure responds, "Make sure his new foster parents rid him of this Christian foolishness."

The words pierce Joseph through his very soul. Anger builds inside of him until he can't contain the words any longer. He opens his eyes and blurts out the culmination of his rage. "I'll kill you," he says, clenching his teeth. Hatred pours from his eyes.

"And teach him to respect the authority of the law," the dark figure adds. With one swift backhand motion, he cracks the boy over the right side of his head with the gun. The boy's eyesight fails as he falls over onto the ground.

CHAPTER 7

Joseph abruptly awakes in a sweat. His eyes are wide open and fully dilated. He stays like that for several seconds, panting hard. His bedroom comes into focus. Realizing where he is, he collapses back into his pillow. Joseph rubs his eyes and looks over at the angry red numbers on his digital clock. It's eight in the morning. Stretching his arms over his head, he lets out a loud yawn.

"I guess it's time to get up," he says as he sits up in his bed. Joseph slips out from under the covers and staggers over to the shower. He lets the water warm up before sliding behind the curtain. Allowing the hot water to run over his head, he tries to wash away the horrible dream. Joseph just stands there for quite a while. Finally, he raises his arm. His hand feels for the shower handle, squeaking it closed with deliberate and forceful turns. The water slows to a drip. Joseph's head is down, and his eyes are still closed. His hand still hangs on the handle as he brushes his wet hair back from his eyes with his other hand. He steps out of the shower and dries off with a towel, which he then nonchalantly tosses on top of the clothes hamper as he passes through the doorway into his bedroom.

He shuffles over to a very ornate dresser. Digging around, he pulls some khaki pants out. As he reaches in to grab his T-shirt as well, he uncovers the edge of a red Bible.

"Tonight's the Bible study," he whispers. A feeling of joy overtakes his melancholy disposition, evaporating it into the air. Even with everything that's happening to him, he still has that to look forward to. That isn't until later tonight though. Today is Saturday. That means H2H. H2H stands for "Hand-to-Hand" combat. It's like a 3-D video game, only much more advanced. Unlike the cities that are still very primitive, the urban areas thrive with the newest technologies from China. The game is based around fighting in different virtual landscapes. From one to four people can play at the same time, either against each other or against the computer program.

Each person wears a helmet equipped with a 3-D viewing screen. They also put on specially designed gloves that interact with the computer system. A computer tracks the player's movements and replicates them in the game. The players also have protective kneepads, arm pads, and a body suit. The pads and the suit are equipped with air bags inside of them. This means that panels pop out against the player's skin, which simulates a blow to the chest, head, or other area. The player can also feel when they successfully block a punch or kick. They accomplish this by activating the air pad. Once activated, it pops out against the area of the body where they block the attack. In addition, the gloves have multiple buttons that support movement or weapons firing.

The players stand on a raised floor panel made up of multiple rollers. This enables them to walk or run in place. They have a full range of motion to move backward, forward, or sideways. Whenever the rollers move, the computer picks up those movements and transfers them back into the game. To simultaneously keep them from falling and from gaining traction on the rollers, each player is suspended from the ceiling by a harness and two cables. The harness is then fastened around the player's chest and shoulders. The cables are attached to the top of each shoulder strap, which supports the player's full weight. It takes a lot of practice for the fighters to learn how to move while suspended in air.

One of the buttons on each glove is used to raise or lower a corresponding cable. If the player wants to duck to the right, then they depress a button on the right-hand glove. This gives them slack in the cables that are attached to the shoulders, which allows the player to duck to the right. The longer the button is held down, the more slack is given. If the player needs to stand up, they depress the button on the left glove, and the cables rise. Jumping works in a similar manner. The player clicks the right button twice in rapid succession. This releases the maximum amount of slack. The player then clicks the left button the same way, which lifts them off of the ground and into the air for several seconds. Advanced players master special moves as well by unlocking secret combinations with the buttons on the glove.

Later today, he's scheduled to fight Zaphin at the Pit. That's their nickname for the virtual fighting arena. Zaphin is a pro at H2H. He slaughtered Joseph during their first match. It isn't that Joseph was a horrible player at the time. Zaphin was just that much better, which is all it took to get Joseph hooked. He's so competitive that he bought a membership to the Pit and practiced for weeks on end until he mastered several fighting styles. They had played every Saturday since then, and Zaphin always won. That was before Joseph found the dikaios breastplate.

Each player has to journey out on quests to earn new weapons or learn new skills in the game. The dikaios breastplate is a secret artifact that he unlocked from a city in the game called Kol. It's extremely rare and hard to find. In fact, no one can purchase or earn it. It can only be given by the unseen king of Kol. As far as Joseph knows, no one has ever met the king. Everyone, however, has heard of his legend and the powerful artifact hidden with him. One of his friends told him of a rumor that he had heard. It was a story of a trial, which was a test of sorts that no one had been able to pass. The tale went that the unseen king had a son who stood at the edge of a great precipice. He guards the entrance of the only bridge across the large chasm to the castle of Kol. It's said that this is where the king can be found. The more his friend told him about Kol, the more he felt compelled to go there.

Joseph scheduled scouting time at the H2H arena that very next Saturday to see if he could find this prince. He didn't have to search for long before he started seeing signs of the king's good works. The kingdom was even more majestic than Joseph had imagined.

He questioned several of the computer-generated people who lived there. Everyone he spoke with sung the good king's praises. The townspeople told him of how he rules. He is a just king and one of unfathomable love. They confirmed that the only way to reach the king of Kol is through his son, the prince. When he asked them, the people were glad to tell him where to find the castle. After traveling a very short distance, Joseph could see the multicolored stone towers rising high above the road. Pristine gold poles topped the pure white rooftops. A strange flag adorned the tallest tower, the two tails of which lapped at the wispy clouds as they passed by. It was some sort of red, white, and gold animal lying against a baby blue background.

The castle seemed to float in the middle of a bottomless pit. As he came closer, he could see someone standing at the entrance to a wide bridge, just as his friend had said. The man wasn't at all what Joseph was expecting. His body wasn't clad in armor. Instead, the man was wearing a white robe that was tied at the waist with a thin brown strap. He didn't have a large sword or a long spear. In fact, he didn't have a weapon at all. When he finally arrived at the bridge, he could make out the shape of the beast on the flag. It had the head of a lion, the body of a lamb, and great white wings, like a giant dove. On top of the animal's head sat a golden-colored crown. The animal was colored red, except for the wings. They were pure white. He brought his attention back down to the man in front of him. Joseph studied the prince's face. It was so peaceful. There wasn't a hint of anger or tension in it. Joseph was confused. He had expected some sort of confrontation. Was it a trick? As he peered across the great expanse, he could now see that the bottom of the pit was filled with molten lava. Fire exploded from the smoldering red lake. Smoke rose continuously from its bowels.

"Are you the prince of Kol?" Joseph asked, turning his attention back toward the man.

"I am the king's son," he answered. "What brings you here?"

His voice was soothing—almost hypnotic. Joseph couldn't help but to feel at ease around this man.

"I want to complete the trial so that I can see the king," Joseph said.

"You will be given a chance in time. First, please allow me to tell you a story."

Joseph nodded his head in agreement. The prince folded his hands in front of him as he began.

"In the beginning, it was only my father the king, the birdman, and I. The birdman is named Parakletos, and he is just as much a part of the family as I. One day, we all decided that it would be good to invite a couple to live with us in the castle. Therefore, the first two people in this realm lived with the three of us across this chasm. At that time, however, the pit you see before you was not here. The couple had fellowship with the three of us and enjoyed our company. They had all that they could ever ask for. The king provided lavish meals and only the finest accommodations. There was an enemy to the king, however. It was a red dragon named Belial. Belial was once one of the king's most loyal subjects. In a time long passed, he too had lived with us in the castle. Although they were good friends, the dragon secretly envied the king's position and power. He let it fester and boil up within him, until one day, he turned on his king. Belial's talons and fire raged against the mighty king, but the dragon was no match for the supreme ruler. That day, the king banished Belial from the castle.

"And it came to pass that one day, this mischievous red dragon secretly flew up to see the people in the castle. He could not enter it without the king's permission, so he swooped up to one of the windows in the tower where the couple lived. Its silver tongue wove a tale of delicious foods and lush gardens beyond the reaches of the castle walls. Belial painted a picture for them of the perfect paradise that awaited them. This was not true, of course, and the dragon knew it. For outside of the walls and deep inside the earth lived a terrifying apparition. The king had already told the couple of this phantom and that he would not protect them from the death spirit if they traveled beyond the castle walls. Therefore, the couple was to stay inside the protective barrier with the king. Death could not capture them there. The dragon's sly words, however, tricked them. Fire spewed from his ferocious mouth as he blasphemed the king. Belial said that the ruler had lied because he didn't want them to know everything about the kingdom. The red dragon told them that if they knew what the king knew, they would be just as powerful.

"So the couple ventured out to find the things that the dragon had spoken of. As they soon discovered, though, the dragon was an ally of the death spirit. When they treaded across the grass, a great rumbling overtook them. The ground shook and trembled underneath their feet. Suddenly, the earth collapsed behind them. They fled away from the castle in terror. Slabs of ground rose up and overturned on themselves, collapsing into what seemed like nothingness. The great hole in the ground encircled the castle. Out from the abyss rose the death spirit, freed from his earthen tomb. The couple screamed as they witnessed this horrifying apparition fly out over the land that still stood. It was a dark being with luminous green eyes. Its formless body floated just above the ground. The black cloak appearing as a shadow that faded into its surroundings. A gnarled skeleton smile hissed from within its ominous cloth hood. The couple scrambled away from it, breaking for the trees. The death spirit chased them across the solid ground. Just before they made it to where you stand now, it struck at them. The couple narrowly escaped. As it slammed into the grass behind their feet, another circle of ground fell away, leaving only a great pit. That is what you see before you."

Joseph gazed upon the landscape. It almost looked like a target used for arrow practice, only made out of earth. The bull's-eye was where the castle sat, a fat pillar of ground holding it up. The ring around the bull's-eye was a deep and wide crevice in the earth. The next ring was another strip of ground that encircled the hole. Outside of that ring was another deep crevice in the ground, and on the outside of that ring was where Joseph was standing.

The prince continued, "And the castle you see on the ground in the center is where my father lives.

"Over time, the townspeople multiplied in the new land. With all the new people, the king decided to give them laws to protect them. Throughout the kingdom, they were to live by these rules, even though they were no longer in the castle. He sent Parakletos, his beautiful white man bird, to fly across the chasm. The bird spirit built a bridge from the town to the middle ledge, but the second chasm was too great to build a bridge between. Although there was no bridge going all the way to the castle, the new bridge allowed people to travel to what was called the *Circle of Plenty*. That is the first ring of ground that you see. There, fruits and water were abundant, and life was much easier than where the townspeople had been. Many of them had tried to travel back to the Circle of Plenty, but the death spirit waited for them on the bridge. It didn't matter who tried, no one could escape the being clothed in shadows. When someone ventured to cross the bridge, the black apparition would appear. If the person had tried to obey the laws of the kingdom, death allowed them to pass to the Circle of Plenty. If the person disregarded the king's laws, however, death would rip them from the bridge and drop them into the fire.

"The king, Parakletos, and I were saddened greatly by what we witnessed. The king wanted to give the people who had tried to follow his laws a second chance. He wanted them to be with him in the castle."

The prince pauses, a troubled look crinkling his brow.

"The only way for me to reach them was to allow death to take me. I stood on the side of the expanse, and the horrible apparition whisked me away from the castle and across to the Circle of Plenty. His sharp, boney fingers dug into my flesh and ripped it as he grabbed me. The pain was so great that I passed out as a dead man. When it dropped me on the Circle of Plenty, I had my senses about me once more. The people there were so excited to see me. They welcomed me with open arms. As I embraced them, I could hear the cries from the people who had been thrown into the lava far below. They pleaded with me to save them, but they had already made their choice. There was nothing that I could do for them. Unbeknownst to the Belial and the death spirit, however, I had secured a rope to my leg. That rope was tied to a bridge that was piled outside of the castle gates and bound to the very foundation of it. I pulled the rope, dragging a bridge across the great expanse from the castle and to the Circle of Plenty. I secured it into the ground and led the people across it. Death tried to stop me from returning to the castle, but I defeated it myself."

The prince opens his hands with a welcoming gesture. "I now stand at the opening of the first bridge. The great death spirit still remains. That is whom you must face. That is the trial you must pass if you wish to see the king."

"I'm ready," Joseph said.

Joseph put one foot out onto the bridge constructed of wood and rope. The sound of many cries came up from the pit as the death spirit appeared.

The prince stretched his hand out toward the ghoulish being. "Behold your opponent. How will you defeat him?"

Joseph recoils. It's even more hideous then he had imagined. The being's glowing green eyes stare right through Joseph. The death spirit's formless body stretches over the bridge. His mouth opens.

A plume of gray vapor puffs out from between his boney teeth, like the snorting breath that escapes a horse's nostrils on a cold day. How could anyone defeat something like that? He knew that no one had killed this monster because no one had been given the dikaios breastplate. Joseph panics. He turns to the prince.

Why did he tell me that story? he thinks to himself. *The answer has to be there.*

Instead of fighting the phantom, he drops his weapon. Joseph falls to his knees before the prince. He doesn't look up but keeps his head to the ground as he speaks.

"Save me, prince, I know it's within your power."

The prince's eyes brighten, and a joyous look overtakes him. "Will you follow me?"

"Yes, I will."

The prince reached down and grabbed hold of Joseph's arm, raising him to his feet. The king's son placed his hand on the teen's shoulder. He was confident yet meek in spirit at the same time. As they began to walk across the bridge, the death spirit circled around them like a vulture waiting for its prey to collapse. Just as a caged lion intently watches passersby on the other side of a thick slab of glass so too the apparition studied the prince and his guest.

After they crossed through the Circle of Plenty, the prince stopped. He turned to Joseph. His voice was still soothing—still calm.

"Do you believe that I alone made this way back to my father, the king?" the prince asks.

"Yes."

"Do you have faith that I will save you from the death spirit and bring you to the castle to be with my father?"

"Yes."

The prince raised his head toward the shadow monster.

"Be gone, for he is mine!" he commanded.

He hadn't even finished bellowing the words before the apparition descended back down into the pit, leaving them alone at the entrance to the second bridge.

Joseph could see the splendor of the castle as they made their way farther across the expanse. It was more beautiful than any that he had ever seen before.

The gates before them were surrounded by what appeared to be thick pearl walls. In fact, all of the walls seemed to be made out of huge solid pieces of precious jewels. "Who requests entry into the castle?" thundered a voice from within.

"It is I, father, your son," the prince answered.

A loud popping noise echoed through the chamber as the gates swung open. Joseph followed the prince into the castle, down a street made out of solid gold. Finally, they came to a great room. At the end of it sat the king himself.

"You must stay here," the prince instructed Joseph.

He nodded his head while the prince continued up to the right hand side of the king's throne.

"This is my father, the king of Kol," the prince announced.

"And what is it that you have come for?" the king's voice was so commanding that Joseph could hardly answer.

"I...that is...I hear...umm. I hear that you have a...uh—"

The king interrupted him. "Since you have followed my son and trusted in him, I would like to give you a present."

The king motioned to Parakletos. The birdman disappeared into a doorway. After several seconds, he emerged once again. His wings were wrapped in front of his body, cradling something. Joseph looked on with great anticipation as Parakletos gracefully walked down the long great hall, appearing to glide across the stone floor. He stopped in front of him, his wings still hiding something. Then he stretched his wings out and back over his head, revealing the dikaios breastplate. The birdman gave the artifact to Joseph. He thanked the king, the prince, and Parakletos profusely before exiting the game. The stories were true. The breastplate could not be earned or purchased. It could only be given. Only through the prince was he able to come before the mighty king and receive the breastplate.

Joseph could hardly wait until his next scheduled training time at the H2H arena. When the time finally arrived, the first thing that he did was equip the new item. He found that attached to the breastplate, there was a very powerful weapon. It's called the spirit sword. This sword is so sharp that it can cut through titanium without even dulling the blade. The handle at the base of the spirit sword is a broad one. It holds the appearance of two black metal cylinders attached in the middle. Above the handle, the two hand guards jut out and away from the blade. The hand guards are adorned with contoured grips. On the tops of each of the grips there are round circles that house thin slivers of metal that curve back and away from the blade.

The sword is a very deadly weapon, but there is yet another use for it. The spirit sword also morphs into two guns. The person wielding it simply grasps each of the two hand guards and pushes downward. As the guards rotate toward each other, the spring-loaded blade collapses in on itself. It disappears into a six-inch silver metal sleeve, which is located just above the hand guards and in between the metal circles. This hides it completely. The metal circles hold the triggers and rotate with the hand guards. Once the blade is fully collapsed, it triggers a mechanism that separates the two hand guards. At the same time, the handle of the sword comes apart, which houses the barrels of two separate guns. The collapsed blade rests on top of the right hand guard. Now all the person needs to do is to spin the guns in their hand so that the barrels are facing forward.

It sounded very complicated to Joseph when he first received the weapon. He practiced with it relentlessly, ensuring that Zaphin didn't find out about his new toy. As he became more adept at using it, he was able to transform the spirit sword into a gun with two swift motions. The reason that he needs the guns so desperately has to do with his opponent's defenses. Zaphin has a shield that can stop a single weapon attack, but if Joseph can shoot him with both guns at the same time, it might penetrate his shields.

"Zaphin's going down," Joseph reassures himself as he opens the door to his bedroom and darts down the stairs. His parents are both sitting on the couch waiting for him. Joseph stops on the landing at the bottom of the stairs. He knows that look. They must have heard him when he came home late last night.

"Big plans today, Joseph?" his mother asks snidely.

"You know, just headed down to the Pit for some H2H action."

"I hope you have a ride, young man," his dad replies.

Joseph's smile melts from his face. His shoulders drop, sagging toward the ground.

"Are you kidding me? I was only like less than an hour late!" he protests.

"We told you what was going to happen, Joseph. You made your choice. You decided to stay out past curfew."

"I—" Joseph starts to explain, but he's cut short by his mother.

"There are no excuses. You're grounded from your car for a month."

"A whole month? That's ridiculous," Joseph snorts at his parents. "You two don't understand anything." Joseph walks past them and out the door.

"Keep it up, mister, and you won't be going out at all," his mother yells over her shoulder, just before Joseph slams the front door closed.

The morning air outside seems colder today. He's greeted by a strong, frigid breeze that blasts against his face. *It won't be long before I'll have to start wearing a jacket,* Joseph thinks to himself. He pauses for a second, reflecting upon what just happened. *Especially if I'm going to have to walk everywhere.*

Joseph pulls out his cell phone and dials up Zaphin's number. The phone rings several times before Zaphin finally picks it up.

"Hello?"

"Hey. What's up, Zaphin?"

"Just eating some cereal. You know, the breakfast of champions."

"Don't get ahead of yourself," Joseph shoots back. "I think there'll be a new champ in town after today."

Zaphin laughs out loud. "Keep dreamin,' rookie."

"I need a favor, Zaphin."

"So the man who has everything needs a favor, huh? Go for it."

"I need a ride to the Pit today. My parents grounded me for being out past curfew."

"What? Did chess club run over?"

"Very funny. I was out with the MagiX tearing up the water park when the R and Gs showed up. They totally annihilated most of the group, including John."

"Wasn't John like Bruce Lee himself or something?"

"Yeah. I thought he was unstoppable, but there was this one captain with the R and Gs that took him out without even breaking a sweat."

"No kidding."

"Straight up." Joseph pauses for a moment, giving Zaphin a chance to ask more questions. He doesn't say a word.

"Anyway, I rode with one of my friends to the park. Since we all got busted up, I had to blade all the way home. My parents must have been up when I got there, because this morning, they grounded me for breaking curfew."

"That sucks," Zaphin replies. "So what time did you want me to pick you up?"

"How about in an hour?"

"Sounds good to me. See you then." Zaphin hangs up the phone before Joseph can thank him.

He closes his cell phone and slips it into the top pocket of his khaki pants. He looks down the left side of the street to the end of the block. Then he looks down the right side of the street, allowing his gaze to travel as far as he can see. It's still so hard to get used to. Saturday mornings used to bring the whole neighborhood to life. The yards would bustle with the sound of children playing tag or football. The streets were filled with kids riding their bikes and walking. Families actually used to do things together outside, but all that stopped when the violence started. Joseph wonders if life will ever be the same or if that time had passed, like the spectacular colors of a sunset that slowly fade into night. After his generation is gone, who would even know the difference? It seems like only yesterday that Joseph was a little boy, playing in the front yard with his mother and father. They were a real family then, not like now. Why can't he be with his real mother and father? It just isn't fair. His life up to this point has gone by so quickly. He weighs the balance of his life in comparison to the time that has already passed. How quickly will the rest of his life go by? *Our lives really are like vapors disappearing into the wind,* he thinks to himself.

Joseph turns and walks back up to his house. He sits down hard on the stairs, feeling sufficiently bored and depressed. He pulls the cell phone out from the pocket of his khaki pants again and flips it open. Joseph starts thumbing through his long list of contacts. He scrolls down until he comes to the name *Sarah*. He puts his finger over the send button, but he quickly flips his phone closed instead. "Snap out of it," Joseph whispers to himself as he shakes his head. He lies back on the stairs and looks up to the sky. A canvas of brilliant blue reaches out across the heavens. Fluffy white clouds glide slowly across it. "Please give me strength today, Father," he asks, still staring straight up into that blue abyss. Joseph sits there for quite some time, just relaxing and enjoying the view. He is roused from his peaceful rest by the sound of a car pulling up.

    He stands up to get a better look over the porch rail. It's Zaphin. Joseph grins with anticipation. He hops over the railing and off of the porch in a single bound. Casually, he jogs up to Zaphin's car and pulls on the door handle. As soon as the door swings open, music explodes from the vehicle. Zaphin always listens to hard rock, and he likes it loud. Joseph sits down in the seat and slams the door shut. Zaphin looks over at him, his eyes hidden by a pair of stylish sunglasses. He displays a thin smile from the corner of his mouth. Joseph smiles back and gives a slight nod of approval to his friend. Then he turns and gazes out the window. His foster parents still haven't come outside. A weight seems to lift off of his shoulders as the car pulls away from his house. He watches it in his side mirror. It shrinks into the distance until it is a small speck. When they turn a corner, it disappears completely out of view.

CHAPTER 8

Zaphin and Joseph arrive at the Pit. They pull into the entrance to an underground parking lot. Three levels above, a crowd of teenagers have already started to gather at the top of the Pit. That's where the restaurant is. It's undeniably the place to hang out. Inside, the whole area is set up like an arena. There are several gigantic viewing screens in the center of the restaurant. Each one of them shows a live game feed of the H2H challenge currently being played. The floor of the restaurant is built on an incline. It gradually rises from the center where the screens are before hitting its highest point at the edge of the outside wall. Several levels are cut into the gradual slope, which accommodates numerous rows of plush horseshoe-style seating. Translucent tables of varied colors create vibrant centerpieces that flicker off of the patrons' faces. The atmosphere here is filled with electricity, accentuated by the high tech special effects. Blue and green lights randomly explode from one area of the dome-shaped ceiling. They shoot overhead like lightning before dissipating into the top of the outside wall. Purple hanging lights pulsate with the sounds that stream from the thunderous speakers. To the delight of the teens, the sound system also accommodates on-demand music. Reddish-yellow lights line the tables. They dance back and forth in between the plants that stretch across the backs of the horseshoe benches. This stands in stark contrast with the cool colors that the designer chose for the rest of the atmosphere. The yellow and red lights make the seating appear to be an inviting and warm haven.

    Joseph puts on his gloves and secures his helmet. He clicks down his visor as a staff member hooks him into the harness. Since the game hasn't started yet, Joseph's visor projects a live picture of the restaurant. It feels as though he's standing right there in the center of it under one of the big screens. He observes the large number of people who are gathered to watch the battles. A commotion starts to come across the teenagers as they see him appear on the main screens. Joseph, hearing some cheers and clapping, raises his hands and jumps up and down. The crowd feeds into his ego and lets out a roar of approval.

The player two light comes on in Joseph's visor, indicating that Zaphin is plugged in. The shouts that now ascend from the onlookers makes the greeting they gave Joseph seem like a whisper. Joseph puts his hands down and turns to face off with his opponent. He clicks the start button on the back of his glove. Zaphin too turns toward the front of the Pit, pressing his start button. Joseph's view changes to the game mode. Millions of tiny colored dots zip into place as the computer logic builds the virtual world, placing the players in random locations. As soon as the image crystallizes, Joseph runs to a pile of rocks. With his back to them, he crouches down behind the large stones. Joseph studies the landscape, trying to familiarize himself with his surroundings.

"The mountain forest," he says, recognizing the terrain. He's just above the large waterfall at the base of the mountain.

Zaphin is transported in. Identifying the setting immediately, the strategy is clear. He runs down the mountain to a ledge overlooking one of the main passes through the valley. The teen is no stranger to this region. He has played it many times in the past. If he stays on the ledge, then he's almost guaranteed to beat Joseph. Zaphin pulls something out of his armament belt and places it on his hand. It's an MI (mirror image) ring. The MI is an item that enables the wearer to replicate his exact image up to one hundred yards away. One of his common strategies is to project his image, as if he is overlooking the river. That way, his back appears as though it's turned away from the pass through the mountain. Then he waits for his opponent, who inevitably tries to attack his mirror image from behind. This leaves his enemy wide open for a weapon attack. Not to mention that Zaphin also has the advantage of being on a ledge in an elevated location. He settles into position and activates the MI ring, waiting for Joseph to fall into his trap.

Joseph isn't too eager to go and find him, however. He repositions himself closer to the falls, squatting down behind a stout oak tree. He follows the large trunk all the way up to its branches, which are spreading out in the gentle wind. Golden yellow and brilliant red leaves trumpet the season throughout the mountainside. Several of them have already fallen, creating a thick blanket of leaves that cover the forest floor. On the canopy of limbs overhead, a layer of leaves still hang in the air. *It'll be hard to sneak up on anyone in all these leaves,* Joseph thinks to himself. He peers out over the waterfall. An endless rush of frothy white streams down the ledge until it comes crashing against a jagged rock at the bottom. On farther down, the pristine water slows into a tranquil pool that allows only a small stream to trickle from its side. Joseph watches a cloud of mist float up from the bottom of the ravine, glistening in the sun. "Now this is virtual reality!"

After staying crouched behind the tree for a short time and without seeing any signs of movement, Joseph stands up. "So that's the way Zaphin's going to play it," Joseph bitterly whispers as he starts to climb up the mountain. He tries to follow the edge of the cliff as far as it will take him. Finally, he reaches the mountain pass. A fast moving river cuts through the terrain and continues on toward the waterfall. Joseph searches the edge of the winding stream, trying to locate a trace of where Zaphin has gone. Nothing. Joseph carefully continues to sweep through the pass. He moves in and out of the trees with stealth as he advances farther and farther into the woods.

Joseph comes to another large rock that is overgrown with moss. It had fallen long ago and landed so that it is now resting partially in the river. He secures his footing as he attempts to climb it. His fingers can barely grip the extremely slippery surface as he scales it. Once at the top, he stands up to get a clearer view of the river. Just then, he sees Zaphin. Joseph drops clumsily onto the rock. He manages to straddle it, struggling to stay on.

By the way he's sitting, it looks like he thinks I'm going to go around the base of the mountain and attack from the other side of the pass, Joseph thinks to himself. He can see that Zaphin's back is turned to him, but his opponent isn't looking up. Instead, he's looking down into the river. Joseph fiddles with a knob on his belt.

"This should show me what's true and what's not," he says as he studies it intently.

Joseph slides down off of the rock and moves around into position. From the top of the mountain, Zaphin watches as Joseph comes into view around the corner of the pass. He keeps his gun pointing down at the replica of his own image, waiting for Joseph to attack. It's happening just as he had anticipated. He sees Joseph's player with his sword drawn.

What kind of sword is that? he wonders.

Joseph's player rushes to strike Zaphin's mirror image. Zaphin feels the trigger give way to the pressure of his finger, just as Joseph's sword comes slicing down at the decoy. The sound of the weapon pierces the silence as the gun recoils. Zaphin quickly brings his scope back in line with his target, but Joseph isn't there. How could he have missed? He spots Joseph running away from him toward the other side of the mountain. Zaphin quickly jumps up and starts racing after him. He's determined to get another shot in before his victim escapes.

Just as Joseph is about to run into a tree line, Zaphin sees him stop. He's pointing two guns up at the top of one of the trees.

"What the heck is he doing?" Zaphin utters as he focuses his sights on Joseph once again. "And where did he get a double weapon? I've never seen anything like that."

Zaphin stops short. Something in his gut is bothering him about this whole thing. Something's wrong.

"Shields!" Zaphin commands.

A force field comes up around his player. Shots ring out from behind him. Suddenly, his body is propelled forward. Rounds of bullets pelt his back and continue to slam him farther through the air. He lands several feet from where he had been standing. He has lost his weapon. It flew out of his hand when he was knocked forward. He looks to the leaves. The butt of the rifle juts out from one of the piles three feet away. Zaphin looks up to see Joseph coming up the hill and through the trees behind him.

"Nice, Jo…Joseph," he gasps as he pulls himself to his knees. Joseph has beaten Zaphin at his own game. He had flushed Zaphin out of his position by using a mirror image ring of himself. As soon as Zaphin attacked the mirror image of Joseph, his position was exposed. That's when Joseph had moved in for the kill. Zaphin had been chasing a 3-D projection of Joseph.

Pure instinct had spared Zaphin from certain defeat, but he wasn't safe yet. He had seen that Joseph has a double weapon, and he knows that it can penetrate his shields. Zaphin suddenly isn't feeling very confident. His rifle, with its long-range scope, is almost useless at this distance. Zaphin grabs it and puts it back in his virtual inventory. Joseph raises his weapons, preparing to shoot. Zaphin triggers a mechanism on his wrist guards, which launches a barrage of fiery spear-like objects at his opponent.

"Shields!" Joseph commands.

His fortified front shield easily deflects the enemy's large fiery darts. This gives Zaphin a chance to regroup. He pulls a new weapon out—a plasma gun. He springs to his feet and sprints toward the river, unleashing a stream of plasma at Joseph. The weapon slices through the trees with ease as he advances. Joseph opens fire and continues shooting as he flees from the beam of destruction. Trees toppled over in the wake of the plasma gun, leaving only smoldering stumps in its path. Joseph sprints harder, anticipating a way of escape. He leaps onto a tree and runs up it with several steps that seem to almost defy the laws of gravity. The plasma beam slices just inches below the heel of Joseph's foot. He pushes off of the tree, sending it toppling away from him as he flips off of the trunk. He continues shooting at Zaphin, spinning as he floats downward in the air. Joseph hits the ground hard and unleashes another swarm of bullets. They trail behind Zaphin as he retreats toward the riverbank. He slides to a stop at the water's edge, frantically looking for an escape. There's nowhere to go, and the bullets catch him. Bursts of white light appear on his shield in fragments as the bullets reach their target. The force blasts him into the river, destroying his shield. As he splashes into the water, his plasma weapon also shorts out.

Now trapped in the torrent of the fast moving water, he uses his misfortune to his advantage. Regaining his composure, he swims toward the bank. Once he's close enough, he allows the fast rapids to take him farther down the stream. Joseph's eyes advance to see where Zaphin is headed.

"The waterfall!"

Joseph can't let that happen. If he makes it to the waterfall first, then he will be on the high ground. Zaphin can set up his rifle and scope there. Then he will definitely have the upper hand. Joseph isn't about to let that happen. He crashes through limbs and branches as he races back down the riverbank, trying to keep Zaphin in his view. As he nears a bend in the river where it cuts back through the valley, he catches a glimpse of Zaphin's helmet. As quickly as he spots it, the helmet disappears around the mountain and out of sight. Joseph slows down to a jog, breathing hard. There's no way he's going to get there before Zaphin now. He'll just have to try to get close enough so that Zaphin can't use the scope again.

Joseph continues his journey along the river. With a keen eye, he searches for wet spots along the bank. He looks for any indication at all that Zaphin has crawled out onto dry ground, but there's nothing. He knows that he's nearing the waterfall. The sound of roaring water crashing onto the rocks is steadily growing louder. "Where can Zaphin be?" Joseph asks himself. Just then, he sees something move out of the corner of his eye. Joseph drops to the ground. The limb behind him explodes into shreds. He can barely make out the shadow of a person through the cloud of splinters. "It looks like a little girl again," Joseph utters. When the debris clears, there's no one there. A loud explosion thunders across the valley and up the mountain.

Joseph slides behind a fallen tree limb. "It must be Zaphin!"

He rises up to see where his opponent is shooting from. He's lucky that he saw something. If he hadn't have dropped when he did, then he would be out of the game. He searches for anything out of the ordinary across the river. Another branch disintegrates on the log that he's hiding behind, just in front of his head. Again, the sound of a gun blast follows a second later. Based upon the trajectory, Zaphin has to be set up over the ridge with his rifle and scope. He's so far away that the bullets are hitting before Joseph can even hear the shot go off.

Zaphin leaps to his feet, sprinting toward the dense line of trees. Time seems to slow down as bullets silently demolish limbs and ricochet off of thick and rugged trunks. Pieces of bark and wood hang in the air, appearing to be suspended by an unseen force. Some of them begin to hit their mark, causing his shields to flicker and finally disappear. One bullet drills him in the head. Luckily, his helmet deflects it. His head rings as the adrenaline pumps furiously through his veins. Joseph manages to dive behind some trees before any more bullets can find him. A burst of gunshots thunder through the valley again, as if they are calling out for the bullets that they had sent ahead of them into the forest.

Joseph pulls out a pair of binoculars from his virtual inventory. He holds them up to his eyes, gently pushing some brush apart so that he can peer through the opening. He scans the riverbed slowly, being sure not to make any sudden movements that will draw the sniper's attention. He knows that his helmet saved him before, but he doesn't want to take any unnecessary chances.

"There you are," Joseph says as he spots his opponent. Zaphin is also searching the tree line with his scope. He's perched at an elevated position that is located across the river on a stone ridge. The river isn't very wide there, but it's situated just before the enormous waterfall. Somehow Zaphin had been able to cross the strong current there. That's where he climbed to the top of the cliff. Joseph studies the riverbank, looking for some way to cross it without getting picked off.

On the edge of the waterfall, Joseph sees a tall cliff on his side of the river. It's higher then the ridge that Zaphin is on. Joseph analyzes the situation. Can he jump that far? No, it's still too far from the cliff to the ridge. Joseph will never be able to make it. He does have the element of surprise though. Since the cliff on Joseph's side is higher than where Zaphin is, he might be able to sneak up on his opponent. Joseph crawls on the ground behind the brush. When he makes it to thicker cover, he slowly rises to his feet. His shoes tread peacefully on the covering of leaves, declaring the good news to the forest that he's still alive. Joseph is careful as he moves on to avoid any open areas that might give Zaphin another shot.

With every step, he draws closer toward the river. It takes quite a while, but eventually, Joseph arrives at the cliff. He looks up to the top of the hill. A medium-sized oak tree shoots straight up from the edge, towering over the water. There's nowhere to hide from Zaphin though.

Joseph has a plan, and he knows that he's only going to get one shot at this. He grips his gloves, placing his fingers above the buttons.

His shoulders tense. Leaning forward, he starts to walk toward the river. Joseph is completely focused on the tall, thick tree. His walk quickens into a trot and then a sprint. Joseph raises his guns as he advances. He begins to blast both of them in rapid succession, focusing on the base of the tree. Zaphin jumps up in alarm, swinging his rifle around. He aims in the direction of the rapid explosions. Joseph continues firing on the tree, his bullets starting to pierce through the thick trunk. He's coming up on the weakened oak fast, but he has no intentions of slowing down. He leaps onto the tree, his weight forcing the shredded base of the trunk to give way. Joseph continues his forward momentum, dashing up the tree as it falls. The splintered tree cracks and groans as it slowly topples over.

Zaphin spots Joseph running. He begins firing rounds at the moving target as he flies across the tree. His attempts are unsuccessful. He can't get a clean shot at Joseph. The worn tree is falling directly on top of him. Bullets pound the underside of the bark as Joseph runs over the top of it. As he nears the end, his weight accelerates the descent of the tree.

Joseph's whole body extends out as he leaps off of the end of the log. The river runs fast underneath his outstretched body, waiting to devour the falling mass of wood and limbs. As he soars through the air, he begins raining rounds of ammunition down on a surprised Zaphin. Joseph's two weapons merge, locking on to their target. Without the once impenetrable shields, Zaphin is a sitting duck. Joseph swoops over his opponent's head, who has now fallen to the ground. Rounds continue drilling into Zaphin's player. Joseph passes over him and begins a downward descent, plummeting toward the hard ground. Joseph curls into a ball to soften the impact. He rolls several times before his back slams into a tree. The teenager sits there for a second, immersed in the game. Has he won? Has he beaten Zaphin?

Joseph's visor displays a red character. This confirms that he has won the match. Today, the tables are finally turned. Joseph's display switches back from the 3-D view to the camera in the restaurant. The cheering is deafening. Joseph rises to his feet, raising his arms into the air. The arena is packed with teenagers who are chanting his name. He pumps his arms into the air in time with the crowd. Glancing to his right, he barely catches a glimpse of a notification that Zaphin's player is logging off. Finally, he has beaten him.

I wonder how he's going to take it, Joseph thinks.

CHAPTER 9

After both of them get out of the harnesses, they shed the rest of their gear. Joseph and Zaphin arrive in front of the elevator at the same time.

"Good game," Joseph offers. Zaphin halfway smiles back at him, only nodding his head.

"You want to get something to eat?" Joseph asks.

"Sure. It's on me. The loser." Zaphin slaps him on the back, mustering a resentful chuckle as he turns to the opening doors. "We can watch some of the matches while we grub."

Zaphin gets into the elevator first. He turns and faces Joseph but avoids eye contact. Instead, he just gazes up at the ceiling with his hands clasped in front of him. Joseph makes an uncomfortable entrance and presses the button to the topside restaurant level. Zaphin exits first, snagging a booth close to the entrance. Joseph plops down across the table from him. The music provides a relaxing rhythm that seems to calm them both down. The warm lights make the plants appear to glow and sway. It's quite peaceful, and yet, excitement fills the air at the same time.

Immediately, a waitress appears behind them.

"That was intense!" she says, flipping her blonde curly hair over her shoulder. Joseph stumbles over his words a little, caught off guard by the enthusiastic girl. "Um, yeah. I, uh, just try to do my best."

The young girl cocks her head slightly to the side with a playful look on her face. Zaphin turns to Joseph and puts his hand to his face, hiding his expression from the waitress. He smirks and stares at him affectionately.

"I mean, thanks." Joseph tries to recover.

The waitress smiles again. "You've got some moves. Maybe you can show me how to play like that sometime."

Joseph's brain seems to be stuck in pause. He can only offer a sheepish grin.

"What's your name?" she continues.

He knows the answer to this one. "I'm Joseph, and this is Zaphin."

"Zaphin. I like that name," she says as she leans on the table.

Zaphin just ignores her. He's following the flashes of light across the ceiling and back again. The waitress takes out a pad and a sheet of paper. "So what can I get you two gentlemen?"

Zaphin snaps out of his trance. "I want a cheeseburger, fries, and a root beer."

"And for you?" she asks, now leaning in Joseph's direction.

"I would like a cheeseburger and fries too please."

"And to drink?"

"Some tea would be great."

The waitress thanks them and politely smiles as she walks away. Joseph watches her out of the corner of his eye. The blue explosions of light illuminate her face as she crosses the room. She turns the order in at the counter and glances back over her shoulder at them. Joseph quickly breaks eye contact and returns his attention to his friend. Zaphin is now watching the big-screen televisions. He must apparently be oblivious to the waitress' advances. Joseph isn't sure what to say. Zaphin doesn't usually act like this. They both just sit there silently while they wait for their food. The crowd of onlookers begins to yell as the next match starts.

Zaphin gradually calms down enough to start talking.

"That was pretty clever. You using your mirror image on my mirror image was ruthless. You just plain outplayed me," he concedes. "But how did you know it was a mirror image?"

"I have the belt of reality."

"You mean the one that can tell you if something is truly an object in the game or just an image?"

"That's the one."

"I can't believe this," Zaphin protests. "How does it work?"

"It sends out a pulse and tells you on a display screen if the image is real or fake. That way, I'm not basing my game play on false assumptions."

"Unbelievable." Zaphin sighs.

Joseph looks at him. His friend's face is still solemn. "I just got lucky, man."

"Boy did you!" Zaphin exclaims, showing the first sign of excitement since the end of the match. "How the heck did you duck my bullet? It was like you knew that it was coming for your head."

"I saw something out of the corner of my eye."

"What was it?"

"I'm not sure. Whatever I saw, it was gone when I looked up again."

"You are the luckiest person I know," Zaphin chuckles. He slaps the table with the palm of his hand. "So you won because you got freaked out over nothing?"

Joseph frowns at Zaphin and sarcastically says, "So all the other stuff I did, like running over the waterfall on a falling tree and jumping off just in time to get you, didn't have anything to do with my victory?"

Zaphin's face softens. "I'm sorry, man. You did outplay me today. But next time!"

Zaphin doesn't finish his sentence. Instead, they both laugh, letting the tension of the game slide off of their backs.

"Here are your drinks," the waitress says as she puts a root beer and a glass of iced tea down on the table. "Can I get you anything else?"

"Not right now," replies Joseph. The waitress smiles again as she turns and walks back toward the kitchen.

"So we're still on for tonight?" Zaphin asks.

"Yep."

"Can you tell me where it is, or would you have to kill me then?" Zaphin asks with a smile.

"It's just a short walk from your house, but a little closer to the city."

"I don't know how it could be closer to the city than my house," says Zaphin. "My house is practically in the city."

"Does all that fighting ever get to you?"

"No. I'm used to it. I've lived there by myself ever since my last set of foster parents ditched me a couple of years back."

Joseph stops smiling. "I'm sorry."

"Don't be. I like not having anyone around to tell me what to do."

"Here are your cheeseburgers," the waitress cuts in. She puts the plates on the table and moves on to greet another set of customers who have just walked in. Joseph bows his head, praying silently. As he finishes, his eyes meet Zaphin's. He holds a sly expression, his eyes half-closed.

That's a new one, Joseph thinks. *I've never seen that look from him before. I don't get it.*

Zaphin picks up his cheeseburger. Lettuce drops from it as he holds it, strategically deciding where to take the first huge bite.

"One good thing about not having parents—I never get grounded!"

Somehow, the events of the day had slipped over Joseph's anger toward his parents, putting them into a slumber of forgetfulness. Zaphin had just woken them back up. Slightly irritated once again, Joseph takes on a slightly less chipper tone. "Fair enough," he mumbles while shoving some fries into his mouth. He chews them up and swallows hard.

"So I was thinking. Maybe I could just hang at your house tonight. That way, I won't have to worry about curfew."

Zaphin mulls it over in his brain while he finishes off the bite of burger in his mouth. "I don't see why that would be a problem, but only because you whipped me in H2H today."

"Sweet. I'll let *the parents* know that I won't be home tonight." They finish eating their lunch without saying a whole lot.

"Okay, let's get out of here," Zaphin says as he pushes the empty plate away from him.

"Sounds good to me."

Joseph pulls his metallic cell phone from his pocket once again. He opens it, checking for any new messages or missed calls as they get up from the table.

"One New Message" appears on the small flip out screen. *Sarah,* he thinks to himself.

Quickly, he presses the send button. He can't explain why, but for some reason, the excitement is already building within him. He feels like a child getting ready to open a specially wrapped birthday package. Instead of Sarah, however, it's his home phone number.

"Gimme a break," he mumbles.

He pulls up Sarah in his contacts and begins to type a message. Joseph's thumbs complete the sentence and hover over the send button before his mind can even catch up with his body. His eyes follow the sentence several times. "DY wnt2go 2 my hous B4 d Bble stdy 2day?"

Joseph hesitates. He wonders how Sarah will take it. *Is it too forward? What's she doing right now?* he wonders.

His thumb presses against the send button but not hard enough for it to register.

I better not, he convinces himself as he cancels the message and closes his cell. He slides his phone back into his pants.

"You coming?" Zaphin asks.

"Right behind you," he answers.

Both Joseph and Zaphin exit the arena and head back toward their vehicle.

Back at her house, Sarah flips open her hot pink phone. Several of her friends had come over just a couple of days earlier to have a cell decorating party. She wonders if she might have overdone it a little as she examines the fake pink diamonds that now splatter the front of it.

"When are they going to get here?" she whines.

Sarah clicks a few buttons, checking for any possible missed calls. Just then, her phone rings. Sarah jumps, slightly startled by the unexpected ringtone.

"You got Sarah," she answers.

It's her standard phone greeting. She made it all up on her own. She was pretty proud of herself for thinking of something so grown up and casual. It was *so* cool and now.

"Hey, girl!" a voice comes from the other end.

It's her friend, Ashlynn.

"Hey!" Sarah says in a very excited voice.

"So we still on?"

"You know it!" Sarah speaks into the phone with a sassy voice.

"Okay. I'll be there in a second!"

Sarah clicks the end button and stares at her display. It was nice to talk with her friend, but she's hoping to get a call from someone else.

"Give it up, girl," she sighs as she slides off of her bed. She's still wearing her pajama bottoms and a tank top. "Guess I better get dressed."

Sarah opens her closet and peruses the selection. It's filled mostly with T-shirts, hoodies, and button-ups. A few dresses are pushed over to the very edge of the rack. The barely worn relics remind her of when she was a little girl. She used to love wearing dresses. And she especially loved to wear the ones that poofed out on the bottom. She would twirl around in circles, making the bottom of the dress float into the air as she spun. But she isn't a little girl anymore. She doesn't have time for those silly dreams of princes and princesses.

"I guess my parents still see me as that little girl," Sarah utters in a hopeless voice. She pulls the bottom of one of the dresses out to get a better view of it. "What can you do?" she sighs. Sarah lets go of the bottom of the dress, letting it slide back into its place between the other clothes in the closet.

She pulls a T-shirt off of the shelf and puts it on. It has ribbons on it that dance across each other, forming a heart and then separating back out into various designs. Over that, she pulls on a black hoodie and slips into some khaki capris.

When will they be here? she thinks impatiently.

Plopping her head down into her open palms, she stares out of her bedroom window. A sly cat crouches low in the grass; only the slender lines on its striped brown and gray back are visible. Sarah recognizes him. It's the neighbor's pet, Butch. Like a shark moving just beneath the crest of the water, the cat slides through the tall green blades. Sarah follows the movement to see where he's heading.

"I should have known," Sarah whispers.

Butch is moving straight toward the bird feeder. He pounces suddenly, leaping up onto an old wooden bench. The birds scatter, abandoning their lunch. It's no surprise to Sarah. Then, however, she spots something—something still rooting around in the food. It's a very small bird. Butch watches as it twitches and pecks around in the seeds, spilling some onto the ground below. The cat recoils back on his hind legs, waiting and watching. He spies his window of opportunity and seizes it. Butch springs out from the bench; his paws stretched forward with his hind legs trailing behind. His body shoots upward into the air. Gravity, however, overtakes him before he reaches his prize. The cat falls short of the little wooden house, landing in the soft grass. The small bird flies up momentarily but immediately flutters back down and starts pecking away. A defeated but determined cat sits on the ground below the feeder and watches the feathered visitor finish its meal.

All the other birds missed out, Sarah realizes. *The bird got to eat, because it isn't afraid. It trusts that the cat can't reach it, because it's up high enough. The maker of the birdhouse built it so tall that no cat can touch the feathered guests. He designed it perfectly from the beginning so that there's no reason for the birds to fear the cat. The littlest bird trusted that it was high enough up, but the other birds let fear drive them. They didn't get any food at all.*

Sarah continues to let her thoughts drift as she watches the bird eat.

"Sarah, your friends are here!" her mother's voice echoes down the hall.

Sarah opens her door and eagerly jogs down the hall to meet them.

The first person to come through the door is Ashlynn. She's shorter than the other girls, but she's also the prettiest by far. She has a slender and tone build. Her blue eyes are soft and gentle. Sarah always likes being around her, because she's always so bubbly and full of life. Not only is she pretty and funny, but she's smart too. Sarah rushes in and gives her a big hug, her hands disappearing into Ashlynn's long blonde hair.

"Hey, girl!"

"Hey!"

The next person in line is Serenity. In addition to being one of the most popular girls in her school, she's also one of the taller girls in her class. Her straight jet-black hair spills down around her shoulders as she runs her hand through her hair. She only has to worry about the front getting messed up, because her hair tapers up to her neck as it nears the back of her head. She is very slender and has the face of a model with high cheekbones. Usually, Sarah gets along with her well enough, but Serenity is always trying to be the leader of their group. It seems like she's always trying to undermine her. Whenever Sarah comes up with an idea, Serenity is right there to put it down. Sarah gives her a quick hug and then moves on to Bethany.

"Hey, Beth!" Sarah says, wrapping her arms around her friend's wide shoulders.

That's Sarah's nickname for her. They have been good friends since they were in elementary school. Sarah's head fits comfortably on Beth's shoulder. Bethany always referred to herself as "big-boned," but Sarah thinks the biggest thing about her is her heart. Her curly brown hair hangs down just past her neck. Sarah notices the color right away.

She pushes back away from her friend, holding her by the shoulders at arm's length. Looking her up and down, she reaches out and bounces one of the strands between her fingers.

"I love what you've done with your hair!"

"Really?" she asks timidly.

"Yes. That color is perfect with your complexion."

Bethany looks down at the ground, a sheepish grin permanently imbedded on her face. She's obviously embarrassed by the compliment.

"Are you going to let me in?" asks Kris. She's the last one to walk in the door. Although she isn't the most popular girl in school, she keeps gaining status every day. In elementary school, Kris had been what some people consider to be a "tomboy." She got that label because when she was younger, she had the frame of a boy. To compound the matter, she was a natural at sports. She had worn glasses that were a mile thick, and wispy red strings of hair framed her freckle-covered face. Needless to say, she quickly learned how to take care of herself. As she grew older, however, she began to lose her boyish figure. It was just after the first year of middle school that she traded in her glasses for contacts and dyed her hair an auburn color. For the final touch, she started using foundation to fade the freckles that God had sprinkled across her face. Kris gave up playing basketball, which she was quite talented at, and started cheerleading instead.

"You know it. Come on in," Sarah beckons to her friend.

She leads the girls through an entryway into the living room. Her parents are sitting there, watching some game show on the television.

"At it again, huh?" Sarah's father spouts without looking up.

"You can come and rock out with us," Ashlynn teases, in her usual peppy little voice.

"David plays a mean trumpet," Sarah's mother interjects, endorsing her husband.

"Not so sure that would fit in with the band," David protests.

"Oh say!" She slaps him on the leg, slipping him a loving smile.

"Right," Sarah says in a dismissive but still playful manner.

The girls continue on to some stairs leading to the basement. They file in, lugging cases of varying sizes and shapes. Ashlynn is carrying the smallest case of them all. In fact, it's so small that it fits in her hand. It's made of black, soft leather and is approximately twelve inches long by four inches wide. Beth isn't carrying anything but a handful of paperbacked books. Serenity turns sideways as she enters the staircase, maneuvering around the corner with what is clearly a guitar case in her hand. The shape is unmistakable. In true Serenity fashion, it's decorated in pink and black. To top it off, the case is adorned with fake white stick-on diamonds that spell her name across the front. Kris also has a guitar case, but hers is longer and wider then Serenity's. Unlike her friend, she has little trouble carrying the larger case as she descends. They continue on their narrow descent into an open area. The lower level is evidently a view out basement as there are windows on one side of the room about halfway up the wall.

A large set of drums clutters the far corner, opposite of the windows. Ashlynn makes her way across the room to where they sit. She scoots a small stool away from the wall and plops down on to it. Then, opening her case, she pulls out two natural colored wooden drumsticks. Ashlynn starts to tap through each drum in a quick, rhythmic fashion. A keyboard stands on the same side of the room. It must be a good twenty feet away from the drum set though. Beth sits down on the bench behind it. She carefully opens one of the paperback music books that she's been carrying and places it on a black metal stand. Meanwhile, Kris is focused on setting her area up. She bends down next to an amplifier box and opens up her case, pulling out a black colored bass guitar. As she hooks it into the amplifier, it catches the light, reflecting off slivers of neon green that seem to come alive from out of the black painted body. Serenity lowers her case onto a table and gently pulls out her instrument. It's the same color as her case. It wouldn't be a Serenity guitar if it were colored any other way.

Sarah makes her way across the dark brown carpet and heads straight for a wood grain cabinet. She opens it and pulls out a hard leather case. Strings hang from the seams, and the black color is worn off in several spots. It has obviously been used for quite some time. She opens the case and lifts her guitar out of it. Amazingly, the guitar inside is in remarkable shape. It resembles more of a work of art than an old guitar. The pearl-white color illuminates varying shades of violet as the light dances from its polished surface.

Each girl takes some time to adjust her respective instrument. The combined twanging of guitars being tuned and drums tapping create an awkward symphony. Sarah listens to it for a moment. She's never really paid attention to how horrible it sounds when they are warming up. All these instruments create a sweet melody when they are playing in harmony. When they have a joint goal and purpose, each unique instrument complements the other one. The result is a song that sounds more amazing than any of the instruments could have created on their own. With each of the girls just warming up, however, everyone is doing their own thing. The instruments actually have a disharmonizing effect on one another. The key is the music sheet. That's the thing that tells each instrument when to play and how to play. If someone doesn't do what the music sheet instructs, then the song doesn't come out quite as perfectly as it has the potential to.

"Okay, girls. Let's start with our song 'Warned,'" Serenity instructs with a bossy tone.

Sarah winces as the command bellows across her eardrums. Serenity is always trying to assert herself as the leader of their rock band. Sarah thinks that she is supposed to be in that role, but it seems that Serenity is gaining a foothold. It doesn't help things one bit that she's gaining so much popularity. All of her other friends have started looking to Serenity for direction lately instead of her.

I have to do something about this before she appoints herself as dictator, Sarah tells herself. Mustering up her courage, she challenges her friend.

"How about we start with 'Shimmer' instead?" Sarah offers.

She waits for the dissent. Not hearing any opposition, she glances up from her guitar at the rest of the girls. Everyone seems to be nodding in agreement—everyone except for Serenity, that is. Instead, she looks like steam is about to explode from her ears. Just as Serenity opens her mouth to tell all the girls why that is the stupidest idea ever, Ashlynn speaks up.

"I love that song. Let's do it!"

Kris shrugs her shoulders, in true Kris style, and grunts, "Whatever."

Sarah, encouraged by the responses, knows that she needs to act fast if she wants to keep the momentum going in her direction.

"One, Two, One Two Three Four!" Sarah shouts. The group begins to play, and Sarah leads with vocals.

"I know you like to pretend that you're in tha know, but you're clueless when it comes to our super glow…"

As they begin singing the song, Sarah can feel Serenity's stare piercing through the side of her head. She half-expects to see a pink and black guitar coming at her head from behind.

Why can't we both lead the band? she asks herself.

The girls continue practicing "Shimmer" for the next hour. They seem to be really getting it down by the end.

"I think we've got it, girls. Let's give it a rest for the day," Serenity puffs, seemingly satisfied with the performance.

Her tone is a little different than before. It's softer—almost human. She's asking now more then she's telling.

"You're right, Serenity," Sarah agrees.

"Good call," Beth says, giving the thumbs-up from the back.

Serenity smiles, interpreting the agreement from the other band members as a small sign of victory. While the girls put away their instruments, they start chatting about what their plans are for the rest of the day. The teenagers wander over to a living room area with a television and some older furniture.

"Let's go shopping. I really need a couple of new button-ups," Kris suggests in her usual monotone voice. If Sarah didn't know any better, she would think that shopping is a huge hassle for the once tomboy turned Barbie. Sarah does know better though. In fact, shopping just happens to be one of Kris's favorite pastimes.

"I'm down," Beth offers. "I could really use some new clothes too."

Beth loves to shop as well. She has a very good eye for outfits. Sarah really admires her creativity when it comes to fashion. She almost never buys name brand clothes from the shelf. Instead, she's always mixing and matching pieces to make the most stunning ensembles. And the best part is that no one ever has anything like it at school. She's well-known throughout the whole school for her keen sense of fashion and her good taste.

"That'll be loads of fun," Sarah agrees.

Suddenly, she remembers what's going on tonight. It's Bible study night. *Maybe some of my friends will go with me if I invite them,* she tells herself.

"What are you guys doing later tonight?" Ashlynn continues the conversation.

This is the perfect opportunity! Sarah reasons. *I'll just come out and tell them that I'm going to a Bible study. After all, they are my friends.*

"Something boring I'm sure," Kris sighs.

"Well," Sarah begins, "have you ever wondered why the government is so down on Christians?"

The room becomes silent. The group of girls stares back at her with blank expressions on their faces, wondering how they got off on this tangent. Sarah is extremely uncomfortable and nervous now.

"I... I mean, why aren't they going after Buddhists or Hindus or something?"

"Um, hello? Probably because they pretty much were the downfall of our whole entire country," Serenity answers in a snotty tone.

"Wasn't it the terrorists who released that virus on everybody? Didn't they cause the downfall of our nation?" Sarah asks.

"It doesn't really matter why. All that we need to know is that Christians are narrow-minded extremists."

"How do you know? Have you ever spoken with one? Have you ever read a Bible?"

"Of course not!" she gasps. "I'm not a traitor!"

Sarah looks around the room at her other friends. Kris is already sitting down on the only recliner in the room. Just to her right is a plush brown couch that is situated perpendicular to the window. It juts out into the middle of the room, creating a break between the band instruments and a recreational area. In the corner sits a large television inside an old oak entertainment center. Her friends don't seem nearly as offended as Serenity does from all the talk about Christianity.

"So what do you girls think?" Sarah asks, addressing the others.

Beth answers immediately. She's been listening intently with a concerned look on her face.

"I would like to know more about Christians, but they don't teach about them anywhere."

Kris rolls her head onto her shoulder and looks over at Beth. Her eyes squint, and her lips purse together. "No one teaches it because they would either be put in prison or killed. Those aren't exactly stellar options," she says, following up with a cynical laugh.

Ashlynn joins in on the conversation. "But something seems true about it. Somehow, deep down, something about it seems true."

"Sarah!" comes a call from upstairs. "Your pizza is here!"

"Coming!" she yells back.

Serenity grabs the remote and flops down on the end of the plush brown couch next to Kris's recliner. She watches Sarah out of the corner of her eye, who is already headed up the stairs. When she's finally out of sight, Serenity slams the remote down onto the cushion and lets out a huge sigh of disgust.

"Can you believe her?" She throws her hand out in the direction that Sarah went. "She's going to get us all in prison with that junk. If someone finds out that we're down here talking about this stuff, we'll be in major trouble."

"But you know that Sarah's a Christian, don't you?" Ashlynn asks.

"I don't know that," Serenity responds. "I have my suspicions, but I don't know that for a fact. You all better think long and hard about what it's going to cost you if you start this Christianity crap."

Serenity picks the remote back up. She scans through the stations until she hits some sort of rock video. A teenage girl with long blonde hair and pink curls jams on the guitar while her band proceeds to destroy a car in the background. The girls watch it for a few moments without saying a word. Finally, Kris breaks the silence.

"And you can be sure that your dreams of being a rock star like her will be gone if you do that Christian thing. You don't see any Christian stars now, do you?"

The sound of footsteps cuts the conversation short as Sarah appears with two boxes of pizza and some drinks. Beth grabs the cups and containers of pop from her.

"All right. One cheese and one supreme. Dig in!"

She tosses the pizza onto a dark brown coffee table and sinks into the couch next to Serenity.

"So anyway." Sarah searches for words, trying to pick the conversation back up where she had left off. "What if I told you that there was this thing tonight?"

"What thing?" Beth asks.

"A secret thing. Something like you have never seen before," Sarah lowers her voice to almost a whisper as she talks, trying to build the anticipation.

"You mean a Christian thing?" Kris asks bluntly.

Serenity immediately chimes in. "Look, what you do when you're not with us is your business. Don't try to drag us into anything illegal."

Sarah is taken back by the opposition. She thought that she was doing a good job of presenting it as an opportunity to learn about something that no one really understands.

Sarah turns to Ashlynn.

"Oh sorry, babe," Ashlynn apologizes in a sympathetic voice, "I already have plans tonight. Let me know next time though. Okay?"

"No biggie." Sarah shrugs her shoulders, pretending like she couldn't care less one way or the other.

Beth is Sarah's last hope.

"What about you, Beth?"

"I…well…I just really don't feel like going tonight. We'll all go next time."

Sarah grabs a piece of pizza and takes a huge bite. She's so frustrated at her friends. She can't hide the red tint that is starting to creep up her neck. When she gets really upset, it's always her neck that gives it away. The discoloration spreads like a rash up the sides of her face toward her cheeks. Ashlynn can see now that Sarah is about to boil over. She discreetly taps Beth on the leg and signals with her head for her friend to look over at Sarah. Beth holds her hands out, as if to say, "What?"

"Her neck." Ashlynn mouths.

Beth takes a second look; this time she sees the telltale sign.

"Thank you for inviting us," Beth says in an overly nice tone.

"Yeah, we will definitely go next time," Ashlynn adds, even more upbeat then before.

"Like I said, no biggie. You better get some of this before I eat it all!" Sarah giggles through a mouthful of pizza as she grabs another piece out of the box.

The girls eat the rest of the food in record time. Everyone seems to be trying to lighten the mood, whether they are cracking jokes, laughing at the television, or telling funny stories. Even Kris tries to join in, turning the conversation to boys.

"What's up with that Jefferson kid? He's got some serious odor going on there!"

"I know," Serenity agrees. "Every time I see him I'm like, '*Hello?*' It's called de-o-dor-ant!"

Beth laughs. "He needs to take some lessons from John. John smells way yummy."

Sarah's mouth drops open. "Yummy? You seriously just didn't call him yummy."

Beth slightly blushes. "Well, you like that Joseph guy."

"What? Are you insane? No, I don't. We're just friends."

"*Oh,*" Serenity bellows. "I think you hit something there, Beth."

"He is kind of cute too," Ashlynn agrees.

"You know who is really cute?" Kris asks, snuggling back into the headrest of the chair. "Ray Ray," she blurts out without waiting for an answer.

"Ray Ray? Have you seen that old brown truck he drives?" Serenity rolls her eyes as she speaks.

"I don't care about that stuff," Kris says defensively.

"Whatever," Kris quickly adds, realizing her moment of weakness. "Like I was totally joking. Let's just get going to the mall."

The girls grab their instruments and head up the stairs, leaving behind a pile of empty plates, pizza boxes, and cups.

Sarah's father and mother are now in the kitchen, cleaning up from the lunch that they have just finished.

"Headed out already?" asks her father, David.

"Yeah, we're headed to the mall."

"Well, are we going to get to see you today at all?" her mother asks, apparently a little frustrated.

"Mom!" Sarah whispers, humiliated by the line of questioning in front of her friends.

"All right," her mother concedes. "What time are you going to be home?"

"I won't be late. Remember, tonight I'm going over to the Jansen's house after supper."

Serenity suddenly looks pale.

"I'll be getting the car," she mumbles as she flips open her cell phone and scurries out the door.

"Be safe," her mother says very softly, trying not to let her voice carry to Sarah's friends.

"I will, Mom. Later, Dad."

"See you later. Love you."

"Love you," her mother echoes.

"Love you guys too."

The five girls all pile into Serenity's bright red convertible.

"What's this?" Kris asks as she pulls a black helmet with a visor out of the front floorboard.

"Oh, that. That's just something my brother left in here when I was driving him around," Serenity explains.

"Put the top down," Beth pleads.

"No way. That will kill my hair," Kris says as she tosses the helmet back onto the floor.

Serenity starts lowering the top. "We'll put it back up before we get on the highway."

Kris huffs, taking in a big breath and releasing it.

This time of year the days are still nice. The cool breeze has continued on throughout the day, and the bright sun now radiates in a deep blue sky. Clouds drift across the vast expanse, morphing into different shapes as they flow along the gentle wind currents.

Sarah stretches her hands into the sky, feeling the blast of air rush through her fingers. She lets her arms fall forward slightly, trying to balance the weight of them against the force of the wind coming over the top of the car.

What an amazing day God has given us, she thinks. *Thank you, God.*

"Look!" Ashlynn exclaims, pointing at one of the small ranch-style houses as the car halts at the stop sign.

The roof of the house is in need of obvious repairs. It's just one of several ancient homes that line the street. A poorly kept lawn frays out across a sun-beaten yard littered with trash. The sidewalk leading up to the house is halfway overtaken by the brownish-green mat of foliage.

"That's where that Amber girl lives."

"How do you know?" inquires Beth.

"Because we used to be friends in grade school."

Serenity accelerates away from the house, letting out a, "Humph! Let's get out of here then, before she comes out."

"She used to be cool," Ashlynn continues, "but now she's all about getting high."

"That's an understatement," Kris agrees.

"I think it's sad," Sarah offers but is quickly interrupted by Serenity.

"No, duh."

"I wasn't finished," Sarah continues. "It's sad because she's just looking for something."

"Yeah. She's looking for her pusher," laughs Kris.

"No. She's looking to fill something that's inside of her. She just doesn't know what she needs. It's like all those rich people that you hear about. You know, how sad and depressed they are, even with all that money. Or how famous people who have everything that they could ever want end up killing themselves."

"I never understood that," Beth admits. "I mean, what's up with those people. What problems could they possibly have?"

"They have the same problem that every person on earth has. They are missing something. There is a hole in their lives—a void.

And just like a hole in a puzzle, there's only one thing that will fit into and fill the emptiness completely."

"And right now, it's this song!" Kris yells, hearing her favorite tune on the radio. "Crank it, girl!"

Serenity turns the dial. The music blasts out through the car's speakers. It echoes across the street and back from the houses as they whiz by them.

Sarah opens her mouth to tell them the answer. She wants them to know that life doesn't have to be empty. That drugs, money, success, power, and boys don't truly satisfy. She wants desperately to tell them that what they have been searching for their whole lives is Jesus—but she can't. The music is just too much. Sarah can barely hear herself think. She glances over at Beth, who has already disengaged from the conversation. In fact, all the girls are now singing along with the radio, smiling blissfully. Sarah lays her head back onto the headrest and stares up at the sky. It all feels so hopeless.

If only they would read it for themselves. If only they would just look at all the evidence in the Bible. Her thoughts continue as Serenity puts the top up, getting ready to enter the highway. Once they're on it, they drive several miles. As they travel, they continue to sing along to the songs that come across the radio. Finally, they arrive at the mall. As they exit the highway, they put the top down again. Would they listen to Sarah now? She looks around at her friends, but she can see that the opportunity has passed. It would just be awkward now.

The crew of future hopeful rock stars whips into a parking stall right in front of the mall entrance. Serenity closes the drop-top again as the rest of the girls fumble around in their purses. She turns the car off and pulls her keys from the ignition, sliding them into her purse. Mirrors snap shut as they all finish touching up their lipstick, gloss, and blush. Even before they can get out of the car, the frenzy starts to build. What bargains will they find today? Will they run into any cute boys? The girls walk across the parking lot and disappear into the mall.

After several hours, they emerge. Every one of them is loaded down with shopping bags filled with items that they just absolutely had to have. They fill up the trunk and pile in. Serenity drives Sarah home first, dropping her off at the front door. She pulls several bags out of the trunk and slams it shut.

"See you girls later," she says waving good-bye.

"Love ya, girl," Ashlynn shouts as they drive away.

Well, better get ready for the Bible study tonight, Sarah reminds herself. Her parents have supper ready and waiting when she comes stumbling in the front door with her finds.

"Looks like it was a successful hunting trip," her father teases her.

Her mother joins in the teasing. "Did you leave anything in the store?"

"Nope. I pretty much cleared out the whole thing." Sarah laughs.

She dumps her shopping bags in the corner and pulls up a chair at the table. The rest of the family sits down to a nice home cooked meal. They chat about the best thing and the worst thing that happened to them that day as they eat.

"So where are you going tonight, honey?" Sarah's mother asks.

"To the Bible study."

"That's right!" Her mother is genuinely thrilled.

"We are so proud of you," her father says. "This is very important."

Sarah placates her parents with a soft "Ahhh."

"No. We're serious Sarah. You're doing something really important. Just be careful."

"Why don't you come with me?" she asks.

Sarah's parents gaze at each other with a loving and encouraging expression. Her mother reaches out and tightly grabs her husband's hand. "It's time for you to start studying on your own," she explains.

"We've been teaching you, but now it's time for you to start reading the Scripture on your own."

"You can't rely on what we tell you," her father agrees. "The Bible tells us that the Holy Spirit will speak to each of us through God's word."

"So you've been lying to me all this time?" Sarah says in a sarcastic tone.

"Some children grow up in a Christian home," her father begins. "They worship together, they say their prayers in bed, and they try to make their parents proud of them."

"So what's wrong with that?" she asks.

"Not a thing," her mother responds, now grabbing her daughter's hand. "It's just that some children believe that they can inherit their salvation. Like just because their parents are saved, they are automatically going to heaven."

"That's silly." Sarah giggles.

"I know," she continues. "And some children don't ever really get into the scripture and read it for themselves. When others start questioning their faith or their views from the Bible, they don't have an answer. They can only say, 'That's what my parents told me, or that's what I learned in church.'"

Sarah nods, starting to understand their point.

"We want you to be able to study with other people besides us. That way, you can be grounded in the Word and know exactly why you believe what you do."

"You guys are so cool," Sarah says as she gets up. She walks over to her mother first. With a thankful heart, she gives her a great big hug, squeezing her tightly.

"Love you, Mom," she says.

"Love you, sweetheart."

Then she walks around behind her father's chair.

"Thanks, Dad. I love you too."

Her father scoots his chair back and faces her. "I love you. You're growing up to be such a fine young lady," he says. She bends down and wraps her arms around his neck. He pats her gently on the back of her head as they embrace.

CHAPTER 10

Joseph leads Zaphin through a large and well-kept yard. Grand old trees tower over them, casting long shadows on the thick blades of grass. They journey on past a white two-story house and out onto another street. After walking several more blocks, Zaphin begins to hear the faint echo of fighting going on in the city.

"It sounds like home sweet home around here." Zaphin laughs.

Joseph has to admit, it's pretty rough in this neighborhood. This is the worst part of town, and it seems like fighting breaks out here all the time. Old cars litter the street. Some have bullet holes from past skirmishes, while others look like they have been dropped off of a building.

The shadows are getting even longer now. Twilight creeps in as the last rays of sun retreat across the horizon. The air is crisp and cool on Joseph's face. His determined steps start to quicken as he walks off of the street and back into one of the yards. It appears that their destination is an older looking single-level house. The grass has a fresh blanket of dew draped over it that whispers where the boys' feet have tread.

"Slow down! You're not excited to get there or anything, are you?" Zaphin's sarcasm is anything but subtle.

"I just don't want to be late." Joseph slows his walk a little and looks over his left shoulder at Zaphin. "Thanks for coming with me."

"I'm glad you invited me. I'm excited to meet your girlfriend. What's her name—Sarah?" Zaphin's smile starts to break before he even finishes his sentence, anticipating the reaction that he's coaxing from Joseph.

"Shut up! I told you she isn't my girlfriend! It's just casual."

"Sure, it's casual and so is—"

Joseph ends the conversation, not wanting Zaphin to say anything stupid in front of Sarah.

"Shhh… We're here."

Zaphin and Joseph walk up to the front of the outdated house. Structurally, the building looks very fragile. The paint is starting to flake off in several areas, and the base looks like it may have been made out of actual stone at one point.

What a dump. Whoever lives here should just tear the place down, Zaphin thinks to himself.

A carefully planned landscape and the tidy yard, in contrast, are in very good condition. The teens tread up the path to the front porch. Joseph knocks on the solid wood door with his hand, but it only gives off a deadened thud with each rap. The blinds covering the window part just enough to reveal two eyes peering out at them. Before they can see who it is, the blinds snap back together. Everything is quiet. Joseph and Zaphin hear the rattling of a chain and a bolt unlocking. The door swings open. Sarah is standing there in the entrance wearing her warm smile. Joseph can smell the hickory burning in the fireplace from outside.

"Joseph, I am so glad you made it." Sarah gives him a big hug. Even the strong aroma of smoke hasn't erased the jasmine scent from her hair. What a wonderful, sweet smell. She turns her head toward Zaphin.

"Who is this?" she questions.

Sarah stops hugging Joseph and takes a guarded step backward.

"This is my friend, Zaphin, from school. It's okay—he's cool."

Sarah tilts her head, as if she's trying to decide whether or not to let him in. She slides her hands in her back pockets and nervously rocks back and forth from her heels to her toes. Not wanting to appear rude, she slightly raises her right hand, making an attempt at a friendly wave.

"Hey. I'm Sarah."

"Hello. Thanks for inviting me."

Sarah studies his expressions with a watchful eye. Finally, she makes up her mind. "We're about to get started. Why don't you come in?"

As Joseph and Zaphin follow Sarah into the house, the comforting fragrance of the wood burning in the fireplace is even thicker.

Once inside the house, they stand silently while looking around the abode. A soothing serenade of crackling from the hearth is the only noise that they hear. The *décor* of the house is very traditional. The furniture that is scattered throughout the house holds visible signs of wear to the fabric. The room is not brightly lit, but it is adequate enough for reading. There's a circle of folding chairs set out in an open space that is situated in the middle of the living room. An older couple is already sitting there, waiting patiently for the gathering to start.

"Hello," Joseph says.

"Hello there," the two chime in together.

"Thank you for coming," the wife adds. "My name is Kathy Jansen, and this is my wonderful husband, Edward."

"My name is Joseph, and this is my friend, Zaphin."

Zaphin waives to the couple, who nod encouragingly back at the teens from their chairs. To the left of them is the lit fireplace, which supplements the house's inefficient furnace system. To the right of the living room is a doorway. Through it, they can make out some cabinets and a white counter.

Mr. Jansen stands up from his chair, beckoning the teens with his hand.

"Come on in, we're just getting started. Please have a seat." There is a small girl crouched down on the floor of the living room. She looks to be around eight years old. The girl is contently petting a cute white dog with curly fur. Joseph crouches down next to her.

"What a pretty little girl," he says.

The girl looks up and smiles at him but continues to pet the dog. Sarah interrupts the conversation.

"I didn't know you had a dog."

"We're just watching it for tonight. The Nuessens are going to a movie and asked if we would watch their puppy," Mrs. Jansen explains.

Mr. Jansen seems to be getting impatient to start the Bible study. He starts to fidget with his Bible, alternating between tapping his fingers on the cover to a silent tune and wiping his hand across it. "Should we go ahead and start the Bible study?" he asks.

Joseph winks at the little girl. Standing up, he makes his way over to one of the chairs. Zaphin, who has been pretty quiet up until now, plops down onto one of the folding metal seats located closest to the door.

"Let's get our Bible on," he says.

Mrs. Jansen takes her place in a chair next to her husband. The little girl gets up from the puppy and scoots up into a seat beside the old couple. Sarah walks over to the chairs and sits down as well, next to Joseph.

There are still a lot of empty chairs left, Joseph thinks to himself.

"Are you expecting more people?"

"You never know who is going to stop in," Mr. Jansen answers.

"I can't believe how much character this house has," Joseph says, genuinely intrigued by it. He has never actually been inside of their home before.

"Yes," Mr. Jansen agrees as he lays his hand gently on his wife's open and waiting palm. "We've made a lot of memories in this old house."

The couple grins as they both look fondly around at their home.

"We moved into this place shortly after we got married," his wife says softly. Her eyes are focused on some pictures that line the top of their fireplace mantle.

"Is that you two?" Sarah asks. She points in the direction that Mrs. Jansen is staring. There's a photograph there of a couple who apparently had just been married. A fancy silver frame outlines the picture.

"Sure is," Mrs. Jansen replies. "We were so young."

"I don't know what she ever saw in me," Mr. Jansen chuckles. "I'm just glad she didn't wise up before the wedding."

Mrs. Jansen squeezes his hand and shakes her head, as if to say, "You are so ornery!"

"How did you guys meet anyway?" Sarah asks.

"Well, we first met at a soup kitchen."

"You worked in a kitchen together?" Zaphin blabs condescendingly.

"Well, we did work there, but we didn't get paid. We would set up a table in a very poor area with a bunch of cooked food on it. It was kind of like your cafeteria is at school. People would walk through the line, and we would put food on their plate. It's a great way to help people in need, and also a great way to share the message of Jesus."

"How does that share the message of Jesus?" Zaphin asks.

"Have you ever heard the saying that there are no free lunches or that nothing in life is free?" Mrs. Jansen asks.

"Sure."

"Well, this soup kitchen was completely free. We didn't make them come to church or do some work or even stay to listen to the message of Jesus."

"Okay, so it was really free," Zaphin agrees, still failing to see what Mrs. Jansen is trying to get at.

Mrs. Jansen smiles a peaceful and patient smile. She seems to be so delighted with Zaphin's questions. "People also have a hard time understanding what Jesus did for us. God sent Jesus, his only Son, to die for us. His Son is a gift to everyone, and that gift is completely free."

"Don't you have to do good stuff to be a Christian?" he asks.

"What do you have to do to make a gift yours if someone is offering it to you?" she inquires as she lifts her worn Bible off of her lap, holding it out into the air for Zaphin.

"Accept it?" he asks, believing that his answer is too easy to be correct.

"Right!" she exclaims. "And all you have to do is accept the gift that God gives us. Do you know what that gift is?"

Zaphin shrugs his shoulders.

"His gift to us is Jesus. Jesus is God's Son, and originally he was up in heaven with God. Heaven is a perfect place, and God, Jesus, and the Holy Sprit are perfect. Since we all sin, we can't go to that perfect place because then it wouldn't be perfect anymore. God tells us that the punishment for sinning is eternal death to a place called Hell. As a great display of his love for us, however, he sent his only Son to this earth to take our punishment. Jesus was tortured and killed on a cross for our sins, but he rose again. Praise God, he rose again!"

"Don't you have to be a good person before you can accept Jesus and his gift?"

"That's what a lot of people seem to think, but the answer is no. No one is perfect. Christians aren't perfect either. Even after they have accepted Jesus as their savior, they still mess up and sin sometimes. You come as you are, and God will do the rest. You just have to let him by making him the Lord of your life."

"I get it," Zaphin says confidently. He stretches his arms above his head and leans back into the palms of his hands, looking up at the ceiling.

Mrs. Jansen's smile fades into a grin. She looks over at her husband. He can tell what she is thinking. Only Jesus can draw hearts. He gives her hand a squeeze of encouragement. She tried. She presented Jesus, and that was all she can do.

"You sure have done a great job remodeling in here," Joseph says, trying to brush off some of the tension.

The old couple turns and looks at the brick fireplace.

"We had to do something after the heavy fighting broke out," Mr. Jansen starts. "A huge bomb had exploded just down the street."

"It shook the house so hard," his wife agrees.

"When we came out to see if everything was okay, we saw pieces of the ceiling lying on the ground. Some of the bricks had cracked on the fireplace as well," Mr. Jansen explains.

"The floor was a mess too. All cracked and broken up," Mrs. Jansen adds. "So we started replacing the bad spots in the hardwood panels. When we got to the kitchen, we pulled out one of the loose boards to replace it. To our surprise, it slid right out. It had been made in such a way so that it slides right out if you pull up on it. Underneath the piece of wood, there was some sort of compartment. The once hidden space was now open to us."

"And there was something inside it," Mrs. Jansen interrupts her husband, barely able to contain her excitement.

"Yes. There were old documents, going all the way back to the 1850s. One of the documents was a newspaper article."

"What was it about?" questions Sarah. She leans forward in her chair, obviously intrigued by the story that is unfolding.

"It was about a law. This particular law had been put into place by our government a long time ago," Mr. Jansen explains.

"Can we see it?" Sarah asks, almost pleading with her.

Mr. Jansen looks to his wife for approval.

"I don't see why not," his wife says.

Mrs. Jansen slaps her hands down onto the tops of her legs. She leans forward, straining to push up and get out of the chair. The group watches her intently as she crosses the floor to a large china cabinet. The ornate woodwork complements the rich and dark color of the mammoth piece of furniture. She pulls out a drawer located just below the wide glass doors. Reaching in, she carefully pulls out a document. It's pressed between what appears to be two pieces of Plexiglas. Mrs. Jansen cradles it in her crossed arms as she comes back across the wood floor. Several of the boards creak as she passes over them. She sits down, her eyes brilliantly twinkling.

"This is one of the documents that we found. It is a newspaper article outlying the details of something called the Fugitive Slave Law."

Mrs. Jansen carefully passes the document across to Sarah. As she takes it, she notices that Mrs. Jansen is holding another document in Plexiglas.

"What's that one?" she asks eagerly. She hasn't even looked down at the first treasure that Mrs. Jansen has passed to her.

"One at a time now."

Sarah lowers her head. She begins reading the newspaper article that's in her lap, slightly embarrassed by her impatience.

"Has anyone ever heard of this law?" Mrs. Jansen asks.

Mr. Jansen smiles, as if he is the only one that knows the answer to a secret riddle. Everyone else stares blankly back at her.

"Well, let me tell you about it," she begins. "It all started way back in 1850. You see, there were all these folks in the south half of the United States that thought it was okay to own other people. They called those people *slaves*. During that time, if you had black skin, you could be a slave. Well, the people in the north half of the United States just didn't think that was right. Even some of the people in the South knew that it had to be wrong, so those people started helping the slaves escape to the North. In the northern part of the country, those people could be free.

"There were networks of houses and people going all through the country, from south to north, that helped them escape."

Mrs. Jansen pauses, taking a second look around at their old homestead.

"This is one of those houses where they helped people. It was part of what was called the *Underground Railroad*."

"I've heard of that," Sarah interjects.

"Well, the article that you are holding in your hands describes an act that the president and the congressmen passed into law in 1850," Mrs. Jansen continues.

"What president was that?" Sarah asks.

"Well, the original president that they proposed it to was named Zachary Taylor. He was against it though. Unfortunately for the slaves, he died."

Zaphin perks up, suddenly interested in the conversation again. "How did he die?"

"Oh, it wasn't some assassination attempt or anything like that. It actually was pretty silly. The man wore a black high-collared suit for the Fourth of July that same year that the act was introduced. That day, they were dedicating the Washington Monument. Well, it was pretty hot, and they didn't have air conditioning back then. The president got extremely overheated. So he tried to cool off by drinking ridiculous amounts of iced milk and cold cherries. It's believed that he got cholera from those cherries he ate. That is how he died."

"Crazy," Joseph says, wide-eyed.

"Tell me about it," Mr. Jansen agrees, slowly shaking his head back and forth.

"Then the vice president became the president. His name was Millard Fillmore. As the thirteenth president, he had to be unlucky for somebody. Those somebody's were the slaves and abolitionists. Congress passed the bill, and he signed it."

"What is an abolitioner?" asks Zaphin.

"An *abolitionist*," Mrs. Jansen says, stressing the pronunciation, "is a person who wants to get rid of slavery."

"What's so special about the law?" Sarah asks, getting them back on subject.

Mrs. Jansen's smile fades. "The law stated that everyone had to help capture escaped slaves. Even people in the Northern states who were against slavery were required to help return them to their previous owners."

"That's horrible," Sarah says empathetically.

"Yes. If anyone helped an escaped slave by giving them food, shelter, or aiding them in any way, they could be put in prison and fined $1,000. Even if someone just failed to report that they had seen an escaped slave, they would be subject to the same punishment."

"Was that a lot of money back then?" Joseph asks.

"It sure was. That was a full year's salary for a lot of folks. When they finally caught the purported escaped slave, he or she wasn't allowed a trial. So people started accusing free black men and women in the North of being escaped slaves. Since they weren't allowed a trial, slave owners or traders simply brought them back to the South and made them slaves."

Joseph squints into the distance, as if he's trying to read some very tiny print.

"Why would they have ever agreed to that?" he finally asks.

"Because they were afraid. They were afraid of what the Southern states would do. That is why we are so excited that we found these documents. They speak to our current situation."

"What do you mean?" Joseph wonders.

"Our old president wouldn't have ever outlawed Christianity. It was a new president who did that. The people were scared of what the terrorists were going to do; just like the Northern states were afraid of what the Southern states would do. Fear made them turn their heads.

Fear made them ignore the injustice that the government was dictating. And fear is the weapon that they continue to use."

"Show them the letter," Mr. Jansen says, motioning to the document that Mrs. Jansen is still holding.

"This is a letter that we found along with the newspaper article. It is from a slave who escaped to Canada. Apparently, the person who lived here had helped her to avoid being captured."

Mrs. Jansen passes the letter across the room to Sarah. As she reads it, the genuine gratitude of the writer is evident.

> *Dearest friend,*
>
> *Firstly, allow me to extend my sincere appreciation to you for your most generous acts of kindness. Thanks be to the most High for it. If it were not for you, I surely would have never escaped those evil men. I have not seen you since all those long years ago, although I often wonder what had become of you. I was filled with joy to read the letter that you sent. It may be of interest to you to know that I have learned to read and write. As a fact, I am making an attempt at this letter, poorly as it may be written. The Quakers, their help and service only being second to yours, assisted me in crossing over to Canada. They are a kind and generous folk. I remain here, Lord willing, even now. Living is hard work here. You know the difficulty of this country, but I would sooner die here than to give up my liberty and go back to that old way. I pray that someday we meet again before I go on to see the Lord. Please write back if you would be so inclined.*
>
> *Sincerely,*
> *Clara*

Sarah passes the letter along for the others to look at.

Mrs. Jansen starts to speak again. "We want to help Christians, just as the former owners of this house helped slaves. We don't care what the law is."

"Doesn't the Bible say that you are supposed to follow the law?" asks Zaphin.

"Yes," Mrs. Jansen answers, "but there is a higher law. When the law of man contradicts the law of God, we must follow the law of God."

Joseph passes the ancient documents to Zaphin. He skims over the old letter, nods his head, and passes it back to Mr. Jansen. With his rough and wrinkled leathery hands, he carefully sets the two treasures down beside his chair.

"Well then, we should probably start getting into God's Word." Mr. Jansen places the red Bible that he has been fiddling with into his lap as he starts to speak. "Let us pray. Great and powerful Father in heaven, how amazing your unending love is for all of us. We praise you for the awesome sacrifice you gave of your only Son, Jesus. We thank you, Jesus, for dying on the cross and taking the punishment that was meant for us. We ask that you would be with us tonight, that you would teach us through your Holy Spirit, and open our minds to your will. We ask these things in Jesus' precious name."

"Amen," several say in unison.

"Tonight, we will be studying Joshua. Would anyone like to start off by reading chapter ten, verses twelve through fourteen?" Mr. Jansen gives an open invitation to the group.

"I can read it," Sarah says. Thumbing through her red Bible, she hunts for the verses. She clears her throat as she comes to the passage.

> Then spake Joshua to the Lord in the day when the Lord delivered up the Amorites before the children of Israel, and he said in the sight of Israel, Sun, stand thou still upon Gibeon: and thou, Moon, in the valley of Ajalon. And the sun stood still, and the moon stayed, until the people had avenged

themselves upon their enemies. Is not this written in the book of Jashar? So the sun stood still in the midst of heaven, and hasted not to go down about a whole day. And there was no day like that day before it or after it, that the Lord hearkened unto the voice of a man: for the Lord fought for Israel.

Joseph stops reading along and looks to Mr. Jansen.

"What does 'and there was no day like that day before it or after it' mean? Does that mean that God doesn't do miracles like this any more?"

Mrs. Jansen answers instead. "My Bible has a reference in that verse to Isaiah, chapter thirty-eight, verses seven and eight." She turns her Bible to that verse and reads aloud.

And this shall be a sign unto thee from the Lord, that the Lord will do this thing that He hath spoken. Behold, I will bring the shadow of the degrees, which is gone down in the sundial of Ahaz, ten degrees backward. So the sun returned ten degrees, by which degrees it was gone down. This talks about how God moved back time as a sign to Hezekiah that he would be healed from his sickness.

Joseph looks astonished. "So God actually turned back time for Hezekiah?"

Mr. Jansen now chimes in. "We know he made the shadow on the sundial go backward, and God did this after he held the sun in the sky for Joshua. That is a miracle, any way you look at it. I think this verse shows that God still did miracles after Joshua's time. And I believe that he still does miracles today."

"Maybe it means that God will never stop time for a whole day again," Sarah suggests.

Just as she finishes her sentence, an explosive boom thunders against the front door. Two troopers crash through it. Splinters shoot out, some flying into the kitchen. The door rips the chain from the wall that was meant to keep intruders out. The men release the battering ram as they come in, sending it skidding across the floor and crashing into a vase. They are followed into the house by two more troopers, who trample over the busted door that is now lying on the floor. The R and Gs draw their handguns as they continue into the room and surround the startled group. Joseph, Sarah, and Zaphin jump to their feet from the noise. The troopers train their weapons on the teens, who are now standing. Joseph can hear slow and determined footsteps coming up the sidewalk. He is frozen. He can't even move his head. He can't even bring himself to look at the person who approaches. Finally, mustering up enough courage, he turns just in time to see the captain step into the room.

The captain's eyes scan the small house. He appears to be pleased with the situation as he starts to nod his head.

"Sit down!" he commands.

The troopers motion with their guns for Joseph, Sarah, and Zaphin to be seated. As they slowly take their seats, the captain starts to talk again.

"Well, well, well, what's going on in here?"

The captain waits for a response. He hears none. Placing his arms behind his back, he begins pacing around the group. Again, he addresses them. "My name is Slynne. I am the senior captain of this region. The government has given me responsibility to stop treasonous activities, like this Bible study."

He ceases walking and turns quickly on his heel, looking into each of their faces.

"I know that upstanding citizens, such as yourselves, would never dream of breaking the law. Especially for something that is no more than a child's fairy tale. So I am going to give you all a chance to show me that you are not Christian traitors.

"You!" Slynne barks.

He points his long and black glove covered finger at Zaphin.

"I want you to spit on your Bible."

Two of the troopers walk over behind Zaphin and point their guns at his head. The remaining troopers continue to keep the rest of the group subdued. Joseph searches Zaphin's eyes. His friend is studying the red Bible that he holds in his shaking hands. Joseph can see the decision weigh on him. His life, or that Bible. Now is when his true faith is tested. He has to decide whether or not he's going to take a stand. Zaphin slowly raises his head and timidly looks around at the others. The old woman and the old man are staring calmly back at him. He can immediately see, however, that Sarah and Joseph are not so confident. Zaphin catches a glimpse of tears rolling off of Sarah's cheeks. He swallows hard and turns to Slynne.

"Shoot him," Slynne says, showing no emotion.

"*No, wait!*" Zaphin cries out. He spits down upon the red Bible in his lap. Slynne is rather pleased with himself.

"Now go and throw it in the fire," he commands.

This time, Zaphin doesn't look at anyone. Instead, he hangs his head in shame and meekly rises with his Bible. He walks across the living room to the fireplace and turns. Zaphin piers into the flames for a brief moment. He runs his fingers across the cover of the sacred red book in his hands and throws it into the fire. His eyes stay trained on the ground as he returns to the circle and sits in his chair.

"Now you two," Slynne says, pointing at the Jansens. The troopers train their guns on the old couple.

"Spit on your Bibles," he commands.

Mr. Jansen softly and respectfully answers the captain's demands. "We will not spit on the Word of God."

Without opening her Bible, Mrs. Jansen quotes a verse. "Mark, chapter eight, verse thirty-eight says that whosoever therefore shall be ashamed of me and of my words in this adulterous and sinful generation; of him also shall the Son of man be ashamed, when he cometh in the glory of his Father with the holy angels."

An evil smile overtakes Slynne's face.

"Then you will die." Slynne gestures toward the couple. "Shoot them!"

Mr. Jansen looks over at his wife. Her open palm lies on his knee. He places his time-weathered hand in hers once again. She squeezes tightly. Mr. Jansen gently whispers, "Close your eyes, honey." His wife and the little girl close their eyes while he starts to pray. *Crack! Crack!* Two loud bangs ring out in succession. Joseph jumps in surprise. He looks over to see two of the guards lower the smoking barrels of their guns. They move in to inspect the old man and old woman. Giving a nod to Slynne, the troopers let their lifeless bodies slump over onto their chairs. The little girl still has her eyes closed as the guards look to Slynne for some indicating of what to do.

Joseph can't help but feel as though he has been through all this before. *This scene—there is something so familiar about it,* Joseph thinks. The little girl, her parents martyred for being Christians—it all triggers something in Joseph's memory. He flashes back to that day in the city when his parents were preaching. He sees the blurred figure again. The figure shoots twice in the middle of the crowd. He knows that it's his parents who are shot. Welcoming the grief and anger like a long lost friend, he starts to allow the feelings to overtake his rational mind. As reality flees from him, sweat begins beading on his forehead. He's looking down the black hole of the gun barrel. Joseph still can't see the dark figure's face. There is no escape from it. There is no reprieve.

Slynne is starting to say something again. Whatever it is, it snaps Joseph out of his daydream-like trance.

This is no game. These cops are going to kill us all, Joseph realizes. With feelings of fear, sorrow, and rage rushing in on him, he closes his eyes and prays.

Dear Father, please deliver us from this evil. Please protect us and keep us in your hand—Joseph's prayer is interrupted by a huge explosion that shakes the entire house. It's a bomb from one of the militant groups. They must have spotted the police cars from the perimeter of the city. The blast is too much for the old house to bear up under. The decrepit roof gives way from the pressure and collapses. The place where the roof connects to the kitchen holds, but it breaks away from the wall on the other sides of the room. This causes the ceiling to swing down against the floor, crushing everyone who is standing up. Luckily, Joseph and his friends are all sitting down. The roof stops within inches of landing on Zaphin, who ducks and rolls. The captain, on the other hand, is not so lucky. Joseph sees him disappear under a pile of drywall and boards.

The room is filled with smoke and dust. Debris covers the area, and the only light left is what little is coming from the fireplace. Joseph is momentarily dazed. He struggles to regain his bearings. When his reeling mind finally slows, he remembers the little girl. He wipes his eyes and peers through the white cloud. He can't see a thing. Joseph slides his backpack on and starts to crawl over to where she had been sitting.

"Ouch!" Joseph winces as he kneels on something hard. He feels around with his hand. It's one of the troopers' pistols. Joseph slides it into his baggy pants pocket and continues over to the little girl. He finds her standing over the old man's and old woman's bodies. From what Joseph can see, she's in a state of shock.

Joseph scrambles over a pile of drywall and looks up into her sapphire blue eyes. They are open wide and portray a picture of pure innocence.

"What's your name?"

The little girl doesn't answer.

"What is your name?" he asks again as he puts his hand out.

"Giby," she says in a small voice.

Joseph gently grasps her tiny hand. "You have to come with me now, Giby. Your parents aren't here anymore." Joseph looks at her face, trying to gauge her reaction. Giby just stares back at him.

"They are with Jesus," he explains. "Let's go."

Giby shakes her head no.

"Come on," Joseph says reassuringly as he places his hand on her shoulder. "I'm going to get you out of here." Joseph starts to crawl toward the front door, which is open to the outside. Giby pulls away from his grasp. She shakes her head frantically, fighting to stay inside the house.

"Come on, we have to go," Joseph pleads, but Giby still shakes her head no. He whips his head around toward the front door again as he hears sirens coming. Peering out from the smoky room, he can see a light reflecting off of the bushes through the open door. It's police lights, and they're getting brighter as they come down the street. Sarah crawls out from under some rubble, looking dazed as well.

"Joseph?" Sarah calls, straining to see if it is really him. He doesn't answer her. He has to stay focused on Giby.

"Here, how about I give you a piggyback ride?" Giby climbs on and wraps her arms tightly around his neck. Joseph makes his way over to Sarah. Before he has a chance to say anything, Zaphin climbs out of the darkness.

"Wait!" he calls out to Sarah and Joseph, coughing profusely.

Joseph looks back at Sarah and says, "We have to get out of here, more troopers are right outside."

"Follow me," Sarah says as she starts to scurry toward the kitchen. She seems to know exactly where she's going. "There's an access panel in here that leads to a tunnel. Hurry, this way!"

She navigates the piles of boards and drywall as quickly as possible. Joseph and Zaphin follow close behind her. They're heading deeper into the house. Sarah walks through a very old kitchen and heads straight to the back wall. This room is the one that was part of the original building. It has extravagant trim work, solid wood doors, and detailed crown molding above the cabinets. She reaches out with her hand and depresses a circle that is located on one of the corner moldings. The wall directly in front of them opens up with a loud click. Joseph lunges forward and catches the large panel before it springs back shut. A set of crumbling stone stairs disappears into a dark underground tunnel.

Sarah doesn't hesitate at all. The entrance is only open for a second before she descends out of sight. Giby slips down off Joseph's back and starts to go down the stairs. Zaphin moves forward at the same time, almost running her over. Joseph plants a hand into Zaphin's chest, catching him off guard. Zaphin stumbles back a couple of feet and looks down at Joseph's hand. Giby rushes past him to join Sarah. He slowly looks up at Joseph until their eyes meet.

"You can't go with us, Zaphin."

"You can't tell me what to do, Joseph."

"Our ways part now. You sold out, man," Joseph replies.

"I panicked. They were going to kill me. Look, man, I swear," Zaphin puts his hand on Joseph's shoulder. "I *will* stand firm next time."

The teens can hear a lot of commotion in the next room. Six guards come into the house and start pulling debris off of Slynne. He releases a long and painful groan as he reaches up to feel his head. Blood drips from his hair and face, pooling on the floor. The captain wipes his hand across his forehead, revealing a large cut above his right eye. As the rage builds up inside of him, he starts to shake uncontrollably. His fist tightens. Bright red blood squeezes out from between his fingers and runs down his arm.

"Get them!" Slynne yells as he crashes his fist to the ground.

Joseph and Zaphin are startled by the loud noise. They jerk their heads toward the sound. Zaphin takes advantage of the distraction and pushes past Joseph, who is still focused on Slynne's voice. Joseph grabs for his shirt, but he's already halfway down the stairs.

"Zaphin!" he calls out in a loud whisper. No answer returns to him from the empty staircase. The guards are bearing down on him now. Joseph has no choice but to follow his friends. The hidden doorway springs back into place just as the guards rush the kitchen.

CHAPTER 11

Joseph tries hard to focus his eyes, but there is no light. He hears movement coming from somewhere in front of him. Joseph hones his ears in on the noise. It's like the muffled sound of some paper rustling. A spark flashes, leaving a still image in Joseph's head of Zaphin holding out his hand. The click comes again, followed by two more sparks. Finally, Zaphin's lighter ignites. He holds out the flame, pointing it toward Joseph. The whole tunnel lights up from its glow. It amazes Joseph how much of a difference that little tiny light made in the extreme darkness. If he were to expose that same flame during the day, no one would even be able to see any light coming off of it. Around other light sources, it might seem very insignificant. Here in the darkest place though, the tiny flame brings light to the entire area.

Zaphin moves to one side of the tunnel. He holds his lighter out in front of him as he trails behind it. Several flashlights hang from hooks in the dirt wall. Sarah grabs one of them and presses the button. A yellow light slices down through the blackness to the dingy floor. Shadows crawl along the walls as she moves the light up and down the narrow corridor. She directs the beam back towards the remaining flashlight and lifts it off of the hook. After testing it out, she hands it to Joseph.

"Here."

"Where does this tunnel lead?" Zaphin whispers.

"Mr. Jansen told me that it leads to the basement of his shop."

"Where is that?" asks Zaphin.

"It's on the edge of the city," she answers.

Joseph analyzes the roof above them that stretches downward away from the stairs. "Wow! So this tunnel is like the length of a football field or more!"

"If you say so," Sarah replies, not finding it quite so interesting.

The group of teens starts their journey down the dark tunnel. The flashlights are the only things lighting their way. Roots protrude from the cold dirt, reaching out to feel these strangers. Pieces of soil roll down the old walls and break on the worn earth floor. Aromas of mud and mildew intermingle in the poorly ventilated shaft. The tunnel walls are only held in place by wood beams that look half-rotten. Joseph can see that the path slopes down for about thirty feet, and then it appears to level out.

"How the heck did they dig this without anyone knowing?" Zaphin asks Sarah as they walk.

"The tunnel was built here a long time ago. Some parts of this house are actually well over two hundred years old. The kitchen is the original part of the estate that was used for the Underground Railroad."

Joseph chimes in. "Yeah, that's what Mrs. Jansen was talking about. Praise God they restored the kitchen instead of just bulldozing it down." Joseph surveys the walls once again. He imagines what those slaves must have felt like traveling down this very path. They probably felt similar to how he does now—fleeing for his very life.

"So that's what this tunnel was used for?" Zaphin asks.

"Yup," Sarah replies. "Over time, people added on to the house and updated it. The Jansens purchased the house when they were younger. You probably couldn't tell, but they actually invested a lot of money renovating it."

Zaphin looks up, skeptically surveying the dirt roof as he travels beneath it. "Let's hurry and get out of here before this death trap collapses."

Two stories above them, some guards scour an empty field. A trooper with several badges on his chest is walking back to the police cars outside of the Jansen's demolished house. To his back is a barricaded wall. Barbed wire littered with trash coils and tangles along the top of it, ending at the gate to the city. They are at the northern guarded gate. Along with the fence, the gate is supposed to keep anyone from coming into the neighborhood from the city. On the west side of the inner city there are several more roads that lead into the suburbs, but those don't have gates. The rebels and gangs have complete control over the urban west side, and the troopers pretty much leave them alone. To try and prevent attacks, they had set up a perimeter around the suburbs with guarded terminals. These checkpoints were installed in order to ward off any potential militia. This particular trooper's name is Alex. He's in charge of the perimeter for the north area. He arrives at a large van to find a medic attending to Slynne, who now has a bandage wrapped around his head that also covers his left eye.

He salutes the captain. "We can't find them, sir."

Slynne looks up, the anger still burning in him.

"They're on foot, so they can't get too far. Call in every available car and have them set up a five-mile perimeter patrol from this spot." Slynne doesn't look up at the lieutenant as he continues his rant. "They will pay for this."

He raises his hand to his head again, feeling his bandage. He lightly traces the outline of it all the way down to his covered eye. Slynne clenches his teeth and slams his hand down onto a nearby table. Alex winces at the loud crack.

"What are you waiting for?"

The trooper jerks his hand to his forehead in a nervous salute. As he lowers his hand, he pulls a radio out from its holder to execute the captain's orders. Alex marches away from Slynne as he discusses their strategy, unaware that the Christians are less then two hundred feet away.

The teenagers have finally reached the point in the tunnel where it starts going up again. They can just barely make out a door at the end.

"Finally!" blurts out an anxious Zaphin as he jogs up to the door.

Sarah runs up behind him. He's pulling on the door, but it isn't budging. Sarah puts her flashlight down and tries to yank on the handle as well.

"Here, hold this," Joseph says as he shoves his flashlight into Zaphin's chest.

"Well, since you asked so nicely," he comments wryly as he backs away from the door.

Joseph helps Sarah yank on the handle. At first it doesn't move—not one bit. But then, it starts making a noise. The handle squeaks as it turns downward. The large metal door is brown with rust, which causes it to make a terrible screeching sound as it swings out. It opens to reveal a stack of boxes. Joseph squeezes beside them as he climbs up into the room. The place is filled with a hodgepodge of things, from old boxes of paperwork to broken electronics and repair parts. There's a wooden workbench on the other end of the room, and to the left of it are stairs leading up to the shop.

Joseph hops back down and nods to the others, signaling that the room is safe to enter. He holds the door open as Sarah steps up onto the concrete platform, followed by Zaphin, and finally Giby. Once everyone is inside, he too steps up into the room and pulls back on the large metal door with all of his weight. He can barely budge it at first, but it closes quickly once Joseph gets some momentum going. A hollow clank rings out as it latches again. Joseph tries to move the handle, but it appears to be stuck again.

"It must automatically lock from the other side," Joseph says. His statement is met with blank stares. "And I don't have a key," he points out.

Zaphin eventually responds. "Well, if we can't go back into the suburbs, then we'll have to go up. We can't just stay here."

Zaphin walks up the stairs to a newer tan-colored metal door. Sarah and Giby look to Joseph for some direction. He doesn't know what to do either. Shrugging his shoulders, he conveys to them that they might as well go up too. Sarah follows Zaphin up the stairs with Giby and Joseph close behind. Zaphin tries the door at the top of the stairs, but it's locked.

"Now this is a lock that I can take care of," he declares as he whips a butterfly knife out of his pocket. He spins it around in his hand several times. Sarah crosses her arms, tapping her foot impatiently. Obviously having done this before, he pries the knife in between the doorframe and the door latch. He then proceeds to force the already loose lock open. They pile into the shop, looking around as they enter. There are rows of shelves, along with various pieces of equipment on the floor. In the aisles of display racks, there are numerous appliances and small machines. It must be a little shop for new electronics. Judging by the equipment, Mr. Jansen must have done some repair work here as well. Mr. Jansen probably had people drop off equipment at his house and used this area as more of a workshop. Joseph looks out upon all of the aisles and aisles of electronics.

What a waste, he thinks to himself.

Each one of the gadgets has a unique purpose in this world. Each one was made for something specific, but there they sit, week after week, collecting dust. Joseph wonders if some of the equipment can even perform the task that it was created for after being out of service for so long.

They make their way through the store and gather around the front door next to the old register.

"Come on," Sarah taunts. "Work your magic, Zaphin."

Zaphin leans in close to Sarah's face, speaking softly. "It doesn't work on dead bolts, genius." She puts her flashlight closer to the door as she examines it.

"Let me try it then," she insists.

Zaphin pulls out his knife again. This time, he doesn't do any fancy tricks with it.

"Be my guest," he offers as he hands it to her.

Sarah digs into the side of the door with the knife, trying to pry the bolt back into the door. She's getting nowhere. Zaphin is right. There's a dead bolt-style lock that requires a key to unlock it regardless of whether you're on the inside or outside.

"You're doing it all wrong," Zaphin says. "Here." He takes the knife from her hands. Zaphin pushes it into the crack of the door and applies pressure. It doesn't move. He grunts as he pries on it even harder. *Crack!* Something gives, and Zaphin falls into the door.

"Did you get it?" Sarah asks.

Zaphin quietly displays the blade, which is broken in half.

"Perfect," he sneers.

Zaphin throws it to the ground in disgust and walks over to the cash register.

Joseph studies Giby as she starts to walk through the store, wandering away from the group.

It must be hard for her to be here at the store that her parents had owned, he thinks sympathetically. He watches her peruse the checkout counter, touching everything as though each holds a special memory for her. Giby keeps moving from shelf to shelf, leaving the area in front of the register. She picks things up here and there on her way over to look at some electronic toys. Sarah is standing next to her, staring sadly off between the metal bars that cover one of the dirty shop windows.

Zaphin grabs a candy bar out of one of the boxes and starts eating it.

"Zaphin!" Joseph says sternly as he gives him a glare of disapproval.

"What? It's not like the Jansens are going to miss it," he spouts back with his mouth still half-full of chocolate. Joseph grabs the front of his shirt, slamming him backward onto the counter.

"Have some brains, freak! She just watched them die."

Zaphin looks across the room to where Giby and Sarah are standing. Zaphin brings his arms up and slams them downward into the inside of Joseph's elbows. "Get off me!"

Joseph's arms bend from the force, and Zaphin pushes him away. Sarah looks over to see what all the commotion is about. She sees Joseph in a fighting stance, readying himself to square off against his friend.

Zaphin looks down at his clothes and brushes the wrinkles out of his shirt with his hand. "I swear. You better knock that crap off."

Joseph doesn't say a word.

Sarah interrupts the two. "Cut it out, guys. Fighting each other is the last thing we need to be doing right now. I think we can get out of this window." She turns back to the lock and twists it open. "These bars are attached to the window pane. They should slide right up with it." Zaphin struts over to her side, where he continues staring at Joseph.

CHAPTER 12

"I got it," Sarah says excitedly as the window slides up. A high-pitched digital horn alarm starts cycling on and off. Sarah jumps out of the window. "Come on!"

Joseph runs over to Giby just as Zaphin is headed out of the window too. Giby raises her arms toward Joseph. He bends down and pulls her up on his back.

"We've got to go now," he explains. He runs to the opening and slides under the top of the window. The base of the window is low to the ground, allowing him to step right out onto the sidewalk. Sarah and Zaphin have already started to run back toward the suburb when suddenly a trooper car turns the corner, cutting off their escape.

Their shoes skid forward on the road as they try to change directions. Zaphin trips and is able to briefly regain his balance before falling down completely.

"Back this way!" Sarah says, sprinting back toward Joseph.

"They're patrolling the city!" Sarah warns him as they approach. Joseph turns around with Giby still on his back and runs back past the shop. He heads straight as fast as he can until he reaches the street corner, where he turns left onto the next crossroad. Zaphin and Sarah follow them, panting hard. Joseph spots an alleyway two blocks up on the right. "Here!" he calls.

The whole group ducks into the darkness. Joseph arrives first and slides Giby off of his back. They both crouch down behind a dumpster that's overflowing with trash. The stench permeates their senses. The noxious smell makes it considerably harder to breathe. Sarah and Zaphin run right past them.

"Over here," Joseph whispers.

They slow down to a crawl, searching around. Zaphin spots him first.

"There he is!"

Zaphin and Sarah run over beside the pile of refuse and squat down as well. They can see the lights of the patrol car flashing against the red brick. They know he must be close.

The trooper car comes into view. As it slowly passes by the alley, a spotlight beams down the dingy wall and around the dumpster. Everyone holds their breath, fearing that even the slightest movement will pull the bright light onto their location. They all exhale in relief as the car drives on past the building and out of sight.

"What's the plan now?" Zaphin asks.

"I know it's dangerous," Joseph admits, "but we work our way into the middle of the city and head west. We can circle back around the troopers when we get outside of the city. Then we head home. They never guard that side of town. Even these troopers won't drive through the west district at night."

"I know the backstreets in this part of the city," Zaphin says. "Follow me, and stay close." Standing up, he brushes off his pants. He starts walking through the alley in the opposite direction from where they had just come from. Sarah looks to Joseph again. He shrugs his shoulders just like before, as if to say, "Your guess is as good as mine." Sarah reluctantly turns around and walks after Zaphin. Giby starts following behind Sarah, and Joseph again brings up the rear.

When they get to the end of the alley, Zaphin motions for them to wait. A second later, another patrol car drives slowly across the street just a block up from them. It turns another corner and drives out of sight. Once they're gone, Zaphin signals for them to cross the street. He walks toward the other side, cautiously looking both ways as he goes. Sarah waits for a second and then follows quickly behind him. She catches up to Zaphin before he can even make it all the way across.

"Go," Joseph whispers to Giby. Her little feet shuffle across the pavement. She doesn't bother looking left or right. She simply scurries straight across. Joseph jogs behind her, watching for cars all the way. When they get to the other side, they realize that the alley doesn't continue. Instead, it's the start of a new road. With everyone across, Zaphin picks up the pace again. He walks briskly up the one-way street, not even bothering to glance back at his friends, who nevertheless stay close behind him.

They walk several more blocks farther up the street. A cop car suddenly pulls around the corner. Joseph motions with his hand for everyone to go back. Giby, Joseph, and Sarah scramble into a side street that they had passed about ten feet back. They all stop behind the corner, frozen, with their backs against the wall. Just seconds later, Zaphin appears and runs in behind them. Everyone listens intently. Two bright headlights slowly get brighter but then fade away. The silence is deafening. It seems to last for an eternity, but the lights do not return. The car must not have seen them.

"That's the bad thing about being out here. You don't know if you're going to run into the cops or the gangs. Either way, it's bad news," Zaphin comments.

"You said it," Sarah agrees.

"This road seems to turn back north again. Let's go this way," Zaphin says as he heads north.

Eventually, they come up to another alley. With his friends behind him, Zaphin courageously enters in. This alley is eerily dark, long, and full of filth. Papers roll in the wind across the path, and the black of night seems to engulf the passage, even suffocating the light that bleeds over from the street.

"Are you sure this is safe?" Sarah questions. She's very worried. Her steps slow as she progresses foreword. Zaphin chuckles back at her over his right shoulder.

"There's nothing to be scared of," he says with a half-smile while he continues to walk deeper into the alley.

Sarah freezes now, unable to continue. Zaphin stops as well, turning around.

"Come on, Sarah. I promise that nothing is going to bite you in here. It's just dark," Zaphin says.

Sarah looks back at Joseph.

"We have to go on, Sarah," Joseph reassures her. "Just stay close to us." Joseph and Giby walk past her, catching up to Zaphin. Sarah starts to walk again with quick, short steps that are haunted by fear.

She turns on her flashlight and searches what is in front of her.

"Dim that thing!" Zaphin commands. "You can see that light a mile away."

Sarah momentarily appears shocked. Then, fumbling around with the flashlight, she manages to cover the end of it with a corner of her unzipped sweater. The light is dimmed substantially, but it still provides enough illumination for them to see a couple steps ahead of them. Sarah peers up between the two buildings. She can barely make out a star high up in the sky. Suddenly, she hears something behind them. Sarah melts, curling forward and away from the noise. She's too afraid to face it and too afraid to run. It sounds like it's coming from where they entered into the alley. They have traveled a little under halfway between the buildings at this point. Just then, a grimy hand reaches out and grabs Sarah's pant leg from the shadows. She screams and instinctually kicks the hand away.

"*Oww!*" something whines. "Wretched little thing!"

Joseph and Zaphin run over to see what it is. An old bum begins to appear as he emerges up out of the dark and into view of the dim flashlight. His face is weathered, and his eyes are yellow. He has an evil, devious look on his face with a sly grin, which shows what very little teeth he has left. The two that are left are black and decayed. The bum then realizes that this girl is not alone. His expression changes from menacing to one of surprise. Gradually, his face fades into a gentle and humble look that you would expect to see from a nice elderly man.

"I didn't see you, missy. You best be careful in here—it can be very dangerous, you know." A pungent odor spews from his foul mouth as he speaks.

"Leave us alone, old man," Zaphin says dismissively.

"Oh, I'll leave you," The bum's face transforms back into the same evil expression and the devilish grin returns. "But you won't be alone!" he cackles as he shrinks back into the shadows.

"What does that mean, old man?" Zaphin exclaims. He grabs the flashlight from Sarah and shines it in full brightness, but the bum is gone.

"The sooner we get out of here, the better," Joseph's voice squeaks. Sarah rushes up in between the men. She can see that Joseph is worried.

"I agree." Zaphin looks very concerned and confused as well. They start walking again, but this time, a little more cautiously. Sarah can feel something in the black night. Some unseen force is bearing down on them. It's making her queasy. Her clammy palms clench down tighter and tighter inside her hoodie pockets.

"What is that?" Sarah whispers. "I hear noises behind us!" They look back, but nothing is there. Zaphin shines his flashlight down the dark alley. The light is starting to fade now. Zaphin hits it with the side of his hand, hoping that it is just a loose connection.

"The battery must be running out," Sarah says.

Still, they don't see anything. The group of uninvited guests is about three quarters of the way through the alley now. This time all of them hear an overwhelming noise.

Zaphin turns around and shines his flashlight again. What he sees startles him. "Oh crap!" he exclaims.

There are twenty or more bums scampering after them. The group of anemic frames is dressed in rags and full-length coats with hoods. Their eyes are crazed. Their teeth are rotten and missing.

Dirt and grime covers their bodies and clothes, and rage pours from their faces. Some have sticks, while others have actual knife-like weapons fashioned from scrap metal. The worn down and decaying mob is advancing down the alley, like a horde of undead.

Sarah screams then turns and runs. Zaphin is close behind her. Joseph grabs Giby and swings her up on his back as he starts to sprint toward the opening. They easily outrun the mob and break away from the darkness and into the welcomed light of the street. Joseph looks over his shoulder, but nothing emerges from the blackness. It's almost as if the homeless men are trapped there, unable to escape its clutches.

CHAPTER 13

The group is entering gang territory now. Bombs shatter concrete in the distance. Sporadic gunfire echoes in the night. Zaphin is leading the group again as they come up to another corner in the city. A car is on fire there, the flames still dancing out of its bowels where an explosion has ripped through the roof. Two unidentifiable groups of men exchange gun bursts down the street from where they are.

Zaphin bends down and starts walking, making sure to keep his head low. He gets to the end of the burning car and then sprints across to the other side. Zaphin arrives behind the next corner, still bent over. He straightens and braces himself up against the building. Joseph can hear him trying hard to catch his breath. After waiting a moment, he waves his hand in a motion for Sarah to come across. She comes out from behind the building and crosses the dangerous street, mimicking Zaphin's motions. She arrives on the other side of the street without incident. Next, Giby tiptoes out from the building. Joseph is walking close behind her. She turns her head to look over the flaming car and then farther and up the street. Not paying attention to where she's going, she stumbles on some debris and falls down onto the pavement. Joseph bends over to help her up, just as the stray blast of an automatic weapon sprays the top of the car. The bullets pass through the exact place where Joseph had been standing. If he hadn't bent over to help Giby, he would have been toast. Joseph jerks his head down and covers the little girl with his body. The random burst stops, and the gunfire is directed elsewhere down the street again.

Giby hops to her feet and walks quickly across the road. Again, she doesn't look left or right. She walks straight to the other side, seemingly oblivious to what's happening. Zaphin waves his hand in a quick, choppy motion, as if to say, "Hurry up, what are you waiting for?" Joseph ducks his head and walks to the end of the burning car. He peeks around the bumper. In the distance, he can see some of the gang members still shooting at someone. He darts across the street and rests behind the safety of the building. By some miracle, everyone made it across unharmed. They have just started to continue on their journey when the sound of loud sirens reverberates through the night air. The unsuspecting teens jump and spin around to see a police van barreling down the street at them. Everyone scrambles around the corner in a mad dash. They retreat up toward the gangs, turning back north up one of the streets. Halfway down the road, Sarah spots a good place to hide in.

"In here!" she yells as she opens a sturdy metal door and disappears through it. The face of the building has several important looking emblems on it. The architecture is distinguished and resembles that of a government building. Joseph waits for everyone to get inside before slamming the door behind him.

They aren't the only ones that have heard the troopers' car, however. The gangs that were previously shooting at each other have stopped and are now watching the police car speeding toward them. They immediately turn their fire on this new threat. The van screeches to a halt and skids sideways. Bullets rip across the side of it, shredding the metal. The van door opens up, and two troopers quickly deploy with weapons drawn. Slynne pushes the passenger side door open where he is sitting. He hops out and hastily walks to the rear of the vehicle. Swinging the back doors open, he grabs a grenade launcher out of the rear compartment. His troopers have already started to exchange fire with the gang down the street. Slynne quickly walks around the front of the van, his overcoat floating behind him in the wind. There is no deviation in his course. He travels straight up the middle of the street. Bullets whiz all around him, pelting the pavement. He aims at one of the gunmen, who is still firing, and rains down grenades on their location. Four explosions go off in a row, and the building collapses next to where the resistance force is positioned. The enemy fire ceases. In its place, a pillar of smoke bellows up, and fire covers the ground.

Slynne turns to one of his troopers and lobs the grenade launcher back at him with his left hand. The trooper lunges forward to catch the weapon and almost falls over from its weight. Slynne never looks back at them. He snaps his fingers, and two more troopers with dogs rush out of the vehicle. They run to where Joseph, Giby, Sarah, and Zaphin had been. Immediately, the canines start smelling around. The dogs easily pick up the trail, yelping as they pull the troopers around the corner. Several reinforcements fall in behind them, ready to strike at any threats. Slynne follows as well. The click of his boot heels on the cement punctuates each quick, determined step.

Zaphin, Joseph, Sarah, and Giby are making their way through some sort of compound. It's evident the place has been abandoned for quite some time. Steel bars protruded from the floor, cut in half from an explosion. Joseph passes through a second doorway. It appears to have once had a high-tech retinal scan and fingerprint entry, but the inside of the place had been destroyed by some sort of raid or battle.

The gangs must have blown up the secure areas and ransacked the place, Joseph thinks to himself.

The group walks through what would have been two separate security checkpoints. When they start to enter the first area, the lighting comes on in the building.

"What gives?" Zaphin asks.

Sarah explains, "This place must have its own generator. From the looks of it, this is a military compound. I read about these places. The generator probably runs off of a huge underground storage tank of gasoline. They must have sensors that run everything on standby. When the system identifies that someone is in the building, it must switch everything to full power. Just like this elevator," she says as she pushes the circular button with the down arrow. It illuminates with a warm yellow glow, and the door immediately opens. "See—it works!"

At the same time, the troopers are coming up to the entrance of the building. The R and Gs burst through the metal door with guns drawn. The trained men tiptoe as they progress, surveying the area for any possible ambushes.

"We need to get off this floor. Everyone get into the elevator," Sarah instructs.

Zaphin rushes in first. He turns to his right, searching for the buttons. Joseph and Giby jump in and head for the back of the elevator, while Sarah is the last to enter. Just like Zaphin, she immediately looks for a button—any button that will get them away from the police. The controls are directly in front of her. There are three levels below them that are underground and six levels above them. Sarah presses the button for the lowest level, and the elevator door closes.

"Why didn't you go up?" Zaphin asks.

"Because I hit the down arrow when we were outside. Besides, they would expect us to go up," she replies.

Joseph looks at Giby. What a night this has been for her. She seems unaffected by everything. Joseph watches her as she looks around the elevator. She's standing between him and Sarah. Joseph squats down on the floor and looks up at her again. Her curly brown hair hangs down, surrounding her face. It dances up and down around her pink cheeks from the vibrations of the elevator. Giby peeks at Joseph from between the swinging locks of hair. Their eyes meet, but she quickly looks at the floor again. She is once again lost in what appears to be intent thought.

"You sure talk a lot, don't you?" he says jokingly.

Giby shakes her head no and continues to gaze at the floor. Sarah looks over at Joseph and smiles. The little girl slides down the wall of the elevator until she's sitting with her knees bent. As she joins him on the floor, she lays her head on one of her legs. Again, as if drawn by some unseen magnet, she stares down at the floor. This time, she's looking at the corner of the elevator. Something is there. It's something shiny. She stretches her tiny finger out at the object. "Look, Joseph, what is that?" she asks.

Joseph looks over and sees something shimmering in the dull light. It's just barely sticking out from under a wood panel. He pulls his own keys out of his pocket and wedges the small item out of the crack. "It looks like some sort of access key," Joseph says.

"There's a keyhole in this elevator panel," Sarah replies.

Just then, the elevator doors open. They are at the basement. Joseph gets up and steps to the front of the elevator. He puts the key into the keyhole and turns it. "This is definitely what it goes to."

The panel opens, revealing a single red button. Joseph looks to the others. "Should we press it?"

"I'm not sure that's such a good idea. We don't have any idea what that does," Zaphin answers.

"I'd rather take my chances with the button than with the police." Once again, he turns to the button. He hesitates at first, but finally commits as he smashes it down with his thumb. The doors close, and the elevator takes a quick drop. Everyone slightly loses their balance. Joseph's face morphs from one of determination to one of uneasiness. Giby slams her hands flat on the floor to steady herself. Sarah braces her body with one hand above the buttons and the other hand behind her on the other side. Zaphin doesn't appear to be happy either. He glares at Joseph as he grinds his shoulder into the wall.

The elevator is slowly picking up speed. It's going so fast that he starts to doubt whether it's going to stop or not. The cable finally begins to slow down again before coming to a complete stop. The doors open up into a pristine white hallway. Joseph doesn't know exactly how far down they are, but they have to be pretty deep. Zaphin steps out first and triggers the lights, which turns on all the equipment as well. He is standing in the long hallway. Everything is white, from the hard tile to the painted walls. Fluorescent fixtures line the tall ceilings. It reminds Joseph of a hospital. To his left is the short end of the hallway, which jogs back to the right after about ten feet. To his right is a fifty-foot long hallway, with one hallway leading to the left about fifteen feet away. A second hallway at the far end of the long corridor leads to the left as well.

Zaphin walks down the short hallway to the left, following it until it jogs back to the right. He stops in the middle of the hall, leery of what may be waiting around the corner.

"What's the matter? Are you scared of the boogeyman?" Sarah taunts as she strolls past Zaphin. She tosses her hair over her shoulder and smirks at him. His face turns a little red, embarrassed at the thought of a girl showing him up.

"I was just thinking," he shouts down the hall after her. Sarah turns the corner and continues to the end of the hall. Zaphin cautiously follows her from a distance, making sure to give himself enough time to run if anything unexpected happens.

Joseph closes up the panel and locks it again. He presses the first floor button and jumps back out of the elevator before the door closes. This way, the troopers won't be able to tell where they are. The elevator makes a grinding noise as it quickly returns to the main level. He takes Giby by the hand and leads her down the long hallway to the right.

As they walk, he wonders where Sarah and Zaphin have run off to.

They come to the first corridor. Joseph can tell that it leads to some sort of control room. He can see that there is a small window in a door at the end of the hall. By the dim glow of the emergency lighting, he can make out some monitors on the wall.

"Let's check it out," Joseph coaxes. Giby seems to be all right with the idea. When they get to the door, he opens it. The little girl shuffles in, and he closes it behind them.

Along the wall are numerous cameras, monitors, and other controls. For some reason, this equipment doesn't automatically come on with the lights.

"I guess not everything is automated," he mumbles as he feels for the switch on the wall. "Found it!"

He raises it and everything flickers for a minute before the charge reaches full power. When the monitors come on line, he can see different areas of the facility. Joseph easily locates Sarah and Zaphin in the R & D room. That's where their hallway must lead to. It's an old assembly room with high-tech robotics and other sophisticated gadgets. Joseph can see them talking, but he can't hear what they are saying.

"This must have been the military's secret R & D facility for new weapons," Zaphin says.

"What was your first clue?" Sarah says with an awestruck tone. She opens her eyes wide, mocking him as she looks up and points to a sign over one of the office doors. It reads "Chief Officer—Military R & D."

Zaphin follows the line of her finger and reads the sign.

"So you can read!" he shoots back at Sarah. "You sure are confident for someone who was scared to be in the dark."

"Does it look dark in here to you?" she asks. "I just don't like to be where I can't see what's coming at me."

They both go their separate ways in the room, toying with all the different inventions and trying to figure out what they do. Most of it seems experimental in nature, and they can't even get it to work. Zaphin tinkers with a softball-sized robot with several levers coming off of it. It resembles an octopus lying on its back. He can't get it to do anything though.

Back in the control room, Joseph sees a trooper checking out the elevator. He has two of the dogs with him. The animals are barking and pawing at the door.

Joseph yells down the hall to Sarah and Zaphin, "Come check this out. They have a dog. I think they're going into the elevator."

Sarah and Zaphin run to where Joseph's voice is calling from. They all gather around the small screen and watch as the policeman presses the small round button. The elevator doors open, and the dogs pull him on. Three more troopers pile into the elevator behind him. Joseph scans the monitors until he finds one that shows the inside of the elevator. It's apparent that the police don't know about the locked panel. They watch the troopers go level by level. The procedure is the same for each floor. First, they let the dogs sniff the area outside of the elevator door. Next, they comb the entire level, trying to find the scent of the teenagers. Little do they know that it doesn't exist, except of course in the elevator and throughout the lower level. The R and Gs come to the last floor. They are certain that they'll find them here, but just like every other time before, they funnel back into the elevator, unable to pick up a new trail.

"I think we're safe here," Joseph says reassuringly.

Sensing that someone is staring at him, he looks beyond his friends toward the entrance. It's Giby. She's just standing there in the doorway that leads to the hall. She looks like she's waiting for him, but she doesn't say a word. Joseph studies the monitors again, hesitant to take his eyes off of the soldiers. Finally Giby speaks.

"Come look at this, Joseph," she says abruptly as she starts to move down the hall.

She must have gone exploring on her own while we were watching the troopers, he thinks to himself.

The police are now spread throughout every floor, searching for the teens again.

"Keep an eye on the guards for a little bit. I'll be right back," Joseph instructs.

He follows Giby down the corridor to the last hallway. At the end of it, there is a large, open room. The sign above the door reads "Test Facility B." Giby continues on into the room and stops in front of something resembling two hockey gloves. Joseph inspects the equipment through a glass case. They have a series of electronics hooked up to the top of each one.

"Wow! These are kind of familiar." Joseph looks them over some more. "They're just like the H2H gloves that I use, only they're a lot bulkier. I wonder what they—" Before he can finish his question, Giby presses a button on the monitor's control panel. A display screen next to the gloves comes on, and a video starts to play. An English woman's voice begins with an introduction.

"This is the instruction manual for Adam's Fall, the next generation atom weapon. The gloves are fully self-contained units that can hold a charge for prolonged periods of time without being recharged."

A 3-D image of the gloves comes up on the screen. The simulation shows them being placed onto the docking station where they currently rest. The recorded voice comes on again. "Please choose what you would like to learn about next." A list of options expands from the prompt on the display panel.

Joseph reads them off, "Technical details, functional instructions, maintenance, live training simulation. I guess we'll just go down the list."

Joseph touches the circle that is next to the words "Technical Details" on the screen. Another picture of the gloves comes up, and the female English voice starts to narrate again.

"The technology for this weapon uses specialized magnetic rays to increase or decrease the polarity between atoms. This makes items more or less dense, depending on the setting that you choose. Each glove emits its own unique frequency. When the two rays intersect, the immediate area is magnetized to either become more or less dense."

The online display shows each glove firing a separate ray and then intersecting on an atom.

"By changing the magnetism, the electrons that make up a majority of an atom's mass are either drawn closer to the nucleus or pushed further away. Since all matter is made from atoms, this weapon can make anything disintegrate or solidify."

"This is what we're learning about in science class," Joseph says, remembering their discussion on super atoms.

The display returns to the list of options. Joseph pushes the circle next to "Functional Information." The gloves come up on the display screen again. This time, the screen zooms in on a switch on top of the right glove.

The English woman's voice explains. "This button on the top of the right arm changes the way the two gloves' rays interact. Pressing the switch to the M sets the controls to magnetize items. This makes them more dense. Pressing the switch to the D demagnetizes items. This makes them less dense."

The display zooms in to the palm of the gloves.

"The width of each ray is changed, depending on how many buttons are held down on the palm of the right glove. Holding four buttons down on the palm projects the narrowest beam. Holding no buttons down generates the widest one."

The display switches again to the left glove and shows a button that is accessible by the thumb. Again, a verbal explanation follows.

"The intensity of the beam is changed based upon how hard you hold down the thumb piece on the left glove. By holding the thumb button all the way in, you can make items either extremely more dense or extremely less dense. If you only slightly depress the button, then it will make items only slightly more dense or slightly less dense."

The display returns to the list of options. Joseph presses the "Maintenance" button.

"Adam's Fall is made from highly durable material and can withstand normal shock that would be incurred during hostile encounters. Refer to the maintenance manual for cleaning instructions. The gloves have an advanced power source that must be periodically recharged."

The display shows the right glove again.

"There is a gauge on the right arm that informs the wearer of how much power remains. The only way to recharge the unit is to bring it back to a docking station, as shown."

The screen shows a 3-D image of the gloves being placed in the docking station again, where they are currently resting.

CHAPTER 14

"The police are gone. I checked the phone lines, but none of them work," says a voice from behind them.

Startled, Joseph's eyes widen as he inhales quickly and spins around.

It's only Sarah. Joseph notices that the smile is no longer playing on her pouty lips.

"You surprised me. I didn't even hear you come in. What did you say about the phone lines?"

Sarah looks annoyed. "None of them work," she says bluntly.

"Most of the hard lines in the city haven't worked forever," Joseph replies.

"Yeah, but I thought that since this place has its own backup power, the phones lines may still be up."

Peering over his shoulder, Sarah changes the subject. "What the heck are those?"

"These? They are some sort of weapon."

"Do you think they work?" she asks, pointing toward the gloves.

Joseph picks up the maintenance manual that's sitting by the gloves. He reads a couple of lines before he answers her. "I think so," he replies as he continues to read.

"This is exactly what Mr. Becker was talking about in school. The gloves change the magnetism of the atoms, making them either more or less dense. If these really work, someone can change any atom into a super atom."

Joseph presses the last option on the display screen titled "Live Training Simulation."

"Click access button to retrieve Adam's Fall from the docking station, then proceed to the designated testing area," instructs the automated voice.

Joseph clicks a glowing blue button that is the size of a small marble. The roof of the glass case covering the gloves opens like a bridge parting for a tall ship to pass underneath it. A substantially louder automated warning blares across a speaker. "Only use weapons in designated areas. Please proceed to test area B-1."

As the message repeats again, everyone searches to see where the voice is coming from. It's emanating from a box above a door with a flashing red strobe. The label beside the door reads "B-1."

Zaphin comes running in, hearing the commotion. "What the heck did you guys do?" he bellows.

Sarah faces him with her hands squarely on her hips. "It's some sort of weapon that the military was working on."

Zaphin looks over to where Joseph is standing. His curiosity seems to be a good remedy for his concern as it fades from his face. "Let me see," he demands, walking over to Joseph. Zaphin reaches for the gloves as he bends over the counter. "Let me see what those things can do."

"I'm about to find out myself," Joseph says as he lays the manual down. He snatches up the gloves before Zaphin can grab them. They feel flexible and light—not at all what he was expecting. He slips them over his hands, assessing their dexterity as he rotates his wrists and extends his fingers.

"Feels pretty good."

Joseph walks over to the room labeled "B-1." A proximity sensor opens the door as he approaches it. He's briefly caught off guard by the motion. Zaphin snickers at his friend, following him through the door. Joseph continues on into an even larger space. The lights automatically come on as he enters. He can see a smaller circular structure enclosed in glass that is located in the center of the room. Surrounding the glass room, there are elevated observation seats. Joseph decides to walk down to the enclosure to get a better look. A glass door slides open as he approaches it. Joseph stops just outside of the entrance. He waits for a moment. Nothing happens. He sticks his head inside and peeks around at the strange setting. There are holes in the floor and several mechanical arms jut out from the walls and ceiling.

It's definitely weird, but it looks safe enough, Joseph thinks to himself.

As he clears the opening, the door slides shut behind him. Joseph raises his gloves, eager to try them. They fit well on his hands and arms. Giby, Sarah, and Zaphin have already followed him into the large room. They spot Joseph in the middle, holding up his gloves. The group makes their way down to the front of the enclosure. The door does not open for them this time. Instead, the computer's voice gives a warning.

"Access denied. Testing in progress."

They follow the perimeter of glass around to the left of the door, where they have a clear view of Joseph from the observation deck. Standing outside of the glass walls, they look down into the arena. Each of their eyes are trained on Joseph, waiting with anticipation to see what's going to happen.

The automated English woman's voice starts again. "Welcome to project Adam's Fall. This is the training simulation. To start the simulation, say 'Start.'"

"Start," Joseph spouts while looking up at the speaker.

"You will see vapors coming out of the ground."

Joseph spots what looks like steam coming up from a metal vent in the floor.

The automated voice continues. "The atoms in this vapor are spread very thin, which makes them less dense than the air around them. Use Adam's Fall to temporarily magnetize the atoms, which will draw them closer together and make them more dense. This will cause the atoms to fall to the ground in a solid mass. You should see an effect similar to changing vapor to water and finally to ice. Ensure the setting on the right glove is at M."

Joseph shoots one glove into the vapor, which has no effect on it. He shoots the ray of the other glove out across the room. Holding the two beams on, he converges the rays onto the mist. Joseph's face crinkles in disbelief as the vapor turns into a hard chunk that smashes to the ground. He ceases firing. The pieces of crumbled, solid mass steadily turn back into a mist that evaporates into the air.

The atoms must return to their normal state in a matter of seconds. These are the super atoms that Mr. Becker was telling us about, Joseph thinks to himself.

"Sweet!" Zaphin sputters, in awe of what he has just witnessed. Joseph looks up to his friends, as if to say, "Did you just see that?"

The computer-generated voice comes on once again. "If you are ready for the next training module, then say 'Next.' If you wish to repeat the last training session, then say 'Repeat.' If you want to exit the training session, then say 'Exit.'"

"Next," Joseph says, barely being able to contain his excitement.

"You will see a metal test article come out of the ground."

Something resembling a steel plate rises out from one of the holes in the floor. "Change the magnetize setting on your right glove to demagnetize or set to D. Use Adam's Fall to temporarily reverse the magnetism of the atoms, which will push them apart and make them less dense. You should see an effect similar to changing ice into water."

Joseph toggles the switch on his right glove. This time, Joseph shoots the right glove, following it up immediately with the other. The middle of the metal test plate transforms into a liquid substance and splashes to the ground. Joseph, becoming more adapted to the weapon, points all the fingers of his right hand at the steel plate. This spreads the beam across half the room. The entire plate bubbles and goes splashing to the ground.

"Whoa, dude!" Zaphin exclaims. "That is unbelievable."

Joseph smiles proudly as he looks up at Zaphin, Sarah, and Giby. He walks up to the glass door.

"Exit," Joseph says excitedly.

"Training program terminated. Good-bye." The locked sliding door opens, and a confident Joseph struts up to the stunned teens.

"This rocks," Joseph says calmly. "The next time we meet some troopers, they won't know what hit them."

Sarah shoots a concerned look at Joseph. "We should probably stay here tonight. It's already dark outside, and we are in the middle of the city. Who knows how many troopers, gang members, or criminals could be out there."

Joseph studies his gloves. "Yeah. You're probably right. There were beds and food in the room next to the control area. We'll stay there for tonight."

All of them head back down the hall toward the sleeping quarters. As they pass back through the area where Joseph had found the gloves, Zaphin stops. Wandering over to one of the tables, he begins lifting up papers and opening up cabinet doors. He seems to be combing the area, as if he is searching for something that he has lost.

"What are you looking for?" Sarah asks.

"Some more super gloves," answers Zaphin.

"Ugh. I give up," Sarah grunts while continuing to walk, leaving Zaphin to his quest.

CHAPTER 15

Miles away, far past the vast cityscape lit only by the fires of war and the lamps of oppression, Daniel sits in the cold, dark dungeon of the R and G's police base. Slynne arrives at the old converted church, calling harshly to several of his troopers.

"Well, those little rats got away. A few unarmed, pathetic Christians managed to escape from under gunfire and elude us the rest of the night."

Slynne pauses, staring into his men's nervous eyes.

"A few Christian maggots!" the captain emphasizes loudly.

Every muscle in their necks tightens as they try not to jump at his words. The men continue staring straight forward, afraid to look him in the eye.

"So we are going to go and get their rat friend. I'm sure he is ready to talk by now. He will beg me just to put him out of his misery." The crooked smile returns under his thick mustache as he looks up at the church.

Three armed guards lead the way, and two walk behind their captain, Slynne. They wind down the stairs into the narrow corridor and continue on to the end of the hall. A young looking trooper pulls out a silver key. The other men raise bandanas over their noses, anticipating the gruesome scene that they are about to witness.

"Open it," Slynne commands.

The young guard fiddles with the lock, finally prying it open and removing it. Slynne pulls his hand gun from the polished holster on the side of his hip and turns on the light switch. Stepping forward, he enters into the room. As the other troopers file in behind him and surround the chair, Slynne is frozen by what he sees. The other troopers lower their weapons, unable to comprehend what they are witnessing. This is something that even they didn't expect to see. The mass of red ants is crawling all around inside the bottom of the helmet, but they have not touched Daniel's flesh. He doesn't even appear to have a single bite mark on his steadfast face.

"What is this?" Slynne questions as he scratches his head with the handle of his pistol. "How can this be?" He stands there, just staring at Daniel with a puzzled look on his face. Then, realizing that his men are watching his every move, he projects a pleased look as he addresses them.

"Good," he says slowly. "Now we can use him as bait to catch the other traitors." Slynne leans forward, inspecting the glass helmet and the bugs that swarm along the bottom of it.

"If they had eaten your face, then your friends might not have recognized you." He stands up and instructs his men. "Unstrap him and throw him into one of the cells until we need him."

The men hesitate, however, unable to take their eyes off of Daniel. He appears content to be there in the chair, seemingly without a care in the world. Either the captain's words aren't registering, or they are too stunned to move.

Crack!

The unfortunate trooper that is close enough to Slynne receives a swift slap to the face.

"I gave an order," Slynne scolds the guard.

The rest of the men stumble over themselves trying to unstrap Daniel and pull the torture chamber from his head. Slynne exits the room, leaving the troopers to carry out his orders.

Back at the abandoned military compound, Zaphin is still searching for another weapon. When the others get to the control room, the first thing that they do is check the monitors.

"I don't think they know we're here. If they did, then they would have been back by now," Joseph says.

He opens the door to the sleeping quarters, holding it for Giby as she walks through. Giving Sarah a warm smile, Joseph follows Giby into the room. He lets the door close behind him as they leave her in the control room.

Sarah looks back to the monitors again when something catches her eye.

What is that? she wonders. It's a key hanging next to the door. The shiny, brass object is shaped just like the one that Joseph found in the elevator. She turns back to the camera and sees Zaphin still nosing around some equipment in the weapons room. Sarah stands on her tiptoes and peeks in through the window on the door that leads to the next room. She can see that Joseph is rummaging around in one of the cabinets. Sarah walks over to the key. After watching him for several seconds, she can tell that he's preoccupied with finding some supper.

"This is definitely a key to the elevator access panel." She reaches out and grabs it, looking through the window to the sleeping quarters one last time before slipping it into her pocket. Nervously, she glances at the monitor again.

"Where is Zaphin? He isn't in the weapons room anymore."

"Hey," Sarah hears from behind her.

She turns around to see Zaphin leaning against the doorway, slyly smirking at her. "What's up, Sarah?"

"Um," she stumbles for words. "Nothing really. Joseph doesn't think the troopers know we're here."

"He's probably right," Zaphin says. He hesitates before continuing, taking the opportunity to blatantly look her up and down. "Even if they did know we were here, they would need one of those nifty little keys to open the access panel. Since Joseph has the only one, that won't be happening."

Sarah puts her hand over her pocket, covering the slight bulge of the key. She lets out a nervous, thin laugh. "Yeah, we don't have to worry about that," she says.

"Well, I'm going to go check out our new digs," Zaphin says as he walks past her.

Joseph is still in the other room with Giby. They're both sitting in chairs across from each other. He punctures a can of minestrone soup with a small knife that he found in one of the drawers and wrenches the lid open. Giby smiles at him as he holds out the can in front of her.

"Here, eat this."

She shakes her head no.

"You have to eat something."

"I'm not really hungry."

Joseph doesn't like that answer. He's on the verge of arguing with her, but sympathy convinces him otherwise. What can he do, force the soup down this poor little girl's throat? She's been through so much. He remembers how hard it was when he lost his parents. Everyone says they know what you're going through, but nobody really does. A warm, heartfelt smile drifts across his face.

"You know that it's going to be okay," he says with an easy voice. "I don't pretend to understand how you feel. I have no idea what kind of relationship you had with your parents. I do know a little bit about losing your parents though. I lost my parents when I was little too. You know they were Christians. Do you know what that means?"

"Yes. It means they are in heaven now."

"That's right"

Joseph waits a moment. He doesn't know what to say next, but the words finally come. "I know it doesn't seem like it now, but everything will be fine. You just have to keep breathing, praying, and trusting God. Every day it will get just a little easier. I promise. Just hang in there."

Joseph searches Giby's face for some sort of sign that his words are making a difference. She's still just sitting there looking back at him with those big blue eyes.

"Are you sure you won't eat something?"

"No, thank you."

Joseph puts the can of soup down with the spoon still in it. "It's getting late. Did you want to go lie down then?"

"Okay," she answers.

"Take your pick, there are six beds."

Giby scoots off of the chair and walks over to one of the cots. She hops up on the edge of it and swings her feet over onto the blanket. Letting her head rest back onto the pillow, she stares up at the plain white ceiling.

Zaphin opens the door. He crosses the room to where Joseph has laid out the cans of food on a table. Sarah enters the room. She squeezes the key through her blue jeans again, paranoia forcing her to ensure that it's still there.

"So what's for dinner, Dad?" Zaphin teases Joseph.

"Looks like soup or beans."

"Wow, you sure know how to cook, Joseph," Zaphin replies.

Joseph chuckles as he tosses his friend a can of beans. Sarah sits down next to Joseph.

"Don't eat those!" she calls out to Zaphin. "Those have to be like more than ten years old."

"So?" he puffs.

"So only something canned with a lot of tomatoes or something else really acidic can last that long and still be okay to eat."

Zaphin searches the label on the can.

"Let me see the soup," she demands.

He reluctantly tosses it over to her. She catches it and places it next to the rest of the cans on the table. Sarah views the selection.

"This minestrone soup has a lot of tomatoes. Back in the old days, this wouldn't even be good, but with the advancements in preservatives, they should be fine. The tomato soup should be good too," she adds.

Zaphin snatches the beans off of the table and lobs them back at the supply cabinet. "Fine. I'll take the minestrone."

Joseph tosses him the can of soup. Zaphin catches it with no problem.

"What for you?" Joseph asks.

"Minestrone is great," Sarah replies.

"Give me that," Zaphin instructs, motioning toward the small knife. Joseph picks it up and leans across the table, handing it to his friend.

Zaphin works his can open while Joseph views the tomato soup.

"Can I get that back?" Joseph asks Zaphin as he sets the tomato soup back down.

"Sure."

Zaphin tosses the knife onto the table. It slides across the smooth surface, bouncing back off the metal cans.

"Thanks."

Joseph pries open the can for Sarah and hands her the food.

"Thank you."

He sits down and picks up the can he had opened for Giby.

"Didn't you hear what I just said?" Sarah warns.

Joseph slowly turns the can in his hand, revealing the label with the words *minestrone* on it. He lets out a good, hardy laugh. Sarah punches him in the arm.

"Okay. Okay. Let's pray," he says.

Everyone bows their heads, including Zaphin initially. As Joseph begins, Zaphin periodically glances up at his friends. He's not sure why he feels compelled to look at them. Is it to determine their sincerity, or is it to see if they are looking at him? Perhaps it is just curiosity.

"Jesus Christ, Lord of all the heavens and the earth, we praise you for keeping us safe from the persecution tonight. You are so awesome, God! We don't deserve your mercy and grace, but still, you give it freely. Thank you so much, Father, for your love. Please continue to protect us. We know that everything is in your hands and nothing can stand against you. Thank you for this meal that you have provided for us. We praise you and give you all the glory and honor. In Jesus' name we pray. Amen."

The three hungry and tired teenagers dig into their soup. After they have all gulped down several bites, their hunger subsides enough for a little conversation between spoonfuls.

Joseph stares out toward the supply cabinet in a daze. "I wonder how they knew we were having a Bible study?" he questions.

Sarah stops eating and glances over at him from the corner of her eye. "I don't know," she answers.

"Only a couple of people knew about it. The only two people I invited were Zaphin and Ray Ray," Joseph continues.

Zaphin chimes in. "No one told me that I was in such an elite group." He smiles and starts shoveling his soup in again.

Sarah digs around in her minestrone with her spoon, turning a piece of noodle over and over again.

Joseph adds, "I guess I did tell Bags about it too, but he ditched out on us." He turns toward Sarah again.

"Do you think Raedun is an informant for the troopers?" she asks.

"I don't know. He's part of the MagiX, but some pretty weird things have been happening lately." Joseph scarfs down another spoonful before continuing. "I just don't think he's the type that would mix well with troopers or any type of authority, for that matter. Raedun didn't get the nickname 'Bags' for nothing."

Zaphin enters the conversation again, "That old couple could have told someone."

"We'll never know the answer to that question," Sarah says sadly.

"Daniel knew about it too," Sarah sighs, remembering their friend.

Zaphin asks, "Wasn't that the guy that the troopers hauled off?"

"Yes. There's no telling what the troopers did to him." Sarah looks up at the ceiling, fanning her eyes to keep from crying.

Zaphin plops down his can on the table and leans back in his chair. "I'm beat," he says as he yawns. "I take breakfast in bed at eight o'clock sharp, and make sure you put cream in the coffee." Zaphin smiles again as he stands up, locking his stretched hands over his head. He walks over to the closest cot on the other side of the room and plops down on top of it. Turning on one side, he digs his head into his pillow and closes his eyes.

Sarah props her elbow up on the table and lays her head into her hand. As she gazes lackadaisically at Joseph, the smile is finally restored to her beautiful lips. She leans in a little bit, pushing aside her half-eaten minestrone soup. "I just don't get him. Why did you invite him anyway?"

"He's always been cool with me. We were just hanging out one day, and he told me he was a Christian."

"So he must be, right?" Sarah says sarcastically.

"I know, I know. Some people who say they're Christians don't even know what it means to be a Christian. I asked Zaphin if he believed that Jesus was God's only son, died on the cross for his sins, rose again on the third day, and is the Lord of his life."

"What did he say?"

"He said yes to all of it. He even said that he asked Jesus to forgive all his sins."

Sarah shakes her head. "I shouldn't judge. It's just sometimes he can be a real jerk."

"I noticed." Joseph fiddles with the empty can of soup.

Sarah reaches over and pats him on the leg. His muscles tense. He tries not to act nervous, but the lump in his throat forces him to swallow hard.

"Thank you for watching out for me today. I don't know what I would have done without you," she says.

"I didn't do anything special."

Sarah bends forward to hug Joseph. Even through everything that's happened, her hair still has a hint of that jasmine. He holds her tightly, closing his eyes as he takes it all in.

Sarah ends the embrace. She stands up and through a yawn says, "I'll see you tomorrow morning."

"Good night."

Joseph gets up too. They both walk over to the cots and crawl into them.

After tossing and turning for a while, Joseph flips over on his back. He just lies there in his bed for quite a while and thinks about what a crazy day it's been. It must be some time in the middle of the night, as everyone else seems to be asleep. If he can just get his thoughts to slow down, he might be able to finally sleep too. He can't rest though. His brain won't let him rest. Something is haunting him in the back of his mind. What is it? Something familiar, but yet something he wants to avoid. Joseph fears it. It's something terrifying. He just can't put his finger on it though.

Finally, sleep finds him, and his eyes start to squint. Joseph closes them but then opens them again halfway. Slowly his eyelids droop. This time, they hold fast to each other, sending Joseph spiraling into a dream world.

As he drifts into slumber, the dark figure returns once again. The dream is clearer this time somehow. Joseph is in the street again. He can see the guards rush in, taking down the couple and forcing them to kneel. The dark figure walks up through the crowd and stops directly in front of them. Joseph can clearly see his parents' faces. There's no fear, and there is no sadness. Their expressions are incredibly calm. Two shots ring out and echo in Joseph's ears. Suddenly, he is back looking down the cold black abyss of a gun barrel. The dark figure's face is still blurred but not as much as it has been. He can just barely make out the man's rugged appearance before he's struck on the head.

CHAPTER 16

Joseph jumps up from out of his nightmare. The sweat falls from his face and hair, as if he has just emerged from a pool of water instead of from a soft bed. He glances around the room, searching for images to get his bearings. He remembers now; they're still in the military base. A strange sound is coming from the next room. As he listens more intently, he hears the quick sound of a zipper closing. Joseph gets out of bed and walks into the camera room. Sarah has her back to him. She's glancing at the monitors while shoving some crackers into her hoodie pocket. It's apparent that she's getting ready to leave. He grabs her hand.

"Hey. Where are you going?"

Surprised, Sarah spins around, ready to defend herself. A sigh of relief escapes her lips but is short-lived as she realizes that she's been caught. Sarah nervously shifts her weight back and forth as she decides what to say. She's desperately trying to come up with an excuse for sneaking out so early. She tries to hide her feelings from him. Looking into his eyes, however, her emotions betray her. Joseph can see how helpless she feels.

"My parents!" she blurts. "I must have been in shock last night. I didn't even think about them. I didn't even think about my own parents! I have to go back home and warn them before something happens."

Zaphin walks in rubbing his hair with his hand, still trying to wake up. "Oh. Well, say hi to the troopers for me then. And pick me up some coffee while you're out, will ya?"

Sarah fumes at Zaphin. "Do you always have to be such a sarcastic jerk?"

"I'm just saying that I'll bet the troopers are still out there looking for us. It would be tough for you to make it through the city," he says.

"Thanks for the vote of confidence. Not everyone caves at the first sign of persecution," Sarah sneers back.

Zaphin freezes, his mouth gaping at what Sarah has just said.

Joseph speaks up, "No, he's right. We need to stay here."

Sarah's eyes start to water in frustration as she defends her actions. "Someone tipped the troopers off that we were having a Bible study, so they probably know about each of us. Your parents aren't Christians, Joseph, but mine are. I have to warn them!"

Sarah seems determined to try and get back to her home in the suburbs. The tears that had been pooling in her eyes finally break over the edge of her eyelids and slide down her cheeks. "What are you saying? That we spend the rest of our lives down here? I'm not just going to sit and do nothing while my parents are in danger," she sobs.

Joseph gently puts his hand on her shoulder, speaking softly. "Calm down. We're all in this together."

Sarah sniffles. She puts her hands on her hips and takes a deep breath, trying to regain her composure. "Of course we're not going to spend the rest of our lives down here."

Realizing what she had said, Sarah wipes her left eye and looks away from Joseph. She gives off a mumbled laugh, as if she had let it escape through her lips of its own free will.

Joseph continues. "I'll go into the city until I can get a signal on my cell phone. I'll call your parents and warn them. Everyone else should stay here. Just keep an eye on the cameras, and you all should be safe."

Zaphin objects. "No way, man. You're not going to have all of the fun. I'm going with you."

"Whatever. It's up to you." Joseph doesn't seem to care one way or the other.

He gives Sarah's hand a squeeze and lets go. Venturing back into the other room, he retrieves his phone from the sleeping quarters. Joseph sees Giby lying on one of the beds. She stares right through him.

"Are you okay?" he asks.

She nods her head.

"Well, I have to leave for a little bit, but you'll be safe here. Sarah is going to stay with you. Besides, you know that God is always watching over us and that he loves us. The Bible says that he wants good things for his children… He's always with us." Joseph brushes the hair out of Giby's eyes.

"Are you coming back?" she asks.

"I promise," Joseph says before leaning down to kiss her on the head.

He gets up and walks into the next room, where Zaphin is waiting to go. Sarah is looking down at the security cameras again. She sees him enter the room and reaches out, grabbing his hand. Turning to Zaphin, she apologizes to him.

"I'm sorry, Zaphin. I shouldn't have judged you, and it wasn't right. Thank you for being strong now. Thank you for going with Joseph."

She gives Zaphin a heartfelt smile of appreciation and then reaches out and grabs his hand as well. Zaphin is completely caught off guard. He can't find the words for either a rebuttal or confirmation.

"Let's pray," she says. "Dear heavenly Father, the Creator of everything. I know that all things are in your hands, God, and we know that you love us. We ask that you would give us strength to stand in the face of persecution, we ask that you would give us peace, and we ask that you would encamp your angels around us and keep us safe. Keep us right there in the palm of your hand. We ask these things in Jesus' name. Amen."

Sarah throws her arms around Joseph. She squeezes tightly around his neck, closing her eyes. Letting go of him, she turns and hugs Zaphin as well. He bends over and holds her tightly as he places her chin on his shoulder.

"You two be careful. You know what they'll do to you if they catch you."

"Don't worry about us," Joseph says.

He reaches into his backpack, pulling out the gun that he had gotten from the troopers at the Bible study.

"Here. I want you to take this," he says, holding out the weapon. Sarah steps back and slightly away from Zaphin.

"I don't need that, and I don't want it," she says sternly.

Joseph places the gun on the counter and hugs her again. "I know that you won't have to use it, but I'm going to leave it here, just in case."

Sarah frowns. Eventually, she nods her head, giving in.

As Joseph's backpack hangs open, Zaphin notices that something else is in it. It's the gloves. He's carrying the Adam's Fall. "Are you taking those things?" He makes a gesture toward the gloves.

Joseph holds them up. Playing on Zaphin's words, he says, "These *things* could come in handy." Joseph places them back into his satchel and turns to say farewell to Sarah one last time.

"You'll be safe here, just keep an eye on the security cameras in case those cops come searching for us again. I'll be back as soon as we warn your parents."

"Thank you, Joseph," she replies.

Joseph and Zaphin walk down the white hall, stopping at the elevator. Joseph hits the small round button. It takes quite a while for the elevator to arrive. As they wait, neither one says a word. Both of them just look up at the numbers illuminating one by one above the door. Joseph feels like he has been here before. It's just like the elevator ride that they had taken after he beat Zaphin in H2H.

"Do you still have the key?" Zaphin asks.

Joseph digs around in his pocket and pulls it out. "Got it right here."

"Make sure you don't lose that. It's the only sure way that we can get back in."

The elevator comes to a stop, and the doors open. Zaphin makes sure to get in front of the buttons this time. Joseph steps in after him. He leans against the opposite wall with his shoulder.

"So you really think the troopers are still out there looking for us?" Zaphin asks.

"I wouldn't be surprised. I think some of the R and Gs died at the Bible study. You know what happens if you kill a trooper."

"Do you think they're waiting outside the building?"

"No. They scoured every inch of this facility last night. They probably have patrols set up to try and spot us on the street."

"Do you think Sarah's right? Do you think they know who we are?"

"I have no clue." Joseph watches as the numbers change on the elevator.

"If they know who you are, then aren't you worried about your parents?" Zaphin asks.

"No. You know that my dad has connections. They wouldn't be able to make him disappear."

"Do you think he'll be able to protect you?"

"No," answers Joseph. "Not after what we've done."

The elevator doors open to the main level of the building. Zaphin peeks his head through the doorway and studies the hallway to his right. Nothing. He peers the other way to his left. Still nothing.

He steps out into the main area. His heels echo as they connect with the cold, hard tile. Speckles of dust dance in the few sunbeams that peer through tall windows at the end of the hall. The dust also covers an old reception counter, where phones and sign-in books lie dormant.

"It's all clear," Zaphin says.

Joseph follows him out of the elevator and onto the main floor. It seems so much lighter here than in the basement. He isn't sure what it is. Maybe it's just all in his head, but it almost feels as though he's being set free from a prison of sorts. Joseph thinks about Sarah and Giby, still stuck in that prison. "Oh well. It's the only thing we can do. It's better for them to be safe down there than to be getting shot at up here with us."

The two teens cautiously walk through the building, checking every doorway and corner before moving forward. Finally, they get to the door that leads to the street. "Here goes everything," Joseph says.

He creaks the metal door open and spies through the crack. There's nothing on the street. There are no patrol cars, no gangs, not even a breeze. A supernatural silence clutches the street, squeezing it so tightly that nothing moves, nothing breathes. There is no sound. Joseph pulls the door the rest of the way open, revealing the towering skyscrapers of the city. Joseph exits the building out onto the desolate roadway. Zaphin follows him, glancing around for anything out of the ordinary. The buildings loom over them, casting menacing shadows on the ground. Joseph wonders what lurks in the many rooms of those glass and concrete towers. Are there families still living in them, remnants of a time past? They're probably all empty. What other secrets lay waiting for someone to discover? He shifts the weight of the pack on his back, making sure that Adam's Fall is still there.

"Which way?" Zaphin asks.

"I don't know."

Just then, Joseph spots a cell phone tower in the distance.

"There. Look between those two buildings."

Zaphin squints his eyes, straining to see where it is. He can't see it. "Where?" Zaphin asks, his tone resonating disbelief.

"Right there, way off in the distance." Joseph points at the tower again.

Zaphin's gaze follows the line of Joseph's finger. He squints harder, trying to see it.

"Oh. Okay," he says.

"Just our luck. It's in the west part of town," Joseph says.

"Oh, the nice part of town."

"We better get going."

They both walk for quite some time, cutting through alleys and making sure to stay close to the buildings.

"Looks like I was wrong, Zaphin."

"What're you talking about?"

"I haven't seen a single patrol car. It's like the whole city was cleaned out or something."

Zaphin starts out, "Well, it's not like—"

Joseph interrupts him. "Shhh!" He holds up one finger, signaling Zaphin to be silent. His eyes pan up and down the street. "What's that noise?"

Joseph refocuses his attention on the humming noise, trying to hear what it is. Zaphin tilts his head. Now he can hear it too.

Joseph looks back at his friend to see if he has identified the noise. He's no help though, as he just holds up his hands and shrugs his shoulders.

"It almost sounds like, like—" Joseph realizes what the noise is, but it's too late now. A jet-black helicopter screams over the crest of the building that they are standing beside.

"Back here!" Joseph yells as he runs into the open door of a nearby building. A frozen Zaphin doesn't follow, panic overloading his mind. He stands there in the street, still watching the helicopter. The battle between fight-or-flight paralyzes him for a moment. Turning away from Joseph, he sprints down the street in the opposite direction from his friend.

"No!" Joseph screams, but it's too late. He stands in the doorway and watches Zaphin tear across the sidewalk, heading in the direction of the suburbs. Joseph slams the door shut and looks around the room. The *décor* resembles an old store. If it was a shop at one time, there definitely isn't much there now. This place had been cleaned out long ago. He slides down the wall and sits on the wooden floor. A bank of windows is located just to his right. Still trying to catch his breath, he tilts his head back. What's his next move? Joseph scoots under the opening and stretches his neck up to see out from between the metal bars that cover the glass. He can barely make out Zaphin at the end of the block. Turning a corner at the intersection, he disappears from sight. The helicopter tracks his movement and follows him down the street.

Zaphin slows down to a jog as he comes up to the next cross street. He looks over his shoulder, but no one is chasing him. He turns a corner as the helicopter advances on him. It's still close on his trail. The noise from the blades mask the faint hum of a trooper's engine as it accelerates. The vehicle is hidden from Zaphin's sight; it steadily progresses up the next street, nonetheless. Zaphin continues jogging, looking up and back for the chopper. Just as he begins to cross the intersection, *Thwak!* With no warning, the patrol car smashes into his legs. His body flips over the hood, his skull crashing into the windshield. The surprised trooper slams on his brakes, sliding Zaphin's limp body off of the hood and onto the street.

The trooper hobbles out of his car and pulls his weapon. He holds it on the teenager while fumbling for his radio with the other hand.

"Sir. Sir. Come in, sir."

"This is Damian, over."

"Sir, I just hit one of them."

"Did you manage to keep from killing them? The Captain wants the traitors alive."

The trooper inches closer to Zaphin, examining his body.

"It's the black haired one. He still appears to be breathing sir."

"Excellent. Ask him where the others are."

"I'm afraid that won't be possible, Damian."

"And why not?"

"He's unconscious, sir."

"Bring him to me. Meanwhile, have your men continue looking for the other Christians."

"Yes, sir."

The trooper lifts Zaphin from under his arms and pulls him to the car. His black boots drag across the ground. Breathing heavy, the policeman shoves him into the back of the patrol car.

"It doesn't look too bad."

He feels Zaphin's legs, squeezing them to try and identify if any bones are fractured. They don't feel broken. He pushes the teen's hair back away from his forehead. There's a bump on the side of his head, but nothing serious.

"He'll be fine," the trooper mumbles. He gets back into the front seat of his patrol car and radios in again. "The Christian is still in the city. Be on the lookout northwest of my position at Broadway and Twenty-First."

I have to keep moving, Joseph thinks to himself. *If they catch Zaphin, he'll probably crack like before. I don't want to be a sitting duck when the troopers show back up here.*

He takes a deep breath and releases it with a sigh. Again, he peeks out of the window. Several trooper cars race past the intersection, about two streets down.

"It's now or never."

Joseph lets out a grunt as he turns on one knee and springs to his feet, breaking through the door. He stumbles slightly as his momentum carries him over the sidewalk. Joseph sprints west as hard as he can. Suddenly, a patrol van speeds around the corner and skids to a halt. The vehicle is directly in Joseph's path. The surprised teen changes direction, without even breaking stride. He heads toward an open entrance to a building across the street.

The van door flies open, and four very large dogs scramble out. They lunge against their leashes and devour the ground with their paws. Their brown hair is cut short across their muscular bodies. Their long torsos convulse as they snarl and bark, displaying their razor-sharp teeth. Their eyes are cold, black, lifeless marbles that show no hint of mercy. The Troopers release the savages from their chains. The beasts immediately spot him and quickly pursue their target. Joseph glances over his back, calculating their speed. He knows he can't outrun them. Instead, he bolts through the open doorway. Joseph tries to slam it behind him. The lock's been broken, however, so the warped metal only bounces back open off of the frame. Dogs rush into the building, close on his trail.

He leaps over a railing and runs up a flight of stairs leading to a mezzanine. Joseph flees across the top of it to the other side of the building and starts to go down a set of stairs at the far end. Two of the dogs are now racing across the mezzanine, quickly advancing on his position.

Where did the other two go? he wonders. A pair of blue-colored metal railings lines each side of the staircase. Joseph puts his arms out onto them, attempting to slide down as he lifts his legs. His momentum forces his body to quickly glide over the stairs. As he descends across the railing, Joseph sees the other two dogs enter the bottom of the staircase. He stops short and looks up. He can hear the dogs' paws sliding around on the tile, one level above him.

Joseph is stuck. He frantically looks around. Moving to the edge, he views the floor below. "There's another balcony on the other side of the room!" Joseph exclaims.

The other balcony that he sees is at least twenty-five feet across and only ten feet down. There's no way he can make that jump. Frustrated, Joseph slams his fist into the drywall, breaking through it. He looks down at his hand. The white dust flakes off of it.

"I've got it."

Joseph climbs up on the double railing, opposite of the wall. He takes several quick breaths, pumping his arms up and down. Now racing forward, his heart is about to pound out of his chest. One of the dogs comes down the staircase and leaps for Joseph's leg, barely missing it. *Pong.* The metal rings out with a thud as the dog hits the railing hard and falls to the stairs. Joseph leaps off of the end of the balcony. His legs run in midair while his body soars across the chasm. Twisting his body as he descends, he pulls his arm back and punches as hard as he can. His fist penetrates the drywall, as before. He grasps at the hole desperately while pieces of the drywall crumble off and crash to the floor, twenty feet below. Joseph strains as he braces his hands against the now exposed wood studs. He slowly pulls himself up. Kicking his leg, he breaks another hole in the drywall. Gently, he places his foot in the hole. He carefully rocks up and down on his foot, gaining momentum for the jump. His target is a balcony, five feet above where he is hanging. He catapults up and grasps the edge. His grip begins to slip. The dust is too slick. He adjusts his weight and swings one of his arms up in a last ditch effort. Grasping the metal railing, Joseph pulls himself up to the balcony. He slides over it, resting briefly on the other side as he catches his breath. The dogs are still barking at him. The slobber flies from their fierce mouths, but there is no way they can get to him. He is safe, for now.

CHAPTER 17

Pulling the backpack off his shoulders, he opens the zipper and takes out Adam's Fall.

"I think I'm going to need these."

Quickly slipping them on, he zips his backpack again and secures it on his back. Joseph follows another set of stairs down and out the back of the building. He opens the door and immediately starts running again. One of the patrol cars pulls around to the rear of the structure, and the troopers start to get out. Just then, the driver spots Joseph across the street. He yells at the men to get back into the vehicle. The tires of the car squeal as they take off in pursuit of Joseph, who disappears from sight. The police speed up as they turn down the side street just in time to see Joseph vanish behind another building. This time, he goes down a narrower avenue just off of the main road.

When he turns the corner, there's a makeshift barricade in the way. Without breaking stride, he leaps over it. His legs kick up sideways until they are parallel with his shoulders. He arches his back and clears the top of the bar. Joseph continues to turn his body and drops his legs down, ensuring that he's facing forward. His feet hit the ground, still running. He continues forward as fast as he can go. When he's halfway down the street, the car pursuing him speeds into the alley. It doesn't even slow down. Instead, it easily demolishes the wooden blockade. Joseph is beginning to see signs of life around the city again. He must be getting into gang territory. Makeshift houses litter the corridors and clutter the sidewalks.

The patrol car is now about to catch Joseph. He turns another corner and escapes into yet another alley. Glancing back to see where the car is, he accidentally runs into a bum, who's pushing his shopping cart. The impact throws the bum against the alley wall. The man's shopping cart topples over on its side. Joseph is knocked off balance for a minute, but he's still moving forward. He glances over his right shoulder at the metal cage. Joseph has another idea. He tries to stop, but his momentum carries him a couple steps past the middle of the alley to the other side. The car has to be close. He can hear the engine echoing around the corner.

Joseph aims his gloves at the cart. Its wheels are still spinning from being toppled over. He shoots the metal shopping cart, fixing the rays on it. It starts to compact. As it does, the concrete under it starts to crack. It begins to buckle from the tremendous weight of the increasingly dense shopping cart. The car flies around the corner and rams the cart. The front of the patrol car crunches around the immovable object. It then continues on and flips end over end through the air. Joseph ducks. The car seems weightless as it floats over him. He looks up to see the crushed hood of the car, just feet above his head. The back of the car continues to come over until the vehicle lands on its roof and skids down the alley. Sparks fly as it grinds across the road. It finally comes to rest against a brick wall. Joseph stands up, ready to run. No one gets out of the car though.

He looks around. The bum is still standing there, dumbfounded by what he has just seen. The homeless man realizes that Joseph is now looking at him. He comes to his senses and frantically scurries out of the alley. Joseph starts to exit from where he entered, but more patrol cars come up the street. He ducks back behind the corner. It's too late. The troopers spot him. Cars fly in from both sides, barricading the opening of the alley. Joseph continues running away from them. He jumps up against the concrete wall and pushes off with one foot, clearing the wrecked police car. Troopers swarm the area with guns drawn.

Joseph escapes as far as he can into the alley. "It's a dead end!" he gasps as he frantically searches for a way out. Cornered, he turns to the oncoming army and shoots Adam's Fall. The dial is set to M. He uses the widest and strongest beam that it can produce. The air in front of him starts to thicken as the troopers climb across the overturned vehicle. R and Gs open fire from everywhere. Hundreds of bullets rain down on Joseph. He winces and closes his eyes as the deadly shots come. He braces for the impact, knowing that this is the end. Curiously, however, nothing hits his body. Instead, he hears a strange noise, like bullets ripping into water. He opens his eyes in amazement to see the thickened air slowing the projectiles down. It looks like the troopers are trying to shoot him through a wall of water. Some of the bullets are now starting to ricochet off of the hardened mass, which grows denser by the millisecond.

A silence falls over the troopers as they see their bullets being deflected in midair. The firing ceases. Joseph looks down at his meter. Two of the thin green bars are gone from the power gauge. The battery pack won't keep this up much longer. An engine revs from behind some troopers, who are perched on the overturned car. They all glance behind them to see what's going on. The men hear the screeching of tires and turn, just in time to see smoke rolling from the wheels of Slynne's patrol car. They abandon their spot on the wreckage as his car crashes through the overturned pile of metal.

Joseph seizes the opportunity. Turning toward the building, he flips the switch on his right glove to D, which changes the settings from magnetize to demagnetize. At the same time, he blasts a beam at the red brick wall. Slynne opens the patrol car door and steps out, staring intently at his prey. He turns to his men.

"Well, what are you waiting for? Fire!"

The dazed troopers begin to open fire once again. The bullets still ricochet off of the hard air. Slowly, however, the magnetism wears off. The rounds begin to penetrate again, but are still swallowed by the liquid substance.

Joseph unleashes the full intensity of Adam's Fall on the alley wall. Little pieces of brick dribble down, like drops of mercury. Then, an entire part of the wall melts and comes crashing to the ground. Joseph runs in, just as the bullets start coming through the now normal air.

He vanishes into the building. The bullets completely penetrate, spraying the wall in the place that he had been standing.

Slynne points to the hole in the wall. "Follow him."

Joseph runs through a dingy room and breaks down an old door leading to a hallway. With the police pouring into the opening behind him, he continues fleeing to a stairwell. As witnessed by the old and decrepit furniture, he must be in an abandoned apartment building. He opens the door and looks up to the top of the stairs. It goes all the way to the roof.

He flies up them as fast as he can go. Stopping halfway up, Joseph points his gloves down at the ground. He uses the powerful weapon on the stairwell. The steps slowly melt away and run across the lower levels, like water cascading down a waterfall. He finishes climbing to the top of the stairs. As he pushes through the door, it swings out to the open air on top of the building.

Joseph can hear the helicopter coming from somewhere behind him. He crouches down behind a wall on the roof. The sound of the blades chopping through the air is getting louder, letting him know that the chopper is close.

Suddenly, it appears, cresting over the edge of the building. The pilot radios down to Captain Slynne. "He's trapped on the rooftop, sir."

Slynne's voice comes back across the radio. "Good. I'm coming up. Make sure you keep him entertained, but don't kill him. He has some sort of weapon that I am very interested in keeping intact."

"Yes, sir. We will keep him pinned."

Joseph gets up and starts walking toward the helicopter.

"What is that idiot doing?" the copilot asks.

Joseph looks up at the sleek black hull of the aircraft, with its blades lapping fiercely at the sky. He aims his gloves at the blurred, spinning lines.

"There's something on his hands."

He hones in on the helicopter's rotors as it comes toward him. As he discharges Adam's Fall into the sky, the blades begin to disintegrate in midair. The pilot tries to regain control but to no avail. The heavy machine slowly drops back down to the street. It slams hard into the concrete, knocking out the pilots.

Finding half of the stairs gone in the stairwell, the troopers go back down a floor and enter the hallway again. They comb the area for some way up. "There's a fire escape over here," one of the troopers shouts.

Slynne and four heavily armed men pile outside onto a balcony. They climb the ladder as high as they can go. It ends on the second floor from the top. Joseph closes the heavy metal door that leads to the open roof. It has a solid latch that's made for a lock to go on it. But where's the lock? It's missing! Joseph glances around for something to secure the door with. A heavy steel bolt shimmers in the sunlight, catching his eye. He grabs it and slides it into the hole. It's a perfect fit. Joseph gets down behind the wall again; his mind is racing. How the heck is he going to get out of this one? The troopers enter the building again and make their way back over to the stairwell. They look down at the missing section of stairs, still marveling at the new technology. Above them is one more set of steps, and then the door to the roof. Slynne's men race up the stairs with guns drawn. The captain follows slowly behind them.

Joseph hears the sound of many footsteps coming up the last flight of stairs. He's desperate at this point.

"Please, Lord," he prays. Just then, something clicks in his mind. He stands up and cautiously inches over to the edge of the roof. He looks down at his gloves and then peers out across the wide expanse. The other rooftop is over thirty feet away. A strong, steady wind is blowing, adding to the uneasy feeling that's growing in the pit of his stomach. The street seems like it's ten miles down. He changes the switch on his right glove to M and shoots a narrow beam out in front of him. A piece of the air becomes opaque. It stays suspended for only a second. The air resembles a small, dark, rectangular cloud. The cloud brick, however, can only cheat gravity for a second. The mass of dense air falls to the ground and smashes into pieces. Joseph hears voices at the door. The shoddy metal handle rattles. Silence engulfs Joseph's head as he waits for the inevitable. He prays that he won't hear it—he prays that it won't come, but he knows that it will. *Slam!* The troopers ram the metal door. A dent protrudes out from the dull metal, but it continues to hold solid.

Joseph looks down at the latch on the door and sees that it's starting to give. His toes scoot toward the edge of the roof. Fifteen stories down, the street stares coldly back at him. The wind gusts, challenging Joseph's balance on the narrow ledge. His body wobbles, but he regains his composure. Pointing his gloves several feet in front of him, he shoots a narrow beam again at full intensity. The air immediately forms into a solid brick. Joseph leaps off of the building, through the air, and onto the brick with his right foot while he continues shooting the beam at full blast. His foot lands on the solid mass while his weapon forms another brick for his left foot. As he pushes off the condensed atoms, the brick gives way to gravity and falls from beneath him. He barely has enough time to continue to the next dense air step before it crumbles.

The troopers back away from the door as Slynne arrives at the top of the stairs. He walks up to the barricade and kicks the metal slab with all his strength. The door flies open. The latch wrenches away from the wall. Slynne continues onto the roof, but he stops after taking only a few short steps. The captain scans the area for Joseph. Where can the Christian be? The rest of the troopers spill onto the rooftop, filing in behind him. They create a V formation and drop to one knee. Their guns are drawn and ready. Seeing movement, the armed men spring to their feet, with their sites honed in on Joseph. Bullets fly from the troopers' weapons, trailing behind him. The shots, which were once crisp and loud, become muffled to Joseph's ears. The bullets slide out of the recoiling barrel of the troopers' weapons and creep through the air, slowly spiraling forward toward their destination. They connect with the hardened air and flatten, crumbling the block of dense matter on impact.

From the street far below, a trooper hears the gunfire and looks up at the sheer side of the tall building. He sees Joseph, who appears to be running in midair, cross between the rooftops. The trooper's mouth hangs open as he continues looking up in disbelief. He can barely make out something shattering under the figure's feet. Still in shock, he stands paralyzed as he watches Joseph head to the other building. He is almost safely across. The last obstacle is a three-foot wall that lines the other rooftop. Joseph blasts one more beam in front of him and leaps off of the air brick. Several rounds explode into the dense air, shattering it underneath his foot, just as he pushes off of it. Joseph stretches with his hands reaching far out in front of him. The rooftop is coming up fast. He curls his body as he lands on the other side of the wall, rolling behind a vent. The armed men can do nothing as he disappears behind a white concrete wall across the expanse.

Joseph runs to the edge of the building and races down the fire escape. The R and Gs stand there, unable to comprehend what they are seeing.

"Move!" Slynne yells.

His soldiers trip over themselves, scrambling back through the narrow roof door. The flustered group of men descends down the staircase, forgetting about the missing piece of steps.

"What are you waiting for? I said *move!*" he yells again.

The troopers part, revealing the end of the stairs. Slynne grits his teeth tightly as he reaches the edge and peers down at the two-story drop to where the stairs start again.

With his left hand, he grabs one of the men by the front of his uniform. In one swift motion, he hurls the unsuspecting man off of the ledge. He barely has time to scream before his body slams into the rubble covering the stairs below.

Slynne grips the radio tightly as he calls back to the street level. His First Lieutenant Alex answers.

"Hello, sir."

"He is on the rooftop of the other building. And Alex, do not allow him to escape."

"Yes, sir," Alex responds.

The troopers emerge from the front door of the apartments. They run to the street to see the building next door surrounded by several battalions. Lines of armed men march into the complex.

"Alex!" Slynne yells.

"Yes, sir," Alex salutes the captain, awaiting further instructions.

"I told you to find him."

"We're searching the building, sir."

"No. You are standing here watching your men search the building. Now get in there and help them," Slynne orders.

"Yes, sir," Alex salutes again, before running off to join the hunt.

Meanwhile, Slynne marches over to what looks like a makeshift command center. He sits down hard on his chair and tosses the radio on to a table in front of him.

"Now what, sir?" the man to his right asks. He appears to be a high-ranking officer as well.

"We wait," he says as he props his feet up on the table.

His boots clunk loudly as they drop onto the wood surface. He loosens the bandage from around his head. His fingers trace the wound again. This time, there is no blood on his hand when he looks at it. Slynne tosses the bandage aside. He leans back in his chair and closes his eyes.

CHAPTER 18

Several hours pass while the police search the building. Finally, Alex hesitantly emerges from out of the front entrance. He stops in front of the building for a moment, pulling off his hat and wiping the sweat from his forehead. He squints as he looks up into the sky. Alex takes a deep breath as he puts his hat back on. He proceeds to make his way over to where the captain is sitting. Slynne sees Alex march across the street with his head down. He stands up from his chair to get a better look. As his trooper gets closer, it's obvious that he doesn't have the rebel. The nervous young man avoids eye contact with his waiting superior. He stops directly in front of him.

Saluting the captain, Alex starts to speak. "He got aw—"

His sentence is cut short as Slynne swings his arm. The hard side of his hand crushes the trooper's windpipe. The lieutenant grasps at his throat and falls to his knees. The captain watches him struggle until he eventually falls over dead.

"Imbecile!"

Slynne looks to the highly decorated trooper on his right. Bars and various medals cover the front of his uniform.

"I want that weapon. Contact our spy and find out where the Christian got it and if there are any more."

"Yes, sir," Damian answers.

Slynne turns and looks at him.

"Oh, and Damian, you know how I hate to be disappointed."

"Yes, sir!" Damian turns to walk off, but Slynne starts to speak again.

"On the other hand, I do find that executing troopers tends to alleviate my disappointment."

"Understood, sir!" Damian answers, with his back still facing Slynne. He can feel the heavy weight of the captain's stare bearing down on him.

Damian picks up a handheld radio as he hurries off to a nearby patrol car. Opening the door, he sinks down into the seat.

"Get the informant," he commands.

Damian waits for his contact to come on the radio and begins to speak again.

"What do you know about these weapons?"

Damian listens to the response.

"I see. Does he have any relatives that he may contact?"

Again, he listens to the informant.

"I see. Can you handle that? Yes. Go to her parents' house and see if the Christians try to contact them."

Damian hangs up the phone and stands up out of the vehicle. He studies the horizon, viewing the clusters of buildings that surround him. Like a bloodhound sniffing for a scent, Damian seems to be searching the air for something. His chin is raised ever so slightly, his eyes squinting so much that now they only appear to be slivers.

"Humph," he utters as he hops into the patrol car. The engine turns over. The car rolls slowly down the road. Damian keeps the noise of the engine almost inaudible as he proceeds.

CHAPTER 19

Twenty minutes later, a motorcycle coasts down a neighborhood street lined with tall and stout oak trees. Their branches block the warm sun's rays and cast a thick shadow along the curb. A mysterious figure climbs off of the bike and quietly walks up through a grassy yard, the black helmet catching the sun as it emerges from the oak's shadow. The person is wearing zippered pants, giving away the age. That's the trend nowadays for teenagers. A pair of black boots quietly steps past a ranch-style house and on through to the backyard. The figure ducks low to the ground and scrambles over to the edge of a Victorian-style house. Several birds scatter from some old feeders in the backyard as the visitor rushes past them. Crouching down underneath a window and flipping up the helmet visor, the visitor is able to get a better view. An older woman's voice comes from inside the house.

"Honey. All the birds just flew away. Can you go out and see if that cat is out there again?"

The figure reaches into the inside pocket of their black leather jacket and pulls out a handgun. Gripping it with both hands, the intruder stays poised and ready to spring into action.

"That cat won't hurt anything. Just leave it alone, darling," a male voice comes back.

"I don't want that thing getting one of our birds, besides..." The woman's voice trails off as she moves farther away from the window. The stranger in the helmet crawls around to the side of the house, making sure to crouch under the windows along the side of it. The figure can now hear the man's voice again.

"Okay. I'll go and che—" The phone rings, interrupting his sentence. The spying stranger peers through the window and sees an older couple. The woman answers the phone.

"Hello?" she answers.

It's Joseph on the other end of the line. He's standing triumphantly on top of a parking garage that's situated close to the tower. It's the same tower that he had seen from the other side of town. His hair blows as the wind gusts hard over the top of the desolate parking garage. Only a few cars remain, their owners abandoning them to rot. The upper level is five stories high. There's also no roof on the structure, which allows Joseph to get several bars on his mobile phone.

"Hello, Mrs. Jairus. This is Joseph," he says. "Listen, I don't have much time, but Sarah wanted me to call you—"

Sarah's mother interrupts him. "Sarah! Is she okay?"

"She's fine, and she's safe."

"Where is she?"

"Mrs. Jairus, I need you to listen to me. The police may know that you and your husband are Christians. You both need to leave right now."

Sarah's father grabs the phone from his wife. "Who is this?"

"I don't have time for this," Joseph responds. "You and your wife need to get out of town right now."

Joseph can hear Mrs. Jairus in the background. Her voice is muffled, but from what little Joseph can make out, she's telling him that he needs to listen.

Mr. Jairus responds, "How do I know that Sarah is okay?"

"You're just going to have to trust me."

Mr. Jairus' voice changes from skepticism to one of concern. "All right. I guess we don't have any other choice. We'll leave, but I want Sarah to meet us. You tell her to meet us at her grandpa's old farm east of town. She will be safe there with us."

"All right. I'll tell her that's where you're going to be."

"And she better not be hurt in any way," Mr. Jairus threatens.

"Don't worry, Mr. Jairus. I promise you that nothing is going to happen to her."

Mr. Jairus hangs up the phone and turns to his wife. Tears stream down her face as she begins to sob. She falls, filled with desperation, into his open arms.

"Don't worry. Everything is going to be fine."

"Where is my baby?" she sobs.

"She's going to meet us at Dad's old farm. Hurry, we need to go."

Mr. Jairus steps back a bit. Bending his head down, he looks into his wife's eyes. He smiles gently at her. His tone is firm and reassuring.

"She's going to meet us there, honey. Let's go."

Mrs. Jairus sniffles and wipes her eyes. "I know she is okay. I know. We just need to trust in the Lord."

Mr. Jairus grabs the keys off of the table and pulls his jacket down from off of the coat rack. Hearing this, the stranger gets up to leave. After making sure that no one is watching, the figure quickly makes a beeline across the yard and past the house directly behind the Jairus.' Staying crouched over, the person hurries back to the bike. The engine roars as it starts, and the motorcycle speeds out of the shadows, turning at the first block. Sarah's parents come out of the house. They fumble with the door, trying to lock it. Both of them look very disheveled as they hurry to the car and get in. Mr. Jairus turns over the ignition. Hurriedly, he backs it out onto the street. He then mashes the gas down. The car jerks forward as the engine accelerates, propelling it down the long row of oaks. The stranger on the motorcycle flips a visor down from a black helmet and slowly pulls in after the car. The bike, remaining hidden from the Jairuses, keeps a distance between the two vehicles.

Joseph looks at his phone to see if Mr. Jairus has hung up. The words *call ended* flash back at him. He flips the phone closed and quickly slides it into his front pocket. What is that? He thinks he sees Giby out of the corner of his eye.

"Impossible."

He turns to ascertain what it is that he saw. As he twists his head, however, a quite larger figure is there. Immediately, Joseph projects Adam's Fall into the air in front of him. The figure, who is obviously trying to sneak up on Joseph, quickly draws his handgun and begins firing. The bullets deflect off of the air, just as before. The man lowers his weapon, appearing more interested in the shield of air than in Joseph himself. Joseph, in turn, takes the opportunity to study his enemy. He is a young man, not much older than himself. Of course, he must be part of the police force. There's no mistaking his red and green uniform. He has a thick and muscular build that narrows at his waist. This guy is definitely not one to mess with. His brown hair flips in the wind, lapping at his chiseled cheekbones.

"You must be pretty important," Joseph touts, sarcastically referencing the silver metals that adorned him.

The trooper is taken back by the comment. After regaining his composure, the figure chuckles.

"I finally meet a Christian with a sense of humor," he comments slyly. He pulls the clip from his gun, tossing it nonchalantly to his side and over the edge of the building. Next, he cocks the weapon, releasing the bullet out of the chamber and onto the ground. He holsters his gun once again. Joseph is now the one confused. He releases the magnetism. The air begins to fall and crumble to the ground like sand when it's thrown to the wind.

"What's your name?" Joseph asks.

"Damian," he answers. His green cloak lifts slightly in the wind, as if the mere mention of his name sends a shockwave rippling after it. "And yours?"

"I'd rather not say."

"I see. Well then, let's see what you've got."

Damian walks briskly forward toward Joseph, his upper body slightly leaning forward as he advances. His hands are cupped, but tense. Joseph spreads his legs, stabilizing his stance. He raises his arms up in front of his face. His breath is calm. His eyes focus in on his enemy's waist, trying to determine what blow will come first. That blow is the trooper's left hand. Joseph deflects the uppercut with his right arm. Damian follows through, using the force of the missed uppercut to spin his body around. Kicking as he turns, his shoe lands firmly into Joseph's back. He's propelled several feet sideways and into a car. Hearing his opponent approach, he rolls down the hood toward the front bumper. Damian unleashes rapid punches in succession, trying to catch his escaping adversary. His fists dent the metal, just missing Joseph's head. As he reaches the end of the car, Joseph is on his side. He runs up a small retaining wall on the edge of the roof while still lying on the hood. Spinning on his back, he brings his foot around with tremendous force. It drives into the side of Damian's head, sending him backward and onto the ground.

Joseph jumps from the car to his feet, breathing hard. He shrugs his shoulders. Then he casually straightens his clothes as he prepares for the next bout. Damian covers the side of his head with his hand, popping his neck as he stands up. He winces as it goes back in place.

"You're definitely not like the Christians that I'm used to seeing." He smiles.

"That's because you're used to torturing women and little kids," Joseph pants.

The trooper stops smiling.

"I don't torture anyone, and I don't mess with little kids or women."

"You must be the exception," Joseph says sarcastically.

"Why do you hate other people so much anyway?" Damian asks.

Joseph is surprised. "I'm the one who hates people?" he sputters. "Do you see me trying to kill people, just because they are Christians?"

"You mean traitors," Damian says with a solemn face. "Look around you. All of this is because of you Christians. The reason why America was attacked is because of your narrow views."

Joseph shakes his head. "Don't you get it? See if this is narrow. You're in the military right?"

Damian doesn't answer.

"What if you're in a combat zone at night and you are surrounded by enemies? What if you're in their territory and you run out of ammo? Now, what if a special reconnaissance team shows up and tells you that the only way out of the enemy's territory and certain death is to follow them? Would you follow them?"

"That really is irrelevant," Damian replies.

"Would you?"

"Of course I would."

"You wouldn't say it's too narrow or tell the reconnaissance team that you want to go north instead of south?"

"No, but that's different than saying there is only one way to heaven," Damian argues.

"What's the difference?" Joseph asks.

"I'll tell you," Damian begins. "The reconnaissance person would have had to get to me. He would have already traveled the path that he is going to take me back out through. He would have proven that the path leads to safety, because he walked it first."

Joseph stops breathing so hard, slightly relaxing his posture. His tone softens as he begins to explain.

"That's Jesus. He is the only one that has actually died and rose again. He has walked the path that he is leading you down. That narrow path. He knows that it's the only way, because he's been there. No other religion can say that. Every other religious leader, religious prophet, or teacher is dead. They're in the grave. We are in enemy territory. We are in a world ruled by Satan, and death is waiting for us down every other religious path. Not just any death. It's an eternal death. The only way to life—to eternal life—is by following the only one that has already walked that path."

Damian just stands there, stunned by the wisdom in what this youth has just said. No one had ever laid it out like that before. No one had ever explained it to him like that.

"So you're telling me that everything I know and believe in is wrong? You're telling me that my parents, my friends, even my country are all wrong, and you are the one who is right?"

"Yes," Joseph replies calmly.

Damian runs his hand through his hair, shaking his head back and forth as he does. "Nice try, but you are a traitor, and I'm taking you in."

Realizing that Damian is going to attack again, Joseph decides to take the offensive. With a burst of energy, he flies forward. He leaps from the concrete, first kicking his right foot and then his left. Damian blocks both kicks by crossing his forearms in the shape of an X so that Joseph's ankle strikes where his arms meet. The trooper slices through the air with his right arm repeatedly while holding his hand flat. Joseph moves slightly back with each blow that falls against his raised arms. Damian closes his open hand around one of Joseph's raised arms as the last blow connects. Then, spinning backward, Damian extends his left leg and plants it behind his opponent while pushing against the arm that he is now holding. Joseph topples over his leg, falling toward the edge of the roof. Instead of trying to fight it, Joseph pushes off with his legs, sending him backward and away from Damian's grip. He lands on his hands and uncoils his bent arms, which springs him back up and over the trooper's sweeping leg that's intended to send him over the side. Joseph begins to retreat to the other side of the parking garage in order to regain his composure, but Damian lands several punches to Joseph's lower back before he can completely escape. As he runs, the trooper follows in close pursuit.

Damian is just too strong for Joseph. He can't beat him in a pure fistfight. Pacing himself, he lets Damian catch up until he's right on his heels. Joseph runs up the driver's side of a truck and arches his body as he leaps backward. Damian, realizing that he's in trouble, immediately ducks to avoid the airborne assailant. His cloak flies up as he plants his feet against the ground, trying to quickly stop and crouch down. Joseph appears to hang suspended in air above the trooper. His cloak reaching up to meet the Christian's waiting hands. Joseph grabs the garment and continues his rotation. As his feet reach the ground, he grunts a war cry. He uses all his might and momentum to sling the trooper by his cape. Damian is jerked backward and over Joseph's shoulder. The trooper ducks his head and extends his arm, which drives down onto the roof. Joseph kicks at his head, but the trooper blocks it again with his forearms in an X formation. Damian quickly leaps to his feet. The trooper enters a defensive position this time. He backs up as Joseph continues trying to deliver a barrage of kicks and punches. Each one is blocked by Damian's tremendously powerful forearms.

Now it's Joseph who is on the defensive as Damian resumes his openhanded punches. This time, he alternates between arms. The force again drives Joseph backward. Damian closes his hand around Joseph's blocking arm and pulls down as he brings his knee up and forward into his stomach. Joseph lets out a loud grunt as the wind escapes from his chest. He falls to his knees in front of Damian, who punches Joseph in the head. The Christian spins on one knee, barely avoiding another punch. A dazed Joseph jumps to his feet. He throws several more punches and kick combinations, to no avail. Damian backs up with every move but blocks each one with his crossed forearms. Joseph is tired. He can't continue this much longer. With all his might, he runs forward and jumps, kicking into Damian's waiting forearms. He then extends his left arm straightforward with his elbow down. He sends his fist forward and down like a hammer, landing it into his block again with the full force of his weight. Unexpectedly, Joseph also brings the same elbow forward and continues in an upward motion. This finally breaks Damian's crossed forearms apart from below. Seizing his opportunity, Joseph drives a fist into Damian's chin. He's already off balance from Joseph's attack. The stunned trooper stumbles on the edge of the roof. He tries to catch his balance, his arms grasping at the air. There is nothing to hold on to. Damian falls over the edge of the roof to certain death. As he sees his opponent beginning to topple over, however, Joseph grabs the front of his shirt. He drops to the ground with one arm latched on to his opponent's clothes and the other extended behind him. His hand catches on the small ledge near the edge of the roof. He pulls against it as they both go over the side. Joseph manages to swing Damian back against the edge so that he can grab it as he drops. The two of them hang there for a second before slowly scrambling over the wall and collapsing onto the ground.

"That was stupid of you," Damian comments. He doesn't look up from the ground.

"You're not a bad person," Joseph explains. He wearily stares up at him as he speaks, not sure what he's going to do. "You just need to see the truth."

"Obviously, you're not bad. I mean, you just saved my life." Damian's voice is quiet.

"You know that it doesn't matter what you've done or where you come from. God wants you just like you are. He loves you so much, Damian."

"Look. You may have saved my life, but that doesn't mean that I'm going to betray my country." Damian motions with his hand toward the exit. "I'll leave. I won't tell anyone that I saw you. That's the best that I can do."

The trooper groans as he gets up. Joseph watches sadly as Damian walks across the roof and out of sight.

Joseph blocks the blinding sun with his hand as he looks up, squinting out over the city back toward where he has come from. The military complex where he left Sarah and Giby seems so far away now. How's he going to make it all the way back across the city? A number of abandoned cars are spread out haphazardly on top of the parking garage. Some are smashed in, while others remain untouched. Joseph bends down and looks through the window of one of the cars.

"No keys."

He runs up to the next car and does the same thing, but still no luck. Joseph spots an older car by the exit and hobbles over to it.

"Thank you, God!" he exclaims as he sees keys hanging from the ignition. He slides in and turns the key. Nothing happens. Upon further inspection, he discovers that the needle on the gas gauge is buried below the red line of the E. He slams his hand down on the steering wheel and gets back out of the car.

Joseph looks up into the sky. Somehow, it isn't quite as calming as it was before. It seems colder now, and foreboding. Next to the car sits a broken-down truck. The front end has been smashed in, and the tires are missing. Joseph looks down at it. The wheels start to turn in his head. He looks over the side and into the bed. An old hose is lying under some garbage. He pulls the hose out and unscrews the lid to the truck's gas tank. Taking a deep breath, he sticks the hose into the open hole and sucks hard. A stream of gas fills the hose. Just before it reaches his mouth, Joseph jerks away from it. He spits on the ground, trying to expel the taste from his mouth. Then he places the other end of the hose into his car's gas tank.

When all the fuel is siphoned, Joseph hops back into the driver's seat and tries to start the car again. The engine struggles to turn. It doesn't start. Then it turns several more times.

"Come on," Joseph pleads. The engine sputters, and then starts. Joseph excitedly steps on the gas, revving the engine hard. Smoke pours out of the tailpipe, forming a large cloud that the wind sweeps off of the top of the garage. He pushes in the clutch and shifts the car into reverse. The car creeps backward until the front end is clear from the truck. Joseph throws the car in first and chirps the tires as he speeds down the open lane of the parking garage.

I better go around the city, he thinks to himself. *The troopers are probably expecting me to go through the town to the suburbs.*

Joseph speeds off to the north side of town before finally coming back down into the city. As he drives, he wonders what happened to Zaphin.

He arrives back at the military base. Everything looks quiet. He parks his car next to some other vehicles that have been vandalized and runs into the military base. Arriving at the elevator, he presses the button. The doors swing open immediately, and he steps inside. Joseph reaches into his pocket and digs for the key to the elevator panel. He finds it just where he put it. Opening the panel, he presses the button that leads to the secured level. The elevator shoots down, pushing his stomach into his throat again. It starts to slow and comes to rest at the bottom of the shaft. The doors open to a smiling Sarah and Giby, who are waiting for him.

Sarah runs to him and throws herself into his arms. She backs up and looks over his shoulder with concern.

"Where is Zaphin?"

"I don't know. He bailed when we ran into some troopers. I was hoping that he had already come back here."

"No," Sarah replies with a confused voice. "Maybe he went home." Sarah changes the subject. "Did you get through to my parents?"

"Yes. Don't worry. They are fine."

"Praise God!"

"They want you to meet them at your grandparents' old farm out of town. They said that you know where it is."

"Sure. It's just about thirty miles south off of the main highway. It will take forever to get there though."

Joseph smiles and holds up his hand. He lets the keys drop from his palm and dangle in front of Sarah. "Not with these, it won't."

Sarah smiles and rocks up and down on her heels in excitement. "Let's hurry. Let's go right now," Sarah urges.

"Okay."

Sarah and Giby head toward the elevator while Joseph grabs the gun. It's still sitting exactly where he had left it.

She hadn't even touched it, he thinks to himself.

All three of them get back onto the elevator and return to the main level.

"The car is right outside," Joseph says.

He pauses at the door, cracking it open just far enough to inspect the sidewalks. The city is still again, for the most part. A broken sign hangs down across the street, some of its metal anchors having given way over time. It's the only movement that he can detect as it creaks eerily back and forth in the breeze.

"Okay. Let's go," he says, holding the door open for them. Giby and Sarah hurry out to the street, looking around.

"Where is your car?" Sarah asks.

Joseph lets the door swing closed as he runs out ahead of them.

"It's over here," he says, heading to the curb. Joseph arrives at his car and opens the back door. Giby makes it there first and hops into the back. Joseph puts his backpack on the back floorboard and shuts the door. As he turns around, he sees that Sarah has opened the front door and is sitting in the driver's seat.

"Hey! What are you doing, Sarah?"

"What does it look like? I'm driving."

"Why don't you let me drive?" Joseph asks.

"Because I know the way, now get in."

"Okay. You're the boss."

Joseph hurries around to the front of the car and slides into the passenger seat.

"Make sure you buckle up," Joseph says, looking into the rearview mirror. Giby reaches down beside her and latches the seatbelt together.

Sarah looks over at Joseph and smiles.

"Are you saying something about my driving?" she says as she clicks her seatbelt together.

"No. I'm sure you can give those troopers a run for their money."

CHAPTER 20

Sarah starts the car and makes a U-turn in the street.

"We'll go north and then head southeast around the city."

"So that's where your grandparents live?"

"Yes. I told you that they live just south of town, out in the country. We used to go there every summer for a week or two."

"What did you do there?"

"We would go fishing, camping, and do all kinds of cool stuff."

Sarah looks off into the distance. Joseph asks, "So do your grandparents still live there?"

Sarah's face appears sad as she answers. "No. They died during the pandemic."

"Oh. I'm so sorry, Sarah."

"That's okay. I know we will see them again some day. They were both born-again Christians." Sarah changes the subject. "Are those gloves permanently attached to your arms?"

Realizing that he's still wearing the Adam's Fall gloves, he examines the weapons covering his hands.

"To be honest, I forgot that I was even wearing them."

"So why don't you take them off?"

"I think that I'll wait until we get to the farm. You never know if we will run into more troopers or not."

"What do you think they'll do to us if they catch us?"

"There's no telling."

"What do you think they did to Zaphin?" Sarah asks.

"I hate to think about it. I don't know what he was thinking taking off like that. I mean, you can't run from—"

"Helicopters!" Sarah exclaims.

"Yeah. You can't outrun a helicopter."

"No. *Helicopters!*" Sarah yells, pointing up into the sky.

Joseph leans forward. He stares upward out of the bug-covered windshield with his mouth hanging open. Two more helicopters are headed straight for them.

Sarah mashes her foot onto the brake pedal, pulling the wheel hard to the left. The force throws Joseph against the passenger door. Sarah leans into the turn, letting up on the brakes and hitting the gas pedal. She cuts the wheel back to the right as the rear of the car fishtails around in the same direction. The slender bodies of the black aircraft veer to the left, exposing their engorged underbellies as they tilt.

"We can't out run them," Joseph says as he scrambles to right himself in his chair.

"I can lose them behind the tall skyscrapers over there," she says. About a mile in front of them looms what appears to be a cluster of shimmering glass columns.

"Good idea," Joseph agrees.

The car continues to accelerate, reaching ninety miles per hour. Even slight humps in the road send the car airborne for seconds at a time. Sparks fly as the weight of the car compresses the shocks, forcing the muffler to graze the street below. The two helicopters have almost caught up with them and are directly overhead now. The sound of an automatic weapon rings out. Bullets spray the pavement in front of the car. Sarah pumps her brakes rapidly, sliding around a street corner. She speeds up again as she disappears in between the giant buildings. The helicopters fly by, unable to make the sharp turn in between the tall structures.

"Give me the gun," Sarah instructs.

"What?" Joseph looks astounded.

"Just give it to me," she says sternly.

Joseph just stares at her, still trying to understand what she's going to do with it.

"Look," she says. "You have those glove thingies. You're going to get out and stop those helicopters. I'll park the car across the street to throw them off. I want the gun, just in case I get into trouble."

Joseph pulls the gun from his backpack and hands it to her.

"This little button is the safety," he says, pointing to a small silver button on the side of the pistol. "Push it in to take the safety off. Then point and fire."

Sarah's heart pounds as she cautiously takes the weapon. It's heavier in her hand than she anticipated, causing her arm to momentarily fall under the weight of it. She raises the barrel, pointing it at the roof of the car. The grip feels cold in the palm of her clammy hand.

The helicopters are now moving through the complex of buildings. Sarah veers left onto a cross street. There's a line of shorter buildings on the right-hand side of the street. They are only about five or six stories high and appear to be a lot older, judging by the fronts of them.

"I'm going to park over there," Sarah explains. "When I stop, you run out of sight. Then blast them when they come over these buildings."

Joseph checks on Giby, who doesn't seem to be scared at all.

"It's going to be okay," he says in a reassuring voice.

"I know," Sarah agrees.

A wisp of hair hangs down in front of Sarah's right eye. It bounces up and down on a single curl with every bump in the road. She sticks her bottom lip out and blows it up and away from her line of vision. The car comes to a screeching halt. They're on the side of the street, opposite from the shorter buildings. Joseph swings the door open, slamming it shut behind him as he exits. He can hear the helicopters already closing in on their position. He ducks behind a white stone seven-story apartment building. Setting Adam's Fall to magnetize, he shoots a beam up into the sky. He angles it back slightly so that the particles are starting to form in the air above the apartments.

"What's that?" one of the pilots asks, turning to two armed men in the rear of the aircraft.

"What do you mean?" asks the soldier manning the heavy artillery gun.

"I don't know. The air looks almost … fuzzy or something."

"Pull up, pull up!" a familiar voice yells across the headset.

The helicopter on the right veers up and swerves away from the cloud, but it's too late for the other one. The rotors cut through the extremely dense air, as if they are slicing into the side of a mountain. The blades bend and finally snap, sending shrapnel spinning into the surrounding buildings. The heavy artillery gun flies out of the helicopter, knocked loose from the impact. It crashes into the alleyway beside the building. Dropping from the sky in a freefall, the helpless troopers brace for the impact. The helicopter smashes against the roof and continues to slide forward. The landing bars tear into the tar and gravel as it skids. It doesn't appear as though it's going to stop. The helicopter crashes into a small retaining wall at the edge of the roof. Upon impact, the rear end raises. It's almost standing up completely vertically on its nose. The helicopter is motionless for a split second. With the weight too much to bear, the tail end tumbles back down onto the top of the building. All three guards lie unconscious inside the bent and mangled carcass.

The other helicopter glides around behind a building and out of sight. Joseph watches it disappear. The wind dies down. He can now hear his heart beating rapidly in his chest. He tries to find Sarah, but he can't see her.

"Sarah!" he yells.

Joseph spots a hand waving from inside the car. She must be lying down in the seat. The hand disappears back inside the window. Joseph can see into the back of the car where the little girl had been. She must be lying down too. The chopping sound of wind being beaten and sliced resonates down the street. The helicopter must be close again. Joseph raises his gloves, ready for battle.

Suddenly, the aircraft appears around the corner of a large skyscraper down the street. Joseph begins to shoot Adam's Fall at the target, but he ceases fire. The helicopter is just hovering several blocks away. He can barely make out something hanging halfway out of the door. No. Wait. It's not something. It's *someone*. A voice comes across the expanse from a speaker system. It's very faint, but Joseph can hear Slynne's unmistakable voice.

"I have … so … if you want … to … fire." He can only make out half of the words as he listens. The helicopter continues slowly up the street.

Again, training Adam's Fall on the advancing aircraft, Joseph tries to identify the person that is hanging out of the door. He can now see that it's a man. Slynne is holding onto his shirt, barely keeping him from falling. Joseph recognizes this person. His heart lifts as he sees his friend.

"It's Daniel," he whispers.

"Like I said," comes Slynne's voice again over the speaker. "I have your friend Daniel, so if you want your friend to live, you will hold your fire."

Joseph can now clearly see Daniel's face. He seems to be fine and not too concerned for someone who's being held out of the side of a helicopter fifty feet in the air.

"We are setting down now. If you try anything, then I will be taking your friend's life."

Joseph watches as the helicopter slowly lowers to the ground. A gust of wind from the blades blasts down against the street, sending dust swirling up and into the air. Joseph squints his eyes, blinking rapidly to keep Slynne in his sight.

When the air clears, Slynne is standing behind Daniel. The captain is holding a pistol against his hostages' temple. He drags him out of the open door.

"Here we are again," Slynne begins. "You have caused me quite a great deal of pain with all of your mischief. I hope that your friend here may be able to persuade you to listen to reason."

Slynne pushes the barrel of the gun into Daniel's head, causing it to tilt sideways. "Now you're going to take off those gloves and throw them to me."

Joseph looks down at the gloves on his hands. *Without these, we'll never get away*, he tells himself. He raises his left arm and begins loosening the strap.

"Patience has never been a virtue for me," Slynne warns.

Blam! Blam! Blam! Several shots ring out in quick succession. Sarah ducks back down onto the seat, having fired the pistol into the air to distract the evil captain. Slynne uses Daniel as a human shield, pointing his gun in the direction that the shots came from. Now is Joseph's chance. Without thinking, he instinctively shoots a beam directly into the base of a tall steel lamppost. A long metal arm hangs off of it, stretching over the street. The tip holds a large light that dangles from the end of it. Immediately, the base melts. The weight of the long arm sends the solid pole falling down toward the spinning blades.

Slynne senses the motion of something shifting. He turns his attention back toward Joseph to find the source of the movement. In an instant, he knows that there is no stopping what is about to happen. He pushes off of his prisoner, recoiling back into the compartment of the helicopter. This sends Daniel flying forward and out onto the street. Joseph switches his gloves to magnetize midstream as he redirects the beam above his friend's head. The solid pole makes contact with the spinning blades. A torrent of metal and debris flies from the top of the aircraft and rains down in a fury on the street below. The space directly above Daniel hardens from Adam's Fall's beam, just in time. Pieces of the rotor strike the air above him and deflect off. They twirl into the nearby buildings, shearing brick and mortar as they slice into them. Daniel continues sprinting forward, halfway bent over, with his hands covering his head.

Joseph hears the roar of a car's engine as Sarah accelerates, leaving two black streaks on the pavement as the smoking tires spin. She pulls the car around, heading toward her friends. She stops in front of Daniel.

"Get in," she yells.

Daniel opens the rear door on the driver's side and tumbles in. Sarah continues across the street and pulls in between Joseph and the helicopter. The solid mass of air begins to disintegrate as he stops firing long enough to get into the front passenger side of the car. Slynne takes aim and shoots at the vehicle, but the air is still thick enough that the bullet ricochets off of it. Joseph locks eyes with the captain. His glare does not waver as the car pulls away and starts heading down the street. Again, Joseph fires Adam's Fall at the air, reinforcing the barrier between the captain and their car as they get farther and farther away.

"We got out of there just in time," Joseph says as he spots a group of patrol cars speeding up the street toward Slynne. "Adam's Fall is getting out of range. Stop the car!"

Sarah pulls over to the side of the road. Joseph exits the vehicle and changes the setting to demagnetize.

Seeing that Joseph is turning his attention toward the buildings, the captain recoils his arm. His hand closes into one solid fist. His glove groans as it stretches. With tremendous force, Slynne delivers a punch to the solid mass of air, putting his full weight into it. The dense air scatters, leaving a hole slightly larger than a trash can lid.

He draws his weapon and extends his arms. The rest of the hard vapor above the hole falls in, as there is no longer any mass under it to support its heavier weight. Slynne grips his firearm firmly with both hands and focuses on the small white dot. He takes careful aim at Joseph, who must be three hundred yards away.

Joseph is unaware of what the captain is doing, as his attention is centered on the giant skyscrapers that line the right-hand side of the road. He begins firing at the base of one of the buildings. As pieces melt away, he moves the beam farther along the foundations until he reaches the building directly beside the car. A thundering noise begins to emerge from the structures. It's a terrible groaning sound of metal twisting as it begins to buckle. Dust and debris begins falling from the tops of the giants. Slynne fires a single bullet. The metal assassin slides through the U-shaped hole in the dense air, traveling at an incredible rate. It begins to climb upward and looks as though it will miss its target. Pieces of the building appear to suspend in midair as it threads through an opening. Missing clumps of debris, gravity begins to take over as the bullet crests and starts to fall. Slowly, it comes back in line with Joseph's head. He turns to look at Slynne, hearing the shot. It is eminent. The bullet strikes. Instead of its target, however, it smashes into a single brick that has fallen in the bullet's path from the top of one of the buildings. It explodes only a few feet in front of Joseph. He jumps, stunned and surprised by the accuracy of Slynne's shot at such a distance. The patrol cars pour down the street. They race past the captain, but it's too late. The base of the building gives way, sending the top tumbling over into the street. Joseph jumps back into the car.

"Go!"

Sarah pulls away, just ahead of the thick cloud that bellows out from under the demolished structure. The police cars swerve and stop, crashing into one another as they barely avoid being devoured under the rubble.

"That was some driving," pants Joseph as he looks out of the back window.

"Thanks," Sarah replies.

"Where did you learn to drive like that?" Daniel asks.

"My dad used to race cars on the side. He's a huge car buff. When I was younger, he would let me practice racing with him in the passenger's seat."

"He should have let you race. You would have won for sure," Joseph says.

"Oh. If you think that was some good driving, you should see my dad," she says. "Enough about me. What happened to you, Daniel?" Daniel stares out the window. He takes a deep breath. "I never want to go back there. I will *never* go back…" He trails off, appearing to be in deep thought.

"I don't know of anyone who has made it out of that place the same as when they went in—if they come out at all, that is," Sarah says.

"Yeah. I didn't see anyone else when I was there. It isn't just a prison. It's a sick and demented place of torture and degradation. They treat people worse than animals."

"Are you okay?" Sarah asks with a soft, empathetic voice.

"I'll be fine. I just need some food."

"We'll stop along the way somewhere," Joseph promises. "But first, we need to get away from the city and the suburbs."

"Agreed." Sarah smiles.

Daniel looks surprisingly healthy, given where he has just come from.

"I haven't slept in days," he yawns. "I'm going to get some sleep." He scoots down in his seat, twisting, as he lays his head against the cold window.

Sarah and Joseph sit silently for several minutes, just looking out at the scenery flying by. Sarah glances over at Joseph.

"You look really tired. Why don't you get some sleep too? It's going to take at least an hour to get there."

Joseph rubs his eyes with the backs of his hands and turns his sluggish gaze toward her. "I'm not really tired," he says.

"Okay, tough guy."

Joseph sighs, still looking at her. He can see the sparkle in her blue eyes again. A smile plays across her lips as she teases him.

"So how did my parents sound?" Sarah asks.

That's why she's smiling. She must be excited about seeing her parents again.

"They sounded worried."

Sarah looks away.

"But they were relieved that you're okay," he quickly adds.

"Yeah?" she questions.

"Yeah."

"Aren't your parents worried about you?"

"I was supposed to spend the night at Zaphin's last night, so it's business as usual at the Garrison household."

"Won't his parents get worried?"

"No. He never knew his real parents. He has bounced around from foster home to foster home. As soon as he turned seventeen, he moved out and got his own place." A look of confusion comes over Joseph's face all of the sudden. "I thought that we were going south," he says.

"We are, but that convoy saw us heading south too. I thought that it might be harder for them to find us if we changed directions. You know—keep them guessing."

"Pretty, and smart too," Joseph says jokingly.

Sarah can feel the heat tingling up her neck and knows that the red tint of embarrassment is trailing quickly behind it.

"If we go north, then east, then south, and then west again, then we probably won't run into any troopers." She avoids eye contact with Joseph as she speaks. She tries not to think about how flustered her face is. Instead, she tries to focus on her explanation for going the long way around.

After driving for quite some time, an orange light on the dashboard catches Sarah's eye.

"Crud! We're almost out of gas."

"So pull over at the next gas station. I think there's one up a couple of miles on the right."

"How do you know that?"

"There was an old, faded blue sign a while back. It said there was a gas station in the next three miles or something. I only hope that the station is still there."

Sarah drives for several miles before she spots another old, faded sign standing high above some trees. She scoots forward in her seat, trying to make out the faint wording on the sign.

"I think that's a Big Six."

"That's it," replies Joseph.

Sarah pulls off the highway and follows the winding road up to an old gas station. Surprisingly, there are several cars already there. As they pull up to one of the pumps, two older men deal them a condescending and suspicious look. Their frumpy mouths sag down, accentuating their multiple scruff-covered chins.

Joseph smiles at Sarah. "Grab your gun. There's a fixin' to be some trouble at high noon." He laughs.

"Thanks, Joseph the Kid," she replies through a giggle. Sarah swings open the car door and steps out, stretching her arms high into the sky.

"Hey Sarah, I have to hit the restroom real quick. I'll be right back."

Sarah smiles at him. "Okay. Grab some food, will ya?"

Joseph turns and jogs around to the side of the station and out of sight.

Sarah unscrews the lid to the gas tank and turns to the pump. *Gas went up again,* she thinks while reaching into her pants pocket. Sarah digs around for a while, searching for something. Her hand emerges empty. Looking concerned, Sarah quickly plunges her hand into the other pocket on her pants. She empties it and views the contents in her palm, which consists of a few coins, her house keys, a charge token, and some lint.

"There you are," she says victoriously.

Sarah picks up the charge token and shoves the remaining items back into her pocket. Everything slides back in except for the keys, which fall to the concrete beside the car. She bends down and quickly scoops them up.

Sarah spins back toward the meter as she stands. Unexpectedly, she comes face-to-face with a patrol car that's pulling up on the opposite side of the pumps. Her breath freezes in her chest. Millions of thoughts flash through her mind all at once. Her lips part as she searches for something, anything, to say.

The trooper looks out his window through his cold, mirrored glasses. The gravel crunches under the rubber wheels of the vehicle as it rolls to a stop. Her mind tells her feet to run, but they don't respond. She's stuck there beside it, petrified with fear. The trooper doesn't get out of his vehicle though.

What's he doing? she thinks. *What is he waiting for?*

He pulls out a cigarette and lights it up. Sarah's breath returns as she realizes that the trooper doesn't recognize her. She hurriedly fills up the gas tank of the large car and places the pump back onto its holder. Just as she turns around, Joseph strolls out of the front door to the station with some bags full of chips and bottled water. He can tell by Sarah's actions that something is wrong. Her movements are rushed as she walks to the car door. Sarah gets into the driver side and starts the engine. It's only then that she turns and sees him coming. She has to warn him. Making sure not to draw any attention from the cop, she pretends to fix her hair in the mirror. With her hand facing Joseph, she points backward at the trooper. Immediately, his eyes hone in on the red and green uniform. His heart stops in his chest as well. The trooper peers out of the open window of his car again. This time, it appears as though something has caught his eye. Joseph ducks his head and keeps his eyes on the ground.

Did he see me? Joseph thinks to himself. He can't tell if he's been spotted or not. The trooper's dark reflective glasses prevent him from seeing exactly where the policeman is looking. Joseph quickens his pace as he heads for Sarah.

"Hey!" The trooper's voice rings out across the gravel lot. Joseph keeps walking. He's almost to the car when the trooper gets out of his vehicle, loudly slamming the door closed.

"*Hey!*" he shouts with more authority as he starts walking in Joseph's direction.

He grits his teeth. There's no avoiding it now. He clenches his fist, ready to meet the oncoming trooper.

"Are one of you old farts going to fill up my tank or what?" The trooper asks angrily, walking past Joseph.

"Thank you, Lord," he sighs under his breath.

He can hear one of the old men sitting outside of the station grumpily mumble something. The car door creaks loudly as Joseph gets into the passenger side of the vehicle. Sarah puffs a sigh of relief.

"Tell me about it," Joseph whispers as they pull out of the gas station and get back onto the road.

CHAPTER 21

Joseph fishes out the bags of chips as they continue down the lonely highway.

"Here's some food," he declares, proud of his capture. Holding them up behind his head, he hangs the snacks over the back of his seat. There are no takers. Joseph wonders why until he turns around.

"Still asleep, huh?" he says. Both Daniel and Giby have their heads against the car windows. Unable to see their eyes, he whispers to them.

"Hey. Hey, does anybody want some food?"

"I do," Sarah answers.

Daniel doesn't respond. Joseph looks back at Giby, who is still lying against the window.

"Looks like we'll be dining alone."

Joseph opens one of the bags and hands it over to Sarah. Both of them snack on the meal as they travel down the long stretch of desolate highway. The median is filled with miles and miles of overgrowth. Weeds protrude out of the cracks in the shoulder, bending and swaying in the wind. They stop speaking to each other for several minutes. Both of them seem to be just enjoying the quiet and peaceful ride. Sarah takes the downtime to try and process everything that has happened. She crunches on some chips while she thinks. Her life will never be the same. She has a test coming up on Tuesday in geometry. How will she go back to school after this? What are her friends going to think? It doesn't matter now.

That girl is gone. It seems like ages ago since all this began, but it's only been a couple of days. Really, if she thinks about it though, she's been changing all along. She used to never talk about Jesus with her friends. Jesus wasn't "cool." And oh, how Sarah had longed to be cool. There were the slumber parties, the shopping, the band, and the cheerleading team. As she kept reading the Bible and talking with Jesus though, something happened. It didn't happen overnight.

It was a gradual process. She was becoming bolder in her faith. She was sharing Jesus more and more. Heck, she even joined the Bible study. Sarah suddenly remembered the Jansens.

"What happened to the Jansens is horrible," she blurts out.

Joseph, who's also deep in thought, doesn't register the unexpected statement. "What?" he mumbles with a full mouth.

Sarah restates her comment. "The Jansens. I can't believe that they're really gone."

Joseph looks back at Giby. She's still lying against the door with her eyes hidden. "I know," he responds. "It is horrible. I don't really feel like talking about it."

Joseph closes his eyes for a moment, yawning wide. When he opens them, his blurred vision slowly comes back into focus.

"What brought that up?" Joseph asks.

"I was just thinking about the Bible study," she responds.

"Speaking of the Bible study, I wonder how Zaphin is holding up," Joseph says, shifting his weight in his chair.

"He has probably told them everything about us by now," she answers as she stretches her arms out over the steering wheel. "If he's still alive…" No one has ever escaped from the troopers. No one except for Daniel, that is. Even he had a little help.

"Didn't any of your other friends want to come to the Bible study?" she continues.

"Most of my friends are MagiX—like Ray Ray. I already told you that I asked him to come."

"What did he say?"

"He asked when we were having it and what time we would be there. He said that he'd think about it. He never showed."

"Are any of the MagiX Christians?" Sarah asks, prying a little further.

"Yes. A couple of them are, that I know of."

"Why didn't they come?"

"I don't know. Why didn't any of your friends go?" Joseph fires back.

"*Touché*. It's not because I didn't try to tell them about it or something. I tried to talk them in to coming by pointing out that they really need to see what's going on for themselves. One of my friends, who's already a Christian, even told me *she* couldn't come. I talked to her about it a couple of weeks ago. I told her that Christians need each other. The Bible says that God wants us to worship together. That way, we can encourage and strengthen each other."

Joseph chuckles. "Let me guess—they say that they can worship him at home just as well."

"Exactly. But what she doesn't understand is that it's even more important now than ever to meet with other Christians. We need that support and fellowship so that we can stand in the face of persecution."

Joseph ponders over her insightful words before responding. "It's probably the persecution that keeps people from coming in the first place. I can't say that I blame them too much."

"I know what you're saying, Joseph. It's hard. But just think about the apostles and others that have suffered for Christ. Peter was crucified upside down. James was beheaded. Andrew was crucified on an X-shaped cross in Greece, after almost being whipped to death. He preached for two days while he was on the cross until he finally died. Thomas was speared in India. Matthias was stoned and then beheaded. Mathew was killed with a sword in Ethiopia. Jesus' brother James was thrown off of the temple. He fell one hundred feet. When they found out that he survived the fall somehow, they beat him with a club until he died. Bartholomew was flayed to death with a whip in Armenia for preaching about Jesus. Paul was tortured and then beheaded by Emperor Nero in Rome. And that doesn't include all the beatings, whippings, stonings, or the times that they were imprisoned, just for telling people about Jesus."

"Man," Joseph says. He exhales loudly, sinking down into the cushioned seat. "When you think about how they suffered to share the good news, it really puts things into perspective."

"I know. And some people actually think they were lying about Jesus coming back from the dead or something. You know that with all of them being tortured like that, at least one of them would have come clean if it all was a lie. It's like, 'Hey, just say that Jesus really didn't raise himself from the dead after three days. Just admit that he's not God, and we won't cut your skin off of your body while you're still alive.' You know it had to be true for all of them to be willing to be tortured and die defending Jesus."

Joseph pauses for a moment and then continues. "Sometimes, I want to tell some of the kids at my school about Christ, but I'm afraid that they'll label me a loser for being a Jesus freak."

"I thought that I was the only one who felt like that," Sarah says quietly. "No one wants to be shunned by the popular kids."

"Or even worse, they might turn me in to the red and greens."

"I think that they already have." Sarah smiles.

"I guess that's true. It all seems so stupid now. I'm not going to worry about what other people think anymore. From now on, I'm going to take advantage of any opportunities that God gives me to share the love of Christ."

"Me too," Sarah says reassuringly. "Deal?" Sarah holds her pinky out in front of Joseph. She's almost daring him to take it.

"Deal," Joseph agrees as he wraps his little finger around hers. He doesn't let go. It feels so nice just to be able to hold her hand.

All the conversation about sharing Jesus with friends reminds Sarah about the discussion that she had with Beth and Ashlynn. They really seemed like they were going to go to the Bible study.

She should have told them about Jesus right there in her basement. What's she been waiting for? She should have explained how he has and always will love them. She should have told them that if they die before turning to Jesus, that they will spend an eternity suffering in hell. *I'm going to tell them—if I ever see them again,* Sarah promises herself. Suddenly, she notices just how tired Joseph really is. His eyes are bloodshot. There is no expression on his face, and he looks like he could fall asleep at any moment.

"You need to get some rest," she says sternly, pulling her finger out of his gentle grip.

"I'm fine," Joseph responds.

"No. I have eyes. I can see how tired you are. You really need to get some rest," Sarah says with soft concern.

"How long do we have before we get there?" Joseph asks.

Her eyes squint again as she stares across the upcoming horizon.

"We probably have another thirty minutes or so," she responds.

CHAPTER 22

While Joseph is making promises to tell his friends who Christ really is, they are thinking about him as well. Their friend has been missing now for some time, and the MagiX are getting worried.

"I can't believe that no one has seen Joseph," Ray Ray sighs.

"Are you gonna cry about it?" asks Alex.

"The only one crying will be you when I drill this ball down your throat."

He pushes Alex away from him as they walk onto a layer of fine white sand.

The MagiX are at the lake again. That's about the only place that they don't ever get hassled by red and greens. It's kind of like an unofficial neutral zone—one of the few places that still seem normal. This time of year, there aren't a lot of people swimming. Most of the people spend their time walking along the shore and enjoying the beautiful day. Others are more adventurous. Some are boating, fishing, or tossing the pigskin around. For the MagiX, it's volleyball.

They usually play three-on-three. The teams for today have Ray Ray, Raedun, and Tyler lined up against Jason, Tommy, and Alex. The whole lot of them looks pretty rough after the run in that they had with the troopers at the abandoned water park. Raedun, or "Bags," as his friends call him, is the only one without a bruise or cut somewhere on his face.

"Are you sure you're up to it?" Raedun whispers to Ray Ray. "You just got out of lockdown." Ray Ray raises his eyebrows, puffing up his chest a little. "And your point, Bags?" he asks Raedun. After staring him down for a moment, he can't continue his ruse any longer. Ray Ray cracks a smile.

"Just kiddin' with ya. I'm fine, Raedun."

Bags gives Ray Ray a friendly smack on the back. "Good. We couldn't have you wimping out on us over a little jail time," he says cheerfully.

"John didn't get off so easily."

Both of them look over at their leader. He's sitting on a bench with some friends. He has bandages wrapped around his chest. A cast adorns his left arm. Somehow, he doesn't seem as tough as he did before. John doesn't seem to be in the best of spirits either, as is apparent by his melancholy expression.

"He has to be in pain," Ray Ray grits his teeth, imagining what it must feel like.

A circle of John's friends are gathered around him, trying to cheer him up. He starts to chuckle at something that one of them says but instantly winces from the pain.

"Yeah. He got hit hard," Raedun agrees.

"He's lucky to get away with only some cracked ribs and a broken arm."

"Are you guys gonna play or talk?" Alex calls from across the net.

"You'll wish we were just talking," Raedun calls back.

"Whatever, Bags. Then go ahead and serve already," Tyler responds.

Raedun takes the ball to the back of the court and holds it up with his left hand. He first looks at Ray Ray to his right, who nods, signaling that he is ready. Next, he glances at Tyler to his left. He too gives Bags a nod of approval. Throwing the ball into the air, he leaps up and swings his hand over his head. A loud smack echoes across the court, following the white sphere across the net and downward. The volleyball strikes against Alex's outstretched hands and spins into the air. Tommy nudges the ball up so that it's just above the net. Next, Jason springs up and hits it almost straight down on the other side. Tyler tries to stop it, but the volleyball ricochets off of his hands and flies off of the court. Ray Ray starts to jog after it, when he stops short.

A sandal comes down on the rolling white ball, pinning it against the ground.

"Throw me the—" Ray Ray begins to say until he realizes who is stepping on it. It's one of the troopers that had arrested them, and he has two others with him. Ray Ray stops walking.

"Hey guys," he calls back over his shoulder to his friends.

Like ravenous wolves coming out of a dense forest preparing for the kill, the MagiX slowly assemble around the three young troopers. They form a ring about twenty feet in diameter. The troopers are surrounded.

John stands to his feet. "What do you want?" the MagiX leader yells with a defiant and cynical voice.

"Look, man," comes the response. "We just want a game of three-on-three."

"I was thinking more like twenty-on-three." John grins. A chuckle comes up from the MagiX as well.

"Let's just head out, Damian," one of the troopers says to the young man with his foot on the ball. Damian reaches down and picks up the volleyball.

"A quick game of three-on-three. We play until we lose. The first time that somebody beats us, we'll be out of your hair."

John looks to Ray Ray to see if he's up to the challenge. He starts to shake his head no, but Damian tosses the ball at him. Ray Ray catches it against his chest. A hollow pong echoes out from his body.

"Unless you're scared of getting beat," the trooper taunts. "You were playing with half a team anyway."

"Let's hurry up and play so that we don't have to look at your faces anymore," Ray Ray replies.

"That's more like it."

"But we're not playing three games. Just one game. Winner stays on the court until somebody beats them."

Damian nods in agreement.

"And we change sides at seven points," Tyler adds.

"Whatever, man," Damian replies.

The sea of MagiX parts for the new players, allowing the three troopers to enter onto the court.

Damian pulls his shirt up over his head. He takes it off, revealing a ripped physique. The trooper also has some distinct bruises on his arms and chest.

"Looks like one of us got some good hits on you," Alex calls from the side of the court.

Raedun, who's still standing on the sidelines, calls out to Ray Ray. "Hey. I just remembered I've got something that I have to take care of. I'll catch you guys later."

"Just play this game, and then you can leave," Ray Ray calls back.

Bags glances across the court at the troopers. He slightly lowers his head. "No. I gotta go. See you later."

Alex raises his hand, signaling to Ray Ray.

"I'll play."

"Okay, Alex."

Alex jogs onto the court, glaring at Damian the entire time. He adorns his best game face as he approaches.

"Ugh," Alex grunts as he trips over one of the rails on the ground that holds the sand inside the court. He falls forward. His legs run to try and keep up with the top half of his body, but it's no use. Alex tumbles into the sand, barely saving himself from a face-plant with his hands. Chuckles bubble up from the onlookers. Even Ray Ray can't subdue his laughter.

"Shut up!" Alex commands, peering up at his friend.

Ray Ray walks over to him, extending his arm to help pull him up. Alex ignores the outstretched hand and stands to his feet. He brushes off the sand from his body and glances at his teammates. They're all trying not to laugh, but their faces betray them. Alex shakes his head slowly back and forth. His face is red with anger and embarrassment. He realizes how he must look. The corners of his lips curl upward as he continues to think about the irony of the situation. Here he is, trying to be as tough as possible. Yet, he's brought down by a six-inch railing.

Some of the MagiX are still laughing while Alex declares in a jovial voice, "Okay, okay, it's all fun and games until somebody gets hurt." The incident lightens the mood tremendously as the two teams face off.

Tyler crouches down, shifting his weight back and forth in a swaying motion. Alex takes a similar stance. His smile is gone. He seems to stare right through the players on the other side of the net.

"Zero serving zero," Ray Ray calls out as he tosses the ball into the air. His leg muscles tense as he springs up. He drives his hand down into the middle of the white leather ball. It whizzes over his teammate's heads and floats down toward the ground on the other side of the net.

"That's you, Kapen," Damian shouts out.

A young man with bleach blond hair hops backward and plants his feet. He's extremely skinny, and judging by his albino skin, he doesn't get much sun. That's why Ray Ray sent it to him. Kapen deflects the ball up into the air with ease, stopping its descent.

"Got it," calls Richard. This trooper is well-built like Damian, but he's slightly shorter. Unlike his friend Kapen, Richard is very tan. He likes to spend his summers at the lake doing just about everything, from swimming to water skiing.

He gently pushes the ball up, only using the tips of his curled index and middle fingers. It floats into the sky, hovering just above the net. Damian comes thundering down across the middle of the sand-filled court. Leaping into the air, he extends his body out as far as he can. His raised hand connects with it. The ball soars back across the net. Tyler bends down, caught off guard by his opponents' well-executed play. Leaping into the sand with his hands stretched out in front of him, he barely reaches the ball. It bounces off of his knuckles and flies backward a couple of feet, rolling the rest of the way to Ray Ray.

Tyler looks up at Alex and then back at Ray Ray. His face reveals his surprise. He raises his eyebrows and shakes his head as if to say, "What the heck just happened?"

Alex grabs the ball and rolls it under the net to Richard. The stocky young man passes it along to Damian.

"One serving zero," Damian calls out. He throws the ball into the air and drills it with his right hand. The line serve soars across the net, parallel to the sidelines. Tyler attempts another dig, diving for the well-placed ball. This time, he's able to save it. The ball bounces off of his outstretched forearms. Alex tries to set it, but the pass is less than perfect. He can barely get to it. This leaves Ray Ray no choice but to attack the ball from the backcourt. It's a successful hit. The ball spins across the net, coming down on Kapen again. Clasping his hands together, he leans backward slightly as he bumps it back up into the sky. Richard moves in for the layup, while Damian comes up for the final blow. He drills the ball down on the other side of the court; this time, it's directly in between the two frontline players. Tyler just barely makes it to his feet again. They both just stand there as it lands with a loud thud.

"Come here, guys," Ray Ray calls.

Damian gives high fives to Kapen and Richard, who smile and laugh in a celebration. "Nice kill," Kapen comments.

"Okay. Obviously, these guys have played before," Ray Ray begins.

"I've never seen them around here," Tyler says. "*Right*," Alex says sarcastically. "And our courts are the only ones in the state."

"Funny, man," Tyler responds.

"Well," Ray Ray continues, "Damian is obviously the power hitter. They're always going to try and set him up. We need to start trying to serve to him. That may mix it up a little."

"Sounds good," Tyler says.

"I'm the tallest one out of us all. I'll take on the blocks," offers Alex.

"But what are we going to do with that killer serve?" Ray Ray scratches his head as he thinks.

"Are you going to play volleyball or just play patty-cake all day?" a voice taunts from their opponents.

The three of them look up at Damian. His upper body is a mass of knots, where various muscles are bulging. His arms appear to be the same size as a regular man's leg. The three of them sink back into the huddle.

"We just need to keep his friends from being able to set him up so easy," Tyler suggests.

"Okay. Let's do it!" Ray Ray spouts enthusiastically.

The three teenagers take their positions on the court once more.

"Are you girls ready?" Richard taunts.

They ignore the trooper, focusing intently on the serve to come. Damian again serves the ball. "Two serving zero."

This time, it's a crosscourt serve. Ray Ray bumps the ball up to Alex. He stretches out his fingers and pokes the ball up, delivering a perfect set for Tyler, who is already on the move. He springs up, hitting the ball at its peak in the air. The tall and lanky Kapen jumps as well, attempting to block the shot. His fingers, however, only graze the ball. It veers off of his hand and out of bounds.

"That's what you get!" Tyler yells as he points at the blonde trooper.

"Enjoy it," he replies. "That's the only one you're getting today."

Damian picks up the ball and launches it over to Ray Ray.

"One serving two."

He serves the volleyball again, but this time, he hits with his palm. His wrist quickly snaps over, creating a fast spin. It's one of his favorite techniques, because it usually catches the other team off guard. His strategy is to serve the first one as hard as he can. For the second one, he uses this spin technique. It's similar to throwing a fastball first and then following that up with a sinkerball. Because there's so much spin from the way he snaps his wrists, the second shot usually falls short of where it appears to be heading. The little white ball flies across the net, looking as if it will sail over Richard. Instead, however, the ball suddenly drops. He tries to react, but it's too late. The best that he can do is to clumsily deflect it away from his head.

Richard is infuriated. He stomps over to the ball and picks it up. He hurls it as hard as he can at Ray Ray, who isn't able to hold on to it.

"Stone hands!" Richard called across the net.

Several of the onlooking MagiX inch closer to the court, ready to take on the troopers if they get out of hand.

Ray Ray isn't shaken by the temper tantrum. He examines the layout of the court. Damian, Kapen, and Richard are definitely more alert after losing those volleys. It's on now!

"Two all," he calls out. Ray Ray tosses the ball into the air once more, using his wrist-snapping serve. This time, Richard is ready. He easily passes the ball to Kapen, who sets it perfectly for Damian. The muscle-bound trooper again leaps into the air, crushing the ball. This time, Ray Ray has to go for the dig. He leaps after the plummeting ball. Sand flies into the air as he lands, but the ball bounces off of his hands and out of the court. He looks to see where it has gone. The volleyball has come to rest in the middle of several girls. They seem to be crushing on Damian pretty hard, from the way they are gawking at him and whispering to each other. One of them giggles as she hops up and tries to kick the ball back. It rolls halfway to the court, veering off toward the net.

"I'll go get it," Tyler calls as he jogs up to the ball. He pops it up into his hands with his foot and lobs it back to Damian.

"Thanks, man," Damian says cheerfully.

"Three serving two," Damian calls out, his outstretched body already halfway in the air. At the apex of his jump, he hits the ball. It flies across to Ray Ray like a guided missile. Ray Ray sidesteps to the left, dipping as he swings his locked hands upward. He bumps the ball with his forearms. It travels through the air and comes down on Tyler. Knowing exactly where Alex is, he tips it up.

"Block!" Richard calls out.

Both Kapen and Richard jump, their arms stretch out and angle slightly over the net. Alex spikes the ball, but it deflects off of the defender's arms. Tumbling forward, it lands on the net, still spinning. The momentum carries it on over the side, and it falls into the troopers' side of the court.

"Yes!" Alex extends his arm as he yells. He clenches his fist and drives his elbow back down toward his body. Ray Ray has the serve again.

"Three serving three," Ray Ray declares with a smile. He lobs the ball into the air. This time, he tries a different technique. Using the palm of his hand, he hits the ball squarely. It shoots forward with almost no spin. The unique thing about this serve is that it's very hard to predict where the ball is going to end up. The pale leather ball appears to wobble in the air as it comes across the court. Kapen reaches for it, but it suddenly veers away from him at the last minute. His hands barely touch it, sending it down and into the sand.

"That's seven points. Switch sides," Damian declares.

The six players change sides on the court. Not a word is spoken as they pass underneath the net. They only stare coldly at one another.

"Four serving three." Ray Ray announces the score again before serving. He knows the field well and plans to use this to his advantage. After all, he plays there all the time. Depending on which way the wind is blowing, he knows how hard and how far he can hit the ball and still be in-bounds. Ray Ray starts the serve. It goes toward Damian this time. It appears to be hit too hard. Damian lets it go. He thinks that it will go out of bounds, but the wind drives it down. The volleyball hits the line, sending sand flying everywhere.

"Out!" yells Richard.

"Give me a break!" Tyler yells back.

Damian raises his hand, his mouth open and ready to speak. He pauses, closing his eyes slowly and deliberately. His posture radiates a lackadaisical vibe that seems to calm everyone down.

"It was in," he says, projecting his voice in Richard's direction.

Upon hearing this, Richard clenches his teeth and lowers his head. Ray Ray can see the muscles tensing around the trooper's thick neck.

Damian picks up the ball and passes it again to Ray Ray. Once more, he studies his opponents. Richard is clearly frustrated. *A perfect target*, he thinks to himself. "Five serving three," he declares with a smile, trying to rub it in Richard's face as much as possible.

Ray Ray lobs the ball into the air, taking aim at the livid trooper. The volleyball zooms across the net, spinning fiercely. Richard gets set for the pass. The wind is playing havoc with his game, making it extremely tricky to predict how the ball will react. He isn't used to playing in the wind. The three of them have mostly been sticking to indoor court matches, where they typically dominate. Simultaneously, a big gust multiplies the effects of the spin on the ball and pushes it downward. Richard reaches forward, stretching to get it. The ball thuds against the uneven surface of the court. He just can't react quickly enough. Unable to control his anger, he lays into the ball with his foot. *Thwap!* The little white sphere compresses as it's propelled out into the crowd. Realizing Ray Ray's strategy, some of the MagiX start to clap sarcastically for the failed attempt by the stocky trooper.

Damian trots over to his friend. He puts his hand on Richard's shoulder and lowers his voice so that no one else can hear him.

"Calm down, man. They're just trying to make you lose focus."

"I know. But the wind is messing with my game," Richard protests.

"Don't sweat it. We're just having fun here anyway."

"Yeah," he concedes.

"Six serving three," comes the score.

Richard knows that it's heading to him. This time, he's ready. He quickly gets under the ball, bumping it into the air. Kapen sets it for Damian, who is already in midair. This time, the trooper's opponents, Alex and Tyler, hang back. Damian is surprised that they aren't trying to block it at the net. He connects with the ball, sending it on a fast downward trajectory. Ray Ray dives into the sand, getting his hands under the ball. It bounces back into the air, where Alex is waiting to set it. Tyler begins his approach, getting ready to spike the ball. Alex tips it up, where it seems to hang above the net. Richard clenches his teeth, letting a vindictive smile worm its way through his lips. Now he's going to shove that ball back in this kid's face. Mustering all his anger, he leaps into the air, slanting his hands over the net. Kapen is there as well. A united wall of arms forms a menacing defense. Instead of spiking the ball, however, Tyler tips the ball. Suspended in midair, the troopers watch helplessly as the fragile ball floats up and over their hands. It lands softly on the sand, followed by the loud thud of Kapen and Richard's feet.

"Now that's how you cheat the ball," Ray Ray yells enthusiastically.

This is embarrassing, Damian thinks to himself as he throws the ball across the net.

The tension builds as the game continues on. The MagiX are well skilled at playing in the wind and on the sand, and they use that to their advantage. The troopers just can't play as well in these conditions. They had dominated the inside courts and probably would have easily beaten the MagiX if the wind would have at least died down a little. As it was, Damian's massive spikes were about the only thing that was keeping them in the running. As they near the end of the game, the score is MagiX, 20, and the troopers, 17.

Ray Ray calls out the score before serving. The ball powers over the net and drops to Kapen. The scrawny trooper bumps the ball to Richard, who pushes the ball into air until it's just above the net. Everyone expects Damian to spike it, but instead, Kapen leaps into the air and drives it into Tyler's shoulder. It ricochets off of his body and rolls out of bounds.

"Nice quick hit," Damian praises.

A beautiful girl wearing a white hoodie with a pink tank top under it scoots off of the old wooden bench where she has been quietly watching the game. As she trots over to the volleyball, she tosses her long, wavy blonde hair. The young lady picks up the ball and cradles it against her side with her right hand. Then she turns to look at Damian.

"Your serve," she calls to the trooper. She then throws the ball into his waiting arms. He hadn't seen her when he first arrived. She must have just gotten there.

"Looks like that's eighteen serving twenty," Damian announces.

Keeping the momentum going, he drills the ball again across the court. Ray Ray steadies his stance. He bumps the ball back to Tyler. Easily controlling the ball, he sets it for Alex. Using all of his force, the young teen soars into the air and makes a solid hit. The ball is going crosscourt into the back corner. Damian leaps with his arms stretched fully out, like he's diving into a pool. He rotates his upper body slightly toward the net and brings his arms together. The ball deflects off of his forearms, slowly spinning upward into the middle of the court.

"Got it," Richard yells.

He sets the ball a little higher this time. As Damian goes up to spike the ball, Alex and Tyler go up as well to secure a block. Their opponent, however, doesn't hit the ball. Instead, he pulls his arm back and curls downward toward the ground. Kapen is already in midair before the MagiX realize their miscalculation. The tall, lanky trooper delivers the kill, sending the ball into the dry sand.

"Nice stack!" exclaims Richard, giving his friends props for the well-executed play.

"Well, that must be nineteen serving twenty," Damian says smugly.

He serves the ball. Going for an ace, he exerts tremendous force and follows through on the ball. The muscles tense throughout his whole body. Just then, the wind gusts across the court. Ray Ray dives for the speeding white sphere but doesn't get there in time. It compresses against the sand and flies off into the crowd.

"It's out!" exclaims Tyler.

Everyone turns to looks at where the ball has landed. The victorious smile on Damian's face fades into a solemn one of defeat. Sure enough, the crater that the ball has left in the sand is clearly just outside of the line. It would have been in-bounds if that gust of wind hadn't come through. Ray Ray peers up from the ground, just as surprised as everyone else.

"Yes," he whispers under his breath.

"Nice match," Damian says, congratulating his opponents.

"Yep, good game," Kapen says.

Even Richard nods his head in agreement. Ray Ray, Tyler, and Alex, in turn, all congratulate the troopers on a game well played.

Damian struts off the sand field onto the coarse grass, looking quite victorious. From the way he's carrying himself, one would think that he won the game. His teammates follow behind him, dusting the sand off of themselves as they exit the court. Damian grabs his shirt and puts his arms into the sleeves. Then he pulls it down over his head. As he emerges from the veil of cotton, he's confronted by the girl with the long blonde hair who had tossed him the ball earlier.

"Hey," he says, grinning at the young woman.

"Hi. Nice game."

"Thanks. I think they got a little lucky on that last point though."

"If you say so." She pauses for a second to draw the wisps of hair out of her eyes with the tips of her fingers. Tucking them behind her ear, she begins again. "How come I've never seen you around the lake before?"

"We don't hit the high school scene too much," he answers sarcastically.

She displays an over exaggerated smile. "I'm not in high school." She acts as though even the thought of it is utterly disgusting.

"Oh. My fault." Damian raises his hands up in an apologetic gesture. "So what is your name?"

"Rebecca. What's yours?"

"Damian." Playing it cool, he slides his left hand into his pocket. "I need to start coming here more often though. The scenery is fantastic."

"Yeah. I love this time of year," Rebecca agrees. She shrugs her shoulders as she rocks up slightly on the tips of her toes.

"Since this is my first time here, can you show me around?" Damian asks.

His friends have already gathered all their stuff together and are now standing behind him. He turns to see what they're up to. Richard is halfway turned toward the lot where they parked. He doesn't appear interested in the conversation. Instead, he checks his watch, in reaction to which he displays an unpleasant look.

"You two go ahead and leave. I'll catch up with you later."

"We're outta here," Richard puffs in a contemptuous tone. "Come on, Kapen."

"Later, Damian." Kapen nods as he and Richard head up the path toward the cars.

Damian turns back toward Rebecca. *Wow, does she have pretty eyes,* he thinks to himself. She's not very chatty. The girl is just staring up at him, waiting with anticipation for his next move. She seems to already know what he's going to ask. She doesn't have to say a word. Her eyes twinkle; a smile purses her lips.

"So, like I was saying," Damian continues. "Do you want to show me around?"

Rebecca waits before answering. She doesn't want to seem too eager. Biting her bottom lip, her eyes look to the side, past Damian. Small lines crinkle up on her brow, as though it's a tremendously difficult decision.

"Why not?" she finally responds. "It's not like I'm doing anything else."

"Great. So where's your favorite spot?"

"Let's walk down the shoreline, and I'll show you."

Damian and Rebecca start strolling along the side of the lake.

"Why would a beautiful girl like you be here all alone?" Damian asks, after walking quietly for a couple of minutes.

"Me?" Rebecca looks surprised. "Oh, I'm not alone. I'm here with my little sister and her friends."

"How old is your sister?"

"She's sixteen going on forty." Rebecca giggles. Damian lets out a hearty laugh as well.

"So what's her name?"

"Ashlynn."

"That's a cool name."

"Yeah. It's definitely unique, just like my little sis."

"She sounds like quite a handful."

"I wouldn't say that. She's just different." Rebecca pauses, looking up at the sky. "But in a good way, you know?"

"Like how?" Damian asks.

"She's just such a nice and sweet little girl. She has such a huge heart."

"Sounds terrible." Damian smiles as he gently nudges Rebecca. She stumbles sideways. Regaining her composure, she runs up to Damian. Planting her feet, she uses all her weight to push him back. He laughs as he too stumbles slightly to the side.

"Let me finish," Rebecca protests.

"Okay, okay. Proceed."

"Well, she acts like my mother instead of my little sister sometimes."

"Really?"

"Yeah. Especially lately. She has this friend named Sarah. I guess she's one of those Christians or something, or at least that's what Ashlynn tells me."

Damian's smile fades as he continues walking along. He stares off into the distance as she talks.

"So now, all of the sudden, Ashlynn has been coming at me with this Christian stuff. At first, I was all like, get a grip. That stuff isn't real. I told her that if she messed around with this friend of hers, then she was going to end up in big trouble. But that didn't stop her. This past week has been the worst. It got really intense last night."

"What happened?" Damian asks. He isn't sure that he even wants to know. This girl is way cool. She has a great personality, she's fun, attractive, and she seems to like him. What if she tells him that she's a Christian now? Is he going to have to turn her in to the captain? Damian thinks about this beautiful young girl locked in the bowels of the military complex. He imagines the torture that she would have to endure. He shakes his head, trying to fling off the horrible thoughts.

"I know, right?" Rebecca says. "So she tells me that she was invited to a—" Rebecca looks around before continuing, making sure that no one is within earshot. "A Bible study," she whispers.

Damian stops walking. He reaches out and grabs her hand. Rebecca is surprised at first but then quickly grabs his hand back. Damian's mind is racing. He remembers the oath that he took to protect his country. That same oath that demands he turn in any Christian traitor. This girl's sister sounds like she knows the Sarah that they are after. She might have vital information that could lead to the capture of the traitors. Imagine the accolades that he would receive from Slynne if he single-handedly brought in the Christians. Damian looks deep into her wide-open eyes. She's just smiling at him. There's no sinister plot here. There is just an innocent smile from an innocent and fragile girl. Damian can't do it. He can't turn her in. He returns the smile with a warm, heartfelt one of his own.

"So what happened?" he asks as they begin to walk up a small hill. Damian looks down at their hands, still holding fast to one another.

"Well, she didn't go, but she couldn't stop thinking about it either. She told me that she was going to go next week. I told her like no way should she go, right? But then she starts coming at me with this Christianity stuff. She tells me that I might find out that I need this Jesus guy. Ashlynn says he loves everyone and that he can change my life—so what do I have to lose by checking it out? So I tell her she's acting like my mom. She's all like, 'Just listen to me. I know this is the best thing for you.' Anyway, so that's what I meant."

"This is it," Rebecca says as they step up onto a wooden pier. The entrance is situated at the top of the hill that just finished climbing. The old planks of wood have been worn by weather and the feet of many visitors over time. They stretch about fifty feet out across the water. As they walk farther out onto it, the two of them cross past rows of large gray support beams. They travel farther across the pier and over the lake. They finally reach the end of it and look out over the landscape. The air is cooler here, and the wind definitely feels stronger. Rebecca shivers as she stands there. Damian reaches around her shoulder and holds her tightly to his body. They cuddle there for some time, looking over the water. Endless rows of little whitecaps crest on the tops of small waves, breaking over and over again in an endless dance. White cotton ball clouds seem to drift across the surface, reflecting the brilliance above. Rebecca snuggles in to Damian. She runs her finger across his hand, doodling imaginary shapes onto his skin.

"What's this?" she asks, gently running the tip of her index finger over a deep abrasion on his left wrist.

Damian breaks his soft gaze, looking to the lake again. "This? I kind of got into a scuffle earlier."

He hadn't even noticed it before. He must have gotten it when he was fighting that Christian. He reflects on the incident. Joseph had saved him on the rooftop. In fact, he had risked his own life to save him. They both almost ended up falling off of the side of the building. It's all so surreal. Joseph doesn't seem like a traitor. He seems like a nice guy. Something just isn't adding up. He twists his arm away from her and pulls his sleeve down over the wound.

"Does it hurt?"

"No. It's fine."

"Is that where you got those bruises that I saw earlier?"

"Yes. He got me pretty good." Damian smiles. "He didn't exactly get away without a few cuts and scrapes either though."

Rebecca pulls Damian's hand up to her face. She lovingly kisses it. His heart melts as he looks into this young lady's trusting face. The water gently laps against the strong pillars of the pier. Birds sing hello as they soar through the air. Damian hears all of this, and at the same time, none of it. He can feel his heart beat faster in his chest as he leans forward. Her eyes close, anticipating his intention. Gently placing his hand into her hair, he slides it back away from her face. Damian leans in the rest of the way. His lips brush up against her slightly open mouth. Rebecca closes her eyes as she presses into him. Her breath leaves her body. Her face becomes flustered as they kiss. Damian opens his eyes as he pulls away from her. Rebecca still has them closed, her mouth still slightly open. She's intoxicated by this new feeling swallows her consciousness. Slowly she opens her eyes.

"That was nice," she whispers.

Damian puts his arm around her again, beckoning for her to cuddle even closer with him. They sit there on the pier for some time, gazing out across the lake at the breathtaking view. Damian feels at peace.

"Rebecca!" comes a voice from behind. The couple turns to see Ashlynn running up the hill toward the pier. Rebecca jumps to her feet, startled by her sister's tone.

"That's her," she explains to Damian. "That's my little sis." She lets go of his hand and sprints to meet Ashlynn at the end of the pier. Damian jogs up to them as well.

"Who? Whose parents haven't heard from her?" Damian hears Rebecca ask.

"Sarah!" Ashlynn repeats herself.

"Oh, Ashlynn," Rebecca says softly, wrapping her arms around her sobbing sister. Looking up, she sees her friends coming up the hill close behind her. It's Beth, Serenity, and Kris. "Let's go sit down in the grass," Rebecca suggests.

"O—okay," Ashlynn whimpers.

As they start walking away, Rebecca looks over her shoulder. She nods, beckoning Damian to follow them. The girls sit down on the cool ground, just as their friends reach them. Rebecca can see that both Beth and Serenity have been crying as well. They all plop down in a circle. Damian follows suite and sits down as well.

"Who's that?" Kris questions.

"Don't worry about it. He's with me," Rebecca says.

"Humph," Kris grunts, as she looks him up and down.

Damian awkwardly waves at them.

"So calm down and explain to me exactly what's going on." Rebecca rubs her sister's back as she speaks.

"Well, we couldn't get in touch with Sarah this morning. No big deal, right? Maybe she was just still sleeping. Or maybe she had to do something with the family, but we keep trying her every hour and still nothing. That's weird for Sarah. Even if she's out somewhere, she'll always at least message us back."

"Maybe her parents grounded her or something. Maybe they took away her phone," Rebecca suggests.

"No," Kris says coldly. "We got a hold of her parents. They haven't seen her either."

"They thought she was with us," Serenity adds.

"And she had been talking about that meeting that she had to go to," Ashlynn continues. "So we think that maybe it didn't go so well." Ashlynn starts crying again.

"We know she's a Christian," Beth says sadly. "We think that the R and Gs might have found out about it or something, because no one has heard from her since." Tears start rolling down Beth's rosy cheeks.

Damian inconspicuously pulls his sleeve down further over the wound on his wrist. Feelings of guilt boil up inside of him as he listens to these brokenhearted girls.

"I just keep thinking about what they might do to her if she got taken. It's just horrible," Ashlynn says between tears.

"The worst thing is that she isn't some radical. She cares about people. There isn't anything that she wouldn't do for someone else," Beth says, her head still down.

"I didn't buy into the whole Christianity thing," Serenity admits, "but I started thinking about what Sarah had said. Her message is real. Remember when she asked how we knew that we were on the right side?"

The other girls nod their heads.

"Well, I thought about all the Christians that I have ever known or known about. The thing is that they are all really good people."

"Like Daniel," Beth agrees.

"Yeah." Serenity looks around the circle at her friends' faces. "So how do we know that we are on the right side? Especially with the way that the police act. They torture and kill people. They can take any one of us at any time, even if they just think we're Christians. How can they be the good guys and the Christians be the bad guys?"

Damian grits his teeth. Something that this teenager said has just ripped him in half. He looks around at the group of girls who are all crying over their friend. He stares into Rebecca's eyes. She seems desperate to console her poor little sister. *Sarah can't be a bad person*, he thinks to himself. He remembers the tortures that he has witnessed. He thinks about all the killings that he has seen throughout the years—all done to stop these traitors. But now, he can see that the traitors aren't out to destroy the country. They seem like good people. Suddenly, he gets it. He feels the cut on his wrist through the thin cotton material, unable to forget how Joseph saved his life. He clenches his fist. Damian rises to his feet. His face looks as hard as stone. His resolve is set. He turns to walk away from the group.

"Where are you going?" asks Rebecca.

"There's something that I have to take care of," he answers.

"Wait up, and I'll scan your number," she calls after him as she starts to get up.

Damian stops, holding out his hand as he turns around. "No. Just stay right where you are. You obviously have a lot to deal with right now. If you're here next weekend, then I'll give you my number then."

"Okay," Rebecca sadly replies. "I'll be here next weekend at the same time, right out on that pier."

"See you then," Damian says. He doesn't smile this time. Turning again, he walks down the hill and up the path to the parking lot. Rebecca watches him until he crests the hill. Damian doesn't even turn around once. When Rebecca can no longer see him, she turns back to console Ashlynn.

CHAPTER 23

Joseph rubs his eyes and lets out a big yawn as he arches his back. He stares out the window once again, watching the miles of desolate highway fly beneath the car. They seem to glide over the road. Joseph watches the grass from the side window. As the wind passes over it, thousands of blades move in harmony. It looks like a deep green sea with tiny waves rumbling over the surface. He watches the hypnotic rhythm for a few minutes before he finally gives in to the heavy cloud of sleep in his head.

As he drifts into slumber, he's in the dream again. Joseph is in the street. He can see everything around him. The guards rush in, forcing his parents to kneel. The crowd hides the mysterious figure as he shoots Joseph's parents. This time, Joseph isn't a little kid anymore. He can see himself being held by guards. For the first time that he can remember, he's a grown man facing this terrifying dream. He sees the dark trooper approaching. Is that his face? Joseph can see his face! No—it isn't. It isn't him. It can't be him! Joseph freezes in shock and disbelief as Slynne's face emerges from the shadows. Rage overtakes his body as the hatred boils up within Joseph. He throws the trooper who's holding him over his back and lunges toward Slynne.

Joseph wakes up. He jerks his body hard toward the front of the car, but his seatbelt stops him.

"What?" Sarah exclaims.

He stays there, pressing against his seatbelt.

"What's wrong?" she asks again.

The thought paralyzes Joseph as he realizes what has just happened. His face fills with a mixture of anger, shock, grief, and relief, all at once.

"I know who killed my parents," he finally replies.

"What? I thought you were too young?" Sarah asks.

"I must have been blocking it out of my memory this whole time. I've always had nightmares about that day, ever since I was little, but I could never see who killed them."

"So how do you know who did it now?"

"I finally saw his face."

"Who was it?"

"It was Slynne."

"Slynne? The same psycho Captain Slynne that killed the Jansens? The same one that tortures Christians? The man that is trying to kill us?"

"Yeah."

"What are you going to do?"

"I don't know yet. I don't know."

Joseph leans back in his seat once again, more exhausted from the dream than refreshed.

"I'm sorry," Sarah says sympathetically.

They sit quietly for a while. Joseph is looking down at Adam's Fall. Maybe he has a chance against Slynne with these. He flexes his muscle in the gloves as he makes a fist. The leather slightly squeaks against itself as it expands. With these, he could stop Slynne. He wouldn't be able to hurt anyone anymore.

Joseph is going to kill him. It's the only way that he'll stop hurting people. As he sits in the car, he begins to plot his revenge. But then, a still small voice speaks to his heart. It's the gentlest voice that he has ever heard.

"I forgave you."

That's all that it says. Joseph immediately starts to defend his thoughts. This is different. This is an evil person that deserves to die. Just think about all the Christians he has tortured and killed. Besides, it isn't like Slynne has asked for forgiveness. Maybe if

Slynne got on his knees and begged for it, maybe then Joseph would forgive him. Again, the calm and loving voice comes.

"Father, forgive them, for they know not what they do."

Joseph shakes his head.

"Okay. I know what you're saying." Joseph settles down into his chair, crossing his arms as he grits his teeth. It isn't fair. He doesn't want to forgive Slynne. Joseph needs the hate. It's a part of who he is. It's what drives him.

"I forgave you," the voice comes again. This time, it almost sounds as if it's pleading with him.

How can he ever forgive Slynne? What he's doing is wrong! He shot his parents in cold blood!

Suddenly, Joseph begins to feel warm. Not just from the sun beating down through the windshield either. This is something coming from inside. Something is beginning to happen to him.

"I love you, child, and I am with you." The voice comes and washes over him, like a mother's hand running through her son's hair. Wave after wave of God's love comes upon him and through him, soothing his soul. He begins to cry as the voice repeats over and over again. "I love you, child."

"Are you all right?" Sarah gasps, shocked to see Joseph crying. She's never seen him cry—ever.

Joseph grabs the front of his hair with his hand and buries his head in his arm. He can't control what's happening. All he can blubber is, "I forgive him—I forgive him."

Finally, the warmth subsides, and Joseph is left feeling exhausted. Although he's tired, somehow he feels much lighter than before. He quickly falls back asleep. For the first time in quite a while, he dreams good and peaceful dreams. They are filled with friends, family, laughter, and God. Dreams free from the dark figure. The hate is gone; the torture is over.

Joseph opens his eyes as he awakes from the blissful rest. The car is just slowing down and turning onto a bumpy driveway. He scoots up in his chair and surveys the area. The old dirt path winds up a small hill. At the top of it is a run-down gray house. The pathway is covered with rocks of various sizes, shapes, and colors that have been driven into the ground over time from the weight of cars passing over them again and again. Beside the house sits a huge red barn. It used to be red at one point, anyway. Obviously, no one has done any upkeep on it anytime recently. Now it's more brown than anything. Only a few flakes of the red paint still hang off of the structure here and there. Joseph rolls his window down, taking in all the smells of the country. He's immediately overwhelmed by a blast of hay, followed by the faint aroma of dirt. It's the same smell that comes from a field that has just been turned or from digging up potatoes from Grandmother's garden.

Joseph turns to see that Daniel and Giby are awake now. They definitely got something to eat, judging by the empty bags of chips in the backseat. He grabs the gun from his backpack before they arrive at the farmhouse. Sarah slows down as they pull up in front of the porch. Just as the car is coming to a stop, Sarah spots her parents.

"There they are!" she shouts to Joseph as she throws the car into park. She jumps out of the vehicle and sprints out ahead of Joseph. She forgets about the police. She forgets about the persecution. She forgets how tired she is. Her parents are here now, and everything will be better if she can just get to them.

"Wait," Joseph screams after her. He gets out of the car almost as quickly as she does and chases after her.

Just as Sarah is almost to the porch, a slender figure emerges from the shadows of the garage. He's dressed in black pants and a black leather coat. His helmet shimmers in the sunlight, and the black visor hides his secret identity. Just as Sarah is running past the garage, the masked figure turns the corner. He steps directly in front of her path. Sarah comes face-to-face with the menacing character.

She tries to stop, but her momentum is too much. Her feet slide on the dirt and come out in front of her, sending her crashing to the ground. Her hands cushion the fall as they connect with the gravel. Her legs kick against the hard path as she frantically tries to reverse her direction. The man starts to reach into his coat, as if he's going to pull something out. Joseph raises his gloves up. It's her only hope. He carefully aims the two beams and fires. The air starts to thicken in front of the man. He stops from pulling out whatever he's hiding inside of his jacket. He just looks at the air. Suddenly, the barricade fails. Panicking, Joseph looks down at his gauge.

"Empty? What?" Joseph exclaims. He reaches into his own shirt and pulls out the gun.

"Don't move!" he yells.

Sarah scrambles to her feet and backs up, putting some distance in between them and the man. Her parents are in shock. They stand there dazed on the porch.

"Take off your helmet," Joseph instructs.

"It's me," comes a familiar voice from behind the tinted visor.

It couldn't be. Surely it wasn't—that would be impossible.

"Zaphin?" Joseph asks, lowering the gun.

The figure takes off his helmet and smiles. It is Zaphin!

"Hey, guys." He laughs. "Is that any way to greet your friend?"

Daniel walks up, studying Zaphin's face. Joseph and Sarah just stand there.

"You know this man, sweetie?" Sarah's father asks from the porch.

Sarah remembers why she was running to the house in the first place. She brushes past Zaphin and hurries up to where her parents are. Zaphin steps back; upset by the cold reception. She throws herself into their open arms. Her mother starts to cry while her father successfully fights back the tears welling up inside his eyes.

"Praise God, you are okay!" her mother says.

"Yes. Praise God." her father echoes.

Joseph walks up to Zaphin, who's still just standing there. He displaces a frown with a familiar grin as he places his helmet under his arm.

"What are you doing here, Zaphin?" Joseph asks.

"When we got separated, a cop car ran me over. It must have knocked me completely out."

"And what, they just left you there?" Joseph asks cynically.

Zaphin is taken back by Joseph's skepticism. "Of course they didn't leave me there. They shoved me into the back of the car."

"So how did you escape?" Joseph asks again, in that same steady and skeptical voice.

"I woke up in the back of the trooper's car, and I heard someone on the radio. They were talking about sending someone to Sarah's parents' house."

"Who was talking about going to her parents' house?" Joseph asks.

"I don't know. It was some guy with two first names or something."

Joseph thinks for a second. "I know someone with a name like that."

"Anyway," Zaphin continues, "I acted like I was still knocked out until I could get my bearings. They hadn't put any handcuffs on me or anything. They must have figured that an unconscious teenager isn't a threat. Luckily, they were taking me to a station in the same part of town as my house. When they were almost to their base, I acted like I was going to puke my guts out. As soon as that cop opened the back door to help me out, I made a break for it on foot. The station is pretty close to my pad, so I threw on my jacket, grabbed my helmet, and headed to the Jairus' on my bike."

Joseph remembers where Zaphin lives. It *is* pretty close to a police station. Maybe he's telling the truth.

"When I got to their house, I was going to go inside—"

"Why didn't you?" Joseph interrupts.

"Because I didn't think that they would believe me. I didn't think they would listen," he replies. Zaphin fidgets with the helmet that he's holding. Then he looks up at Joseph again from under the long and thin strands of hair that dangle in front of his eyes.

"A brown truck followed them here. They left when they found out that none of us had gotten here yet. I stuck around to warn you, in case you showed up," Zaphin says.

"Nobody move!" a voice comes from around the corner. A man dressed in all green emerges from around the side of the house. Zaphin is still just steps outside of the garage. The man hasn't spotted him yet. He sinks back inside the shadows and waits for the trooper to pass by him.

"This is scout thirty-four. I have the suspects. Please proceed to the farm as soon as possible," he speaks into a radio as he continues to walk farther around the front of the house. He waves his pistol at Joseph and Daniel, motioning for them to move up toward the house. They slowly back up until they are at the base of the porch. Zaphin can see that Joseph still has the gun hidden down by his side. As the scout passes the garage, Zaphin attacks, striking him over the head with a shovel. The man falls over, unconscious from the blow.

"Zaphin definitely isn't one of the troopers from the compound," Daniel finally says. "I'll never forget their faces for the rest of my life."

"Someone followed us?" Mr. Jairus asks from the porch.

Zaphin turns around quickly. "Yes, and we all have to leave right now—before they come back."

Sarah stops hugging her parents and faces Zaphin. "If it's the troopers that followed my parents, then why didn't they go ahead and arrest them? It's not like they would need backup for just two people."

"I don't know for sure," Zaphin answers, "but I think they're after you two and not your parents at all. They probably left so that you wouldn't suspect anything when you got here. That scout was probably checking on the house to see if you had shown up yet."

"Which one of you is Zaphin?" Sarah's dad bellows down at the three teens.

"That's me," he says as he halfway raises his hand in the air.

Mr. Jairus turns to Joseph. "That would make you Joseph, right?"

"Yes, sir," Joseph responds.

"Thank you for keeping our daughter safe, Joseph."

"I appreciate it, but I had a little help." Joseph looks down at his weapons.

"Why didn't you keep the beam in front of me?" Zaphin asks.

Joseph taps the power gauge. "They're out of juice. I have to go back to the military base and recharge them."

"If it isn't safe, then we need to leave," Sarah says firmly.

"We should go to my brother's house," Mrs. Jairus agrees.

"How far is that?" Joseph inquires.

"It's only about forty-five miles away from here," Mr. Jairus answers. He's already headed to the car before he stops speaking.

Joseph hurries to his vehicle and immediately climbs in. "Sounds good to me. We'll follow you there."

The Jairuses quickly walk to the garage, but Sarah splits off and heads toward Joseph. Joseph is one step ahead of her, though, and is already starting the car.

"Where are you going?" her parents ask in unison.

"I'm going to ride with Joseph."

"Are you sure?"

"Yes. We'll follow you guys."

Daniel, who followed the Jairuses to their car, shouts back to his friends. "I'm just going to ride with them. See you when we get there."

With that, the Jairuses and Daniel get into their car and back out of the garage.

Zaphin gets onto his motorcycle and revs the motor. "I'll be right behind you," he calls from over the roar of the engine.

The Jairuses are the first to pull out. They come out of the driveway slowly, pacing themselves so that their daughter can catch up with them.

"Looks like it's the same old Zaphin," Joseph says. Sarah turns to see Zaphin tearing across the yard, dirt flying from the back wheel. His bike seems to hover as it hops over the bumps in the road. Then, just for the effect, Zaphin pops a wheelie as he turns onto the highway to catch up with his friends.

"On the road again." Sarah smiles.

"Were you expecting something else?" Joseph laughs.

"No, but I hope that those people aren't expecting us," Sarah says, pointing out somewhere to the road ahead of them. Her voice is strained and tired.

Joseph follows the line of her finger out into the distance. A convoy of vehicles is headed toward them.

"It could be anybody," Joseph says, half trying to convince himself. He grips the steering wheel tighter as the cars get closer.

"Just act normal," Sarah whispers.

The cars slow down as they begin to pass Joseph. The driver peers out of the window. Their stares connect. The trooper's eyes widen, realizing that these are the teens that they're searching for. The policeman slams on his brakes and turns on his lights, which had previously been hidden from sight. Joseph watches the lead car swerve and skid as it makes a hasty U-turn in the middle of the road.

"Crap! They spotted us!" Joseph exclaims.

The convoy of police cars follow suit with their sirens blaring. The troopers accelerate as fast as possible up the road.

The trooper in the passenger side of the lead car leans out the window and starts firing at Joseph. One bullet penetrates the trunk, while the second round explodes through the back window.

"Get down!" screams Joseph.

He pulls out his own gun and gives it to Sarah.

"Just shoot at their tires. Try to slow them down."

Sarah grabs the weapon and leans out the window. She takes careful aim at the bottom of the car behind them. The gun recoils in her hand after each shot, until finally, the only response is a hollow click. She misses the tires, but the startled troopers back off a little. The car swerves as they try to avoid the spray of fire. After the bullets stop coming, they speed up again. Joseph veers to the left of the street, avoiding another burst of rounds from the trooper's gun. Giby ducks down in her seat and covers her head. Zaphin ducks his head in between his handlebars as he separates from the group. He jumps his bike off of the highway and speeds through an open field to avoid the oncoming police force. Luckily for him, the troopers are focused on Joseph's car and continue to follow him down the highway.

Joseph looks up in his rearview mirror. He can see Zaphin's bike heading away from the road.

"They're not following Zaphin. I think he was right. I don't think they want your parents either. They want us." Joseph turns to the right onto an even larger highway. The convoy follows his car. The trooper who had been shooting at them ducks back in his car and braces for the turn. Joseph's phone goes off, ringing in the middle of all the commotion. Sarah picks it up.

Mr. Jairus' voice is desperate on the other line. "Where are you going?"

"They're after us, not you two. We'll lose them and meet you at Uncle Dan's."

Gunshots hit the passenger window next to Sarah and blow it out. She ducks down, still gripping the phone to her ear.

"I love you."

Sarah snaps the cell phone shut.

Mr. Jairus is still driving down the highway, watching the race ensue from a distance.

"Sarah, Sarah, are you there?" he screams in desperation. He listens for some response, but his questions are returned by deafening silence. Mr. Jairus pulls the phone from his ear and frantically looks at the display. The call is disconnected. He closes his phone and grips it tightly in his hand. Unable to hold back his anger, he slams his clenched fist into the steering wheel.

Mrs. Jairus says quietly, "Is she okay?"

Mr. Jairus looks over at her. Now he can see the tears that are streaming down her face.

"She *is* going to be fine. They *are* going to meet us at Uncle Dan's."

Mrs. Jairus closes her eyes and prays as they drive off toward the new *rendezvous* location.

"Father, please protect my little girl. She loves you so much, and she still has so much life to live. I pray that you would spare her life, and let her come to us safely. In Jesus' name, Amen."

Meanwhile, Joseph, Sarah, and Giby are still trying to outrun the troopers. Joseph glances again into his rearview mirror. Giby isn't covered up anymore. Instead, she's sitting in the backseat, looking out of her window.

"Train," she says while pointing to something outside.

She seems oblivious now to what's going on. Joseph looks out to where she is pointing. A very long train is bellowing down the tracks. Up ahead, he spots a road that looks like it crosses paths with the train tracks. The road is an old dirt road that winds back around after a mile and heads away from the highway. From the looks of it, it doesn't get used very much. Joseph looks out at the long stretch of concrete in front of him, melting into the horizon. The road is broad, and it appears as though it would be easier to drive on. He turns again and looks at the train barreling down the track.

"Hold on, I'm going to take that narrow path."

"What?" Sarah exclaims. "Are you crazy? What if we get cut off by the train? I'm not even sure that you can make those turns."

"I know that it won't be as easy, but if we stay on this open road, eventually they will catch us and kill us. The other path is the only one that's going to save us."

Sarah grabs a hold of the handle protruding from the roof of the car and braces herself. He turns hard to the right, onto the road. The car fishtails a little from the momentum.

As Joseph accelerates toward the train, he knows that it's going to be close. He mashes the pedal to the floor. The train and car get closer and closer to the intersection. The massive chain of metal boxes is unaware of the race that's taking place. Just then, the engineer sees the oncoming car. He tugs on the horn, unable to halt the inertia of the speeding mass of metal.

"We have to make it," Joseph exclaims as the car begins to jump over the tracks. They're directly in the path of the train. The engineer braces for impact, ducking his head and wincing as he looks on. Joseph's tires appear to be spinning very slowly. The car glides past the train engineer's window as his adrenalin explodes. Small rocks and dirt roll off the tires of the car and seem to drift in the air. They pelt the windshield of the train as Joseph's rear bumper barely clears the tracks. The troopers are following too close behind. They hit their brakes, but the lead vehicle can't stop in time. The train crushes the front of the police car and spins it around. The conductor slams on the brakes to try and avoid causing any more damage, but the momentum of the huge titan pushes the train forward several hundred more yards. When the train finally comes to a halt, Joseph's car is shrinking into the distance. The police vehicles are lined up behind the clump of mangled steel that used to be a police car. The road is now completely blocked, and there is no way for the troopers to follow them.

One of the troopers gets out of his car, straining to see where Joseph is going. He reaches into his pants pocket and pulls out his cell phone. Flipping it open, he slowly brings it to his ear.

"They got away."

The trooper nods his head.

"Yes, sir. We'll head that way."

CHAPTER 24

Joseph, Sarah, and Giby drive off into the stretch of country.

"I'll drive for a little bit," Sarah offers.

"If you insist," Joseph concedes as he pulls over on the side of the road. They switch places and buckle up before taking off again.

Sarah notices that Joseph is squeezing his gloves again. He appears to be in deep thought.

"What are you thinking about?" she asks. She hopes that it's not Slynne.

"I need to go back to the military compound to recharge Adam's Fall."

"Why, do we still need it?"

"I have a feeling like they aren't going to just give up on us. With these, we have a chance."

Sarah looks at Joseph's phone. It's out of bars again. They must be getting close to the edge of the city.

"Let it go," Sarah finally says.

"What do you mean?" he asks.

"Everything. We don't need to go after Slynne."

"I know, Sarah. I'm not planning on it."

"Then why worry about the weapon?" she questions.

"It's for protection—that's all."

"Okay," Sarah finally concedes. She knows that this isn't a battle that she's going to win. Instead of arguing, she decides to let the subject rest a little bit. After all, there's no harm in recharging the gloves.

The road stretches on for a very long time. As time passes, Joseph begins to grow impatient.

"Are we ever going to get there?" he complains.

Just then, they crest a hill, revealing the outline of skyscrapers rising up from out of the mist far in front of them.

"See," Sarah says in a matter-of-fact way. "You just need a little patience."

Joseph pretends to cough.

"Shut up!" Sarah teasingly laughs as she punches him in the arm.

"It's broken," Joseph taunts her right back. "I can't move it. Call an ambulance."

Joseph turns back toward his beautiful chauffer. Sarah is staring at him. She had stared at him before, but this is different. There is a different light in her eyes—a different glow around her smile. He holds the stare, finally breaking it when the moment becomes uncomfortable for him.

Does she actually like me? he thinks to himself. *Not just like me, but really like me like me?*

The silence is too awkward for Joseph to bear. Finally, he musters up the courage to say something.

"We'll call your parents as soon as we get back into cell phone range."

"Sounds good," she says.

They sit there for some time again until Sarah speaks.

"Look how beautiful the sunset is!"

Joseph looks out at the sun. The sky has begun its nighttime transformation. The sun is turning orange in the sky. Its rays paint the clouds that float above it in brilliant colors of violet, pink, blue, and orange hues. The beauty of nature presents itself, making a distinct contrast against the cold, hard city. They're just starting to enter its outskirts as they both gaze at the vivid colors that God is painting across the heavens.

"I know," Joseph says, after taking it all in. "It's amazing—just totally amazing. Just think—God created this for us. There really is no reason for the beautiful sunset. He just made it for us. Just like when God was creating the universe. After he created each thing, he said it was good. That's because he was thinking about Adam when he created all that stuff. He was thinking about how good it was going to taste to Adam the first time that he ate a cherry. He was thinking about how much it would blow his mind the first time he saw all the stars in the sky."

"Or how Eve would like the smell of a rose," Sarah adds.

They sit quietly again.

"Thank you, God," Sarah whispers.

The teens continue making their way up the back streets on the northeast side of town. They're still about fifteen minutes away from the abandoned military base. It's dangerous this time of night, although the gang activity seems to be virtually nonexistent as they plunge deeper and deeper toward the heart of the city. They pass by the rows of tall buildings. Not a single window bears light. Joseph can't help but wonder if there are people living in those buildings, lonely and scared. There could even be Christians like them hiding in the city. Of course, there isn't really any food source, so if there are people, they would have to be getting meals from somewhere. He tries to picture what it must have been like when the city was at its prime—before America turned. All the people would have been walking this very street. The shops would have been full of customers, and people would have been working and living in what are now empty brick and steel tombs.

"A roadblock!" Sarah exclaims as she turns a corner.

Just two streets away, the flashing lights illuminate the sky. They're coming up fast on a cross street, just before the barricade. Sarah begins to turn to her left, but patrol cars emerge from behind the building. In the rearview mirror, more lights appear. With the road to the left of her blocked, the one straight ahead of her closed off, and more troopers coming from behind, her only option is to take the road to the right.

"Hold on," she warns as she makes a hard turn.

Sarah realizes her folly as the rest of the street comes into view. Just before the next intersection are three more heavy armored cars blocking the road.

"It's a trap!"

Sarah quickly brakes. When the car comes to a halt, they just sit there with the engine idling. The squadron of vehicles pulls in behind them, blocking their escape. The troopers file out of their cars and draw their weapons.

"Out of the vehicle!" one of the troopers commands. Joseph looks at Sarah. He can tell that she's frightened. He turns his head and sees Giby. Her head is down, her hair covering her face.

"Stay here," Joseph instructs as he begins to exit the vehicle.

Sarah reaches out, grabbing the sleeve of his arm. Joseph briefly stops. He gives her a pat on the hand and gently pries it loose. Giving her a reassuring smile, Joseph opens the car door. He knows it's over, but he has to be strong for them. He turns, facing toward the back of the car, as he gets out of his seat. He stands up. The lights blind him.

"Everyone!" the voice comes again.

Joseph's mind races. What is he supposed to do? There's no way to escape. Please, Lord.

"There is no way out of this for you. Give up, or we will take you by force."

There's nothing for Joseph to do. He's out of cards, and the troopers have the better hand.

The sound of a heavy-duty vehicle approaches.

It sounds like they're bringing in a tank or something, Joseph thinks to himself.

He signals Sarah and Giby to get out of the car. The sound is getting louder. It's coming from behind him somewhere. Joseph peers over his shoulder to see what it is. As his eyes adjust to the darkness, he can see some of the troopers starting to back away from the armored vehicles. Without warning, a massive heavy-duty truck comes into view. Its ten oversized wheels grip the road as it accelerates. Judging by the olive green paint, it has to be a military vehicle. The front of the cab tapers up from the wheels, coming to a point in the front. The mammoth head of the beast then slants back and upward over the driver. The rear of the vehicle is flat like a trailer, as though it's meant to carry something on it. As it nears, Joseph can tell that even the lowest part comes up to the shoulders of an average-sized man. Heavy armor completely covers the vehicle.

Like cockroaches scurrying out from under a rug, the troopers abandon their posts at the blockade. The crowd of troopers in front of Joseph turns their attention to the oncoming juggernaut as well. The front end crushes one of the armored vehicles with tremendous force. Panels and debris fly as the front tires of the large military truck briefly come off the ground. The front of the smaller vehicle swings around, smashing into another section of the blockade. Sounds of metal shredding fill the air as the drab olive green truck continues pushing through the blockade. As it finishes ripping a hole through the troopers' vehicles, it continues on past Sarah and Giby's car. The driver cuts the wheel hard, sliding the back end around. It comes to rest in between the troopers at the back of Sarah and Giby's car and Joseph. The driver turns his face toward Joseph.

"It's Damian!" Joseph exclaims, unable to move. He can't wrap his head around it. What made this commander switch sides? Is it because he saved his life? Is he returning the favor? It has to be more than that. Joseph had planted the seed, but someone else must have watered it. God must have sent someone else to minister to him. Damian nods at Joseph, raising his thumb in approval. Joseph gives him a thumbs-up as well. Mouthing, "Thank you," he heads back toward his car.

"Fire!" comes the delayed command of the leader.

The street is filled with strobes of light as the R and Gs unload their weapons. Bullets ricochet off of the trailer, which shields Joseph and his friends. Joseph reaches the car and gets in. Sarah is already pulling away before he can close the door. They race toward the opening in the blockade and pass through it easily. Joseph looks back at the military vehicle. Damian starts to follow them, almost oblivious to the projectiles ripping into the reinforced panels. He pulls back through the hole that he had made coming in. Damian stops just after the cab clears the end of the wreckage, plugging the hole with the back of the trailer. Just before Sarah turns the corner, Joseph turns to see Damian bail out and start running away.

After maneuvering around some backstreets, they finally pull up to the old military building. There aren't any new cars around. The place is just as they left it—lifeless and barren. Joseph parks the car next to the front entrance. He gets out and opens the back door, letting Giby out. She jumps from the backseat onto the battered street. While stretching her little arms in the air, she does a quick little hop.

"Ready to go?" Joseph laughs.

"You said it," Sarah calls from across the car.

Giby smiles and nods, signaling that she is ready to go.

Joseph reaches into the backseat and grabs his backpack. The three continue on into the building. It seems quiet enough. They travel down the corridor to the elevator and press the down button.

"Let's hurry and get this done," Sarah says nervously.

"We'll be out of here in no time," Joseph assures her.

The elevator arrives with a "ding." Sarah, Giby, and Joseph enter as the doors open.

"I've got the key," Joseph declares as he pulls it out of his pocket. He inserts the key into the panel and turns it, revealing the button once again.

"Hold on," he says as he pushes it.

Like before, the elevator starts picking up speed as it races toward the basement level. This time, none of them are caught off guard. The elevator descends just as quickly, but they barely flinch. Instead, Sarah reaches over and inconspicuously slips her hand into Joseph's. It seems very hard to breathe for a moment. He tries to casually look over at her. She's beaming again. This time, he doesn't hold back his smile. It's already there, warming her heart. She smiles back shyly and looks at her shoes for a moment before gazing back up at him. Her head tilts sideways, playfully expressing her affection with her eyes.

After coming to a sudden stop, the elevator opens up. Sarah gives Joseph's hand an extra squeeze and lets go as she steps out of the open doors. She turns to the right, headed back to the charging station. Abruptly, the loud crack of a gunshot rings through the hallway. Sarah looks down in disbelief as blood starts to saturate the front of her shirt. She staggers backward, looking up to see captain Slynne standing there. His gun is still drawn as he begins to walk toward her.

"*Sarah!*" Joseph yells as he sees her starting to collapse. Sarah manages to stumble back into Joseph's waiting arms.

He grabs her body, which has gone limp, and drags her back into the elevator. He smashes the lobby button with one hand while still dragging her into the elevator. The metal doors shut just before a group of troopers come in from the right. Joseph can hear more shots being fired. They ricochet off of the outside of the doors. The elevator starts to ascend to the lobby level.

"It was a trap," Joseph utters. They'll surely be waiting for them on the lobby level.

He hits the stop button on the panel. There's nothing else that he can do.

Giby stands back in the corner, looking sadly at poor Sarah. Joseph lets Sarah's body down slowly as he slides clumsily down the elevator wall. He lays her head in his lap and strokes her head with his hand. Joseph begins to sob as he holds her dying body. She struggles to breathe and begins coughing up blood.

He feels helpless. Utterly useless. Sarah fights to keep her eyes open as death takes hold.

"Sarah, hold on, Sarah! Don't leave me here, don't you die," he blurts out in between sobs.

Sarah gives up the battle, closing her eyes. Her body becomes limp in Joseph's hands. A lone tear slides out from between her closed eyelids and glides down her cheek. She is dead. The sun outside has now set. Its brilliant and vibrant light has been extinguished, so too Sarah's light is gone from this world. Joseph knows that she's in heaven. He knows that just because we can't see the light of the sun anymore, doesn't mean that it's gone. It still exists. He knows that just because Sarah's body has died, and he can't see any sign of life in her, that her soul lives on. He knows that she's in heaven, but it's still too much for him to bear.

"No! No! *No!*" Joseph screams.

An eerie voice comes echoing up the elevator shaft at him. "There is nowhere to run, Joseph. Yes, I know your name. I know all about you and your pathetic plight. Your friend told me all about it."

"Shut up!" Joseph screams.

"Don't you wonder how we found out you were having a Bible study in the first place? Our Lieutenant Zaphin led you right into our trap. Zaphin, tell your friend to come out. If he gives up, we might let him get away with just a little jail time," Slynne coaxes.

Did he just say Zaphin? Joseph thinks. *It was Zaphin all along? No. It's another trick.*

Then Joseph hears another familiar voice reverberate up through the metal chamber.

"You better come out, man. They have troopers on the top floor too. The only way out of this alive is to give up," Zaphin says.

"But it can't be you," he says in denial. "You could have just turned us in at any time."

"No. No, I couldn't have. You had those gloves. You would have just used them on me, and I would have never seen you again. That's why I had to take out that scout. I had to convince you that I was on your side. I knew it was only a matter of time before you laid the gloves down or something."

"It doesn't make any sense," Joseph sobs.

"I knew exactly where you were headed," Zaphin continues, "when you said you had to recharge them. I already had a key to the elevator too. Earlier, I had seen Sarah put that spare key in her pocket in the control room. Then I stole it when she hugged me good-bye."

"Sarah's dead because of you!" Joseph screams.

He waits for a response, but none comes. There is only a somber silence that permeates his ears between each shallow breath.

"Why did I have to come back here?" Joseph cries. "Why didn't God make these last longer!"

He holds his arms up into the air with Adam's Fall still attached to them.

"Oh why, dear God, why couldn't you have made them work just a little longer?"

A different voice comes to Joseph now. This is a soothing voice. It's the beautiful voice of a little girl. Joseph looks to see who is speaking. It's coming from behind him where Giby is standing, but it doesn't sound like her.

"Because doing that would not have glorified God," she says gently, laying her hand on Joseph's shoulder. Joseph remembers that the little girl is in the elevator, looking over at her hand on his shirt. He follows the line of her wrist, and then her arm, until he sees her face. She is glowing. Not just glowing, but light is radiating from her face. It's as if her skin has been placed over a light as bright as the sun itself. Joseph is speechless. It's as if he is hearing her voice for the very first time.

"How long have you relied on your weapons?" she asks. "Rely on God instead. Remember how God turned back the shadow on the sundial for Hezekiah?"

Joseph flashes back to the Bible study. He remembers the Jansens reading about God turning back time. How he had, indeed, moved the shadow back on the sundial. Mrs. Jansen's voice rings out in his ears as he remembers her words.

"I believe that the miracles are for today."

Gloriously and unexpectedly, wings of light begin to unfold from the little girl's back. Brilliant pure white surrounds her and flows from her mouth. It's so bright that Joseph has to cover his eyes from its wonderful radiance.

"Ask your father in heaven, and he will be faithful, for this will bring glory to his name," she instructs.

Joseph's mind races. How can this be? Is this the same little girl?

His mind flashes back again. This time he remembers when he first met her. It's as if he is there in that room again, only he can see himself speaking. Giby is not there. He sees himself say, "What a pretty little girl," to the dog.

"I didn't know you had a dog," Sarah replies to Joseph's comment.

"We are watching it for the Nuessens," Mrs. Jansen replies.

They all thought he was talking about the dog. They could never see Giby. She wasn't their child.

He flashes back to the first time they were in the elevator. Again, he can see himself, as if he is an outside onlooker. Giby isn't there either. Joseph looks up at Sarah.

"You don't talk much, do you?" Sarah smiles and looks down at the ground again.

Sarah thought he was talking to her. She couldn't see Giby either.

Once more, he flashes back to when they had arrived at the compound. He sees himself open the back door of the car, but again, Giby is not there.

"You ready to go?" Joseph says.

"You know it," Sarah responds.

He sees himself grab his backpack out of the car and close the door.

"They could never see you," Joseph whispers in awe. You were always there, always helping me, but they couldn't see you. I was the only one that could see you.

"Ask him, Joseph," the beautiful voice comes.

"Ask him for miracles. Miracles that will bring him glory. Ask him for the miracles of Hezekiah and Joshua."

"Yes," he mumbles. "Yes, I will," he says more boldly as he begins to pray. "Dear heavenly Father, I am so sorry for relying on myself and not on you, my God. You made the moon and the sun; you made the heavens and the earth. Nothing is beyond your control. You have always been and will always be. You live outside of time itself. I pray dear God that you would turn back time for me, just as you turned back time for Hezekiah, so that it will bring glory to your name. I beg you, my father. I beg you."

A wonderful, loving, and powerful voice echoes inside of Joseph's mind. "I do this miracle so that the Lord your God may be glorified in heaven and that my children that I have called will believe."

Joseph stands to his feet. Giby pulls on his shoulder, guiding him to the back of the elevator. Outside, the brilliant colors return to the sky as the sun floats back up above the horizon and hangs above the city. Joseph sees himself praying and then holding Sarah again. The events that occurred are unraveling themselves as time spins into reverse. Sarah flies back out of Joseph's hands and back out into the hallway. The bullet withdraws from her body and slides back into the barrel of Slynne's gun. Sarah walks backward into the elevator once again, and the doors shut. All this is happening in Joseph's sight. His eyes are witness to it all. He refocuses them, and he is standing there with Sarah, holding her hand.

The doors open again, and Sarah lets go of his hand. She starts to walk out, but this time, Joseph grabs her hand and pulls her back into the elevator. Sarah is shocked and confused as the doors close behind her. Suddenly, she is face-to-face with Giby. Her countenance is still glowing in all its radiance. Sarah falls down on her knees beneath the outstretched wings.

"Where did you come from?" Sarah gasps. "Are you an angel?"

"Yes, Sarah. I have always been with you."

Sarah sits there, bewildered by what is happening. Joseph lays his hand on her back. "It's going to be all right," he reassures her. "She's helping us."

Joseph kneels down beside Sarah and begins to pray. "Dear God. I pray that you would give me the strength to defeat my enemies. I pray that you would hold the sun in the sky, like you did for Joshua. I pray that you would give me your strength, and I pray that your will be done."

The sovereign voice comes again. This time, it shakes Joseph to the very core. He bows lower to the ground as the voice begins to speak.

"I do this miracle so that the Lord your God may be glorified in heaven this day and so that my children that I have called will believe. You will have victory this day, Joseph."

"Thank you, God. I praise you, Jesus," Joseph whispers. He kneels there on the elevator floor for a moment. Then, looking up, he sees Sarah and Giby staring at him.

"You stay here," he says to Sarah.

Sarah, still in shock, manages to nod her head in agreement. Joseph gets up from his knees. His actions are determined. His demeanor is confident. His purpose is clear. Joseph walks up to the elevator doors and opens them. He moves to go out into the hallway, but Giby exits first. She slowly walks across the hall and turns to face Joseph. Her stare is fixed on him as if she is beckoning him to come—calling him to fulfill his purpose. Joseph exits the elevator. He sees Slynne down the hall to his right. The captain fires the shot that was originally meant for Sarah. Joseph jumps back into the elevator, anticipating more rounds to follow. To his amazement, he sees something floating through the air. It's moving slowly, like a tiny hummingbird steadily advancing toward him.

Joseph leans forward to get a better view. He is taken back as he watches, realizing that the object is a bullet. It's the bullet that Slynne has just fired. His eyes meet Giby's as the projectile passes between them. She is calmly looking back at Joseph, as if miracles like this happened every day. The tension goes out of Joseph's shoulders. His face relaxes. He knows what he must do.

Emerging from the elevator, he sees more troopers. They have just rounded the corner and are in his path. They are in front of the captain, who has ceased fire for now. And who is leading the pack? It's none other then Zaphin himself. Joseph advances on the men. Zaphin attempts to clock Joseph in the face with a right hook, but God is slowing the fabric of time itself. His actions appear extremely slow to Joseph. He looks up at the arm coming toward him. Moving to the side, he dodges it easily. Then he looks back at Zaphin again. Joseph purses his lips as he swings with his left hand at Zaphin's head. The punch connects directly with the poor teen's chin. The force of the blow spins Zaphin around 360 degrees. Before he even finishes spinning, Joseph is recoiling his right hand down and back. He releases it upward, just as Zaphin finishes spinning and is facing him again. His right fist crashes into Zaphin's stomach. The uppercut sends him flying across the hallway.

Another fist comes at him from the side. He quickly spins around, delivering a roundhouse to the dazed red and green soldier. Time seems to accelerate as his limp body flies to the floor. The two last advancing troopers reach for their weapons. One of them manages to draw his stick just before Joseph reaches him. He swings, and Joseph blocks the attack. Meanwhile, the other one has drawn a handgun. Joseph turns his attention to the armed man. He slices through the air with his hand, connecting just at the trooper's wrist. The gun topples to the floor. The other trooper follows up with a combination kick and punch, but Joseph easily thwarts his attempted attack.

More guards come from the hallway on the left. They immediately pull their guns to fire on Joseph, as he is unaware that they have entered the corridor. Giby, who has stayed out of the battle until now, puts her hands out in front of her, as if she is holding something. Light bursts from her hands and flows upward in a straight line. Shimmering pieces of luminous objects spin off and overflow from the solid beam, like a giant sparkler. The light starts to widen and take shape. As the beam begins to fade, a sword slowly comes into focus. Effortlessly, Giby brings it to the ground and swiftly slices upward into the trooper's guns. Time slows again as the blade goes through the barrels with laser precision. Three severed, hollow black cylinders float upward and away from the guns. As they rotate from the sheering force of the sword, two silver projectiles slide out from the end of the barrels. A third continues upward with the cylinders, the bullet splitting in half in midair. The sword has cut through all three barrels, catching one of the bullets before it has even left the gun.

Slynne begins to panic. The once fearless and ruthless captain now appears terrified. His hand shakes as he lowers his gun. It's almost as though he has forgotten that he is holding it. Joseph spins and extends his leg out, sliding it along the ground. He drives the troopers' legs out from under them, knocking both them off of their feet. Time has slowed so much that Joseph actually comes back around before their bodies hit the ground. Their weightless torsos float through the air as Joseph uses his momentum to hit one of the troopers. He clasps his hands together and drills the man with the force of his arm's combined strength. The trooper's body hurls toward the other trooper. Joseph flips forward into the air, allowing his leg to follow his full body weight. He comes down as the first trooper's body connects with the second. Joseph's leg pummels them both down onto the hard floor.

Time speeds up again as Joseph continues down the hall. Now it's just him and the captain. Joseph looks up at Slynne. Their eyes meet. The captain frantically pulls his gun up to fire on Joseph, who is already running toward him. Time strains and images vibrate rapidly until they almost completely come to a halt as Joseph sees God slow time once more. The captain's finger compresses the trigger. Again, his gun recoils. Joseph ducks, avoiding the oncoming bullet. He grabs the captain's arm and leans backward as he begins to sling Slynne over his head. As he pulls down on the captain's hand, the gun shoots again. With his hand pointing downward, the second bullet travels on a trajectory toward the elevator. Joseph continues rolling backward onto the floor, using the captain's arm as leverage to hurl Slynne down the hallway. His helpless body flies over the bullet, which is continuing slowly down the hall. The captain lands sitting on the floor in front of the elevator. He is facing Joseph. A look of complete shock crumples his face. Time slips as it speeds back up to normal. The bullet that the captain meant for Joseph zips down the hall and plows into Slynne's own heart. The captain's expression changes from one of shock to one of pain and confusion. He looks down at the bullet wound in his chest and falls over onto the cold, hard tile.

Everyone is still. Even the remaining troopers stand down. Zaphin, who has been viewing the whole thing from the ground, slowly gets up. Holding his stomach, he staggers against the wall. Sarah comes out of the elevator and looks down at the captain. Giby walks over to the dying man as well. There is no emotion in her face. She simply watches him. One last breath escapes through his lips as he dies. Her face morphs into one of fury. She wields her sword of light over the dead body. Her face is tense, like she is expecting something. The other troopers groan as they hobble to their feet, struggling to see what's going on. An eerie silence falls on everyone. Suddenly, what looks like a thick shadow emerges from Slynne's body. The horrible demon shrieks as it comes up and hovers in the air. The menacing dark terror peers at Joseph with its red eyes. It begins to strike out at him, the edges of its black form extending out like snakes. Giby moves in front of the dark angel—her sword raised and ready to deliver a blow. The ferocious demon lunges at Giby. She spreads her wings as far as they will go. Light explodes from them as they expand. Now, even the troopers can see Giby. The men squint as they witness this intense scene. Giby stares into the demon's eyes and swings her sword. The demon recoils, letting out a shriek that is even more terrifying than the first one. Several troopers cover their ears, wincing at the sound. Reluctantly, the demon finally flies up through the roof of the building and out of sight.

Joseph walks over to the captain's lifeless body. He then turns to the angel that has just saved their lives.

"Is Giby really your name?" he asks.

"God is beside you. That's all you need know," she replies.

Everyone gathers around the angel, including the troopers. Those who still have weapons drop them. Zaphin, who has made his way up to her, falls to his knees. Upon seeing this, all the other guards follow suit and bow down as well.

"Do not worship me," Giby explains, "but instead, worship God—worship Jesus. For God sent his only Son, Jesus, into the world to die for your sins. That you should not perish but have eternal life. No man comes to the Father except through Jesus. It doesn't matter how good someone is, how bad they are, or what good works they have done. For all have sinned and come short of the glory of God, and the punishment for sin is death."

Joseph joins in, "But you can be cured of this disease called sin. The cure is Jesus. God sent Jesus as a gift to all of us. As a cure for sin, and all one must do is accept the gift."

Zaphin raises his head. "How can we accept this gift?"

"By believing that Jesus died for your sins and that he rose again," Joseph answers. "You must then ask Jesus to forgive you for your sins, and make him the Lord of your life."

"I do believe in Jesus, and I want him to be the Lord of my life," Zaphin admits in a humble voice. He looks to Joseph, the man they have been trying to kill. "What else must I do?"

Joseph replies, "Whatever he asks us to—whatever he asks."

The old man leans back in his plush, overstuffed green chair. He looks around at the crowd of children and adults. They are all riveted, leaning forward in anticipation of what's going to happen next.

"What did Zaphin do?" a young man asks.

"He ended up accepting Jesus. He eventually ended up starting a Bible study too."

"Is he alive today?" the curious boy asks again.

"Yes. I am Zaphin," the old man says proudly.

Whispers and murmuring fill the room as the people listen on in wonder and amazement.

"I'm not proud of what I did, but I am proud of what Jesus did in me. He continues to do miraculous things to this very day."

A young girl in the front of the Bible study pipes up, "Did Joseph ever use those cool gloves again?"

He takes his glasses off and lays them on the side table beside the paper.

"Why yes, he did," he replies with a suspenseful grin.

He scoots forward in his chair and leans in close to the little girl, as if he is going to tell her a secret.

"We need to start Bible study now, but I'll tell you about that story next time."

DISCUSSION STARTERS

Is America promised success?	Page # 12-18
Creation	Page # 26
What do you have faith in?	Page # 27-28
Daniel and the lions	Page # 48, 181-182
The Trinity	Page # 79
Adam & Eve	Page # 79
Death before Jesus' sacrifice	Page # 80-81
Jesus' sacrifice and victory	Page # 82
How to enter Heaven	Page # 83-84
Righteousness cannot be earned	Page # 85
Life is short	Page # 88
Armor of God	Page # 95-98
Trust in Jesus	Page # 109
The music sheet and God's plan for us	Page # 112-113
There is a cost to being a Christian	Page # 117
Jesus is the only one who can fill the hole	Page # 121-122
We can't inherit Christianity	Page # 124
Read the Bible to know for yourself	Page # 124
The gift of Jesus is free / come as you are	Page # 132
Obey God or the government	Page # 138
Standing in persecution	Page # 141-142
Light shines brighter in the darkness	Page # 148
Pew potatoes	Page # 152
Men agape darkness	Page # 159-161
God knows what we need before we ask	Page #167, 187, 208
One way	Page # 221-222

Love your enemies	Page # 224-225
Sometimes change happens slowly over time	Page # 244-245
Christians need fellowship	Page # 246
Apostles testimony about Christ must be true	Page # 246-247
What is really important	Page # 247-248
Some plant and some water	Page # 265, 269, 270, 291
Forgiveness	Page # 274-275
The broad and narrow paths	Page # 284
Overlooked gifts from God	Page # 288-289
The body dies, but we live on	Page # 294
Rely on God	Page # 295-298
Miracles are for today	Page # 299-301
Only worship God	Page # 302-303
God can change anyone	Page # 303-304

listen|imagine|view|experience

AUDIO BOOK DOWNLOAD INCLUDED WITH THIS BOOK!

In your hands you hold a complete digital entertainment package. Besides purchasing the paper version of this book, this book includes a free download of the audio version of this book. Simply use the code listed below when visiting our website. Once downloaded to your computer, you can listen to the book through your computer's speakers, burn it to an audio CD or save the file to your portable music device (such as Apple's popular iPod) and listen on the go!

How to get your free audio book digital download:

1. Visit www.tatepublishing.com and click on the e|LIVE logo on the home page.
2. Enter the following coupon code:
   02ff-e66a-4deb-2216-01c4-4f30-27c1-3c8f
3. Download the audio book from your e|LIVE digital locker and begin enjoying your new digital entertainment package today!